TO SAVE A SINNER

ADELE CLEE

Copyright © 2015 Adele Clee
All rights reserved.
ISBN-13: 978-0-9932832-1-5

Cover designed by **Jay Aheer**

CHAPTER 1

LONDON, 1820

It took a certain type of gentleman to bring a ballroom to its knees, Helena Ecclestone thought, as her gaze drifted up the stairs to the sinful-looking rogue located at the top.

Descending with a slow, predatory grace, he acknowledged the stunned crowd with a smirk and the name Lucas Dempsey floated past her ear on a breeze of muttered whispers.

"So, the gossip is true," Amelia said, patting her hands together with excitement.

Helena raised a curious brow. "What, that Lucifer vowed to don an evening coat and torment us with his presence?"

"No, that Viscount Harwood has brought his brother back to the fold after years of living in exile." When Helena appeared unimpressed, Amelia added, "You do know Mr. Dempsey killed a man. Though I don't suppose it matters when you have a face like that. Is he not the most handsome man you've ever seen?"

Helena glanced across the room. She had to admit there were not many men who could claim to be as handsome as Lucas Dempsey. Although upon further reflection, his features lacked a level of compassion and kindness she found particularly desirable. His rigid jaw looked as though it had been carved from a smooth slab of marble as a perfect example of defiance. His angelic blue eyes were just a mask for a cold and cynical gaze, and his black hair hung in a rebellious wave over his brow. Indeed, Lucas Dempsey looked every bit the master of his own world; a world where rules were for the weak and integrity for fools.

"It appears Lady Colebrook is equally impressed," Helena announced with mild amusement. "She is practically hanging from his coattails. Let's hope he doesn't quickly change direction as she'll find herself skating across the dance floor."

"I've heard that Lady Colebrook is his mistress." Amelia gave an exaggerated sigh and trailed her fingers along the neckline of her gown. The movement suggested the idea of being on intimate terms with a murderer was more than pleasing. "Although I believe he's not short of ladies offering to step into the role."

Yes, and Amelia dreamed of being one of them.

"Where do you get all your information?" Helena asked, deciding to test the theory that her sister had concocted the story for her own amusement or at least added the odd embellishment.

"From Millicent," she said, her lips forming an exaggerated pout. "Her brother is a friend of Viscount Harwood." Amelia glanced across at Lucas Dempsey as though the gods of Olympus had opened up the heavens and delivered their most coveted disciple. "Millicent said he has come back to England to find a wife, and I find he has much to recommend his suit."

"And you're happy to overlook the fact that he killed a man?"

"He killed a man in a fight, Helena," Amelia said, flicking her fan in frustration. "I'm sure he wouldn't dream of killing his own wife."

It appeared Amelia's logic knew no bounds. So she decided she ought to quash whatever idiotic notion had entered her younger sister's head.

"Mr. Dempsey is not looking for a wife," Helena scoffed, sneaking a glance at the man in question.

"How do you know?"

"Because he seems thoroughly disinterested in everyone and everything, as though he has already experienced all life has to offer, and nothing else could ever meet with his lofty appraisal." Helena pursed her lips to suppress a snigger. "Look, even Lady Colebrook with her generous bosom is struggling to hold his attention." Feeling relatively pleased with her assessment, she added, "He does not want to be here, Amelia, and he is certainly not looking for a wife."

"You're just saying that because you know he wouldn't even consider you." Amelia's gaze flitted to the sleeves of Helena's dress. "I don't think anyone would consider you, not while you're wearing that dress. You have so many ruffles I believe if you flapped your arms you could fly around the room." She put her hand to her mouth and chuckled, obviously pleased with such a witty observation.

Helena sighed.

It was easy to judge when blessed with natural beauty and when it came to Amelia she would always pale in comparison. While Amelia's honey-gold hair shimmered in the candlelight, Helena's was a dull, muted brown, styled with excessive curls to disguise her elfin features. Amelia's blue eyes were as rich as lapis lazuli while hers were so light a green they were often mistaken for grey.

Indeed, while Amelia needed no trinkets or adornments to enhance her features, their mother insisted that Helena wear a band of roses in her hair. Nestled amongst the curls, the pale pink roses drew out the natural tones; the dark green leaves enhanced the depth of her eyes. The frilly sleeves gave the impression hers was a more robust, more voluptuous frame, as opposed to the slender, willowy form she was born with.

"When one does not possess natural beauty, a way must be found to cultivate it," her mother had said.

Helena did not have the strength to argue. What was the

point of discussing the merits of character over beauty when it only mattered to her?

Awakened from her reverie by the sound of a playful shriek, Helena followed Amelia's gaze to Lady Colebrook and the portly gentleman who'd stolen a grape from her elaborate coiffure and dropped it down her impressive cleavage. Helena had no idea who the gentleman was but noticed that Lucas Dempsey had disappeared.

"What happened to Mr. Dempsey?" Helena asked, a little surprised the words had fallen from her lips. "Let me guess. He turned into a three-headed dragon and flew off in the vicinity of the ornamental gardens."

"Obviously not," Amelia said, standing on her tiptoes and raising her chin. "I lost him between the stone pillar and the doors to the terrace. Perhaps he *has* gone for a stroll in the garden or to get some air."

Helena imagined him on the hunt for something far more satisfying than fresh air.

"Perhaps someone should tell Lady Colebrook," Amelia continued, "as she seems oblivious to the fact and is using every tactic possible to attract his attention." Amelia turned to Helena, but her expression grew grim as she spotted something in the distance. "Mother is making her way through the crowd and is heading in this direction," she said with a mild sense of panic. "No doubt she intends to chastise us for hanging back like wallflowers while our adversaries dance with all the eligible gentlemen."

Helena turned to scan the sea of heads but being somewhat smaller in stature could only see two ostrich feathers sticking out of a pea-green turban. When her mother eventually broke through, her exaggerated scowl reminded Helena of Aunt Augusta's pug.

"Have I not stressed the importance of making yourself available?" Esther Ecclestone complained. "How do you expect to attract attention when you're huddled in the corner like a couple of old matrons?"

Her mother's reproachful gaze fell to Helena's slippers before drifting up to her hair.

"You more than anyone must make a good impression," she continued. "I am not averse to you standing with your sister. On the contrary, Amelia has always been adept at attracting a gentleman's eye, but I expect to see you in the company of at least one eligible gentleman this evening. Surely, that is not too much to ask," she said, the words accompanied by numerous sighs and tuts. "Now, I believe your sister has just escaped through the terrace. Find her and make haste else the night will be over before either of you have had a chance to dance."

Helena turned sharply, but the only thing standing behind her was a potted fern.

"Well, off you go." Her mother shooed her away like a mangy dog. "You do not have all night."

Amelia would feel the sharp edge of her tongue for abandoning her, Helena thought, as she stormed out onto the terrace. But other than Lord and Lady Fanshaw, who were only concerned with staring into each other's eyes and giggling like children, the terrace was empty.

Helena muttered an unladylike curse.

How was she supposed to catch the attention of a suitable gentleman when she spent most of her time traipsing about after Amelia?

She walked to the top of the steps leading down into the dimly lit garden, placed her hands on her hips and scoured the shadows. Surely, Amelia was not silly enough to walk in the garden alone. Then Helena remembered that was where she thought Lucas Dempsey had gone. What better way to glean a marriage proposal than to be caught in an illicit embrace.

Compelled by a sudden wave of panic, Helena stole down the steps and out into the garden in search of her wayward sibling.

CHAPTER 2

Lucas Dempsey sauntered through Lady Colebrook's ballroom and examined the wide eyes of those he had once called his friends.

As expected, his attendance received a rather varied response. There were those who reacted with shock and disbelief: the idea that Lady Colebrook would extend an invitation to the man responsible for killing Lord Banbury was abhorrent. From the more dissipated gentlemen of the *ton*, he received a knowing smirk or a respectful nod—while some would not dare to look in his direction.

The hostility in the air clawed at his shoulders, and he brushed it off like a speck of dust on a new coat. In retaliation, he flashed an arrogant smile which never failed to rouse a reaction. The respectable matrons gathered around their daughters like ewes protecting lambs from a wolf. And the more *seasoned* ladies, particularly the widowed Miranda Colebrook, stepped closer, lured by the thrill of dicing with danger.

"Mr. Dempsey. How wonderful it is to see you again," Miranda Colebrook chirped, rushing to greet him with outstretched hands and a lascivious grin.

He brought her fingers to his lips, his mask of indifference concealing his disdain. "I found that I could not stay away," he lied, quickly dismissing the memory of her writhing and panting beneath him.

She raised a seductive brow and inhaled too deeply, causing her breasts to rise and expand before his eyes so that her chin was almost lost between the bulging mounds. "I am so pleased to hear it."

Purely out of respect for his host, Lucas gazed at the inflated spectacle, and she gave a coy smile before introducing him to a group of people: a Lady Altwood, Major Dunstable, and two other guests whose names he did not care to remember.

"Mr. Dempsey has just returned home from Boston," Miranda informed the group in a tone that suggested he'd been living amongst savages and deserved some recognition for his plight.

"I returned a few weeks ago, albeit reluctantly," Lucas replied, feeling the need to correct any misconception. He did not find it necessary to add that he regarded Boston as his home now.

"I take it you're not referring to Boston, Lincolnshire?" Major Dunstable chuckled, placing a hand on his portly stomach to stop it shaking. "After a stint across the water, it must feel splendid to experience refined society once more. I say, have they finished building that cathedral?" He turned his attention to Lady Altwood. "It is just a cruder version of our own St Paul's. The blighters are even stealing the name, but what else can one expect from such heathens."

Lucas flexed his fingers; a way of alleviating the urge to punch the man on the nose. "I do not think crude is the right word," he said in a tone that would frighten the devil, "less pretentious perhaps. Thankfully, they do not feel the need to impress themselves on others through exaggerated displays of grandeur."

Dunstable's stomach wobbled like a perfectly set blancmange. "Yes, yes ... indeed," he mumbled causing saliva to bubble between his lips. "I just meant that ... that ..."

Lady Colebrook cleared her throat. "What do you think of my coiffure?" she said, gently patting the sides of her golden locks without disturbing the fruit. "Is it not a remarkable piece of craftsmanship, Mr. Dempsey?"

Lucas wanted to say that he had never seen anything so ridiculous in his life. But Lady Altwood was cooing over such a creative ensemble, amazed at the ingenuity of fixing fruit to hair combs, that he found his attention diverted and gazed around the room in search of more stimulating company.

The fact that his brother was the only person who captured his interest was telling.

Stepping back from the group, Lucas made his way across the crowded room but did not have to barge and push his way through the throng as others had done. On witnessing his approach, people instinctively stepped out of his way, thus creating a narrow aisle leading to his destination.

"You could at least give the appearance of being more affable," Anthony said with some frustration as Lucas joined him. "You look like a fallen angel, brooding after being cast out of the flock."

"Trust me, I am not disappointed about being cast out of this particular flock," Lucas replied. "I see little has changed. Society still bows its head to gossip and deceit. I am only sorry that you forced me to return."

Anthony sighed as he placed his hand on Lucas' shoulder. "I did not force you, Lucas. After four years, I assumed you'd want to see your mother. You didn't say goodbye to Father, and I did not want you to make the same mistake."

The last thing Lucas wanted was his brother's advice or pity. "There was no mistake," he informed Anthony bluntly. "As far as I'm concerned my father died four years ago when he packed my trunk and cast me aside. Coming back would not have made any difference." Lucas shrugged while his expression remained emotionless. "I'm afraid the caring and compliant brother you knew died that day, too."

Indeed, on that fateful day, he became the man everyone believed him to be: a liar and a libertine.

"I don't believe that," Anthony whispered through gritted teeth. "I refuse to believe that." He nodded across to the other side of the ballroom. "There are still some members of Society who are willing to overlook your past. It will not take long for others to follow suit."

Lucas put his hand on his chest and snickered. "Please tell me you're not referring to Lady Colebrook. After what happened with Lady Banbury, do you honestly think I care for such shallow opinion? Like everyone else, she sees a handsome face and nothing more."

Anthony was silent for a moment and then said, "You have always been more than that to me."

The comment rebounded off the iron breastplate Lucas had worked years to craft, leaving nothing but the faintest scratch. "Perhaps, but it's a little too late to partake in sentiment, four years too late. Besides, what is one opinion worth amongst many?"

Anthony opened his mouth to protest, but Lucas raised his hand to silence him. "Understand this," Lucas continued with a level of vehemence he had not fully intended. "I'm here because you requested it and because I had a desire to see my mother. Do not expect me to conform to your notions of propriety and respectability, as they no longer apply to me. If you want to save my soul, I suggest you say an extra prayer in church on Sunday." He moved to walk away, but stopped and added, "And as for my relationship with Lady Colebrook, it is nothing more than an easy bit of sport."

Leaving his brother standing at the edge of the ballroom, his eyes wide in disbelief, Lucas stepped out onto the terrace and away from the hypocritical pomposity he had grown to detest.

He could not linger there for too long. When it came to voracious appetites, the ladies in London Society were no different from those in Boston. Where he was concerned, taking a walk or seeking some air was an invitation to partake in another form of exercise. In a matter of moments, he would be joined by at least one lady looking for some vigorous amusement. And so he moved swiftly down the steps and across the lawn until hidden safely behind an eight-foot topiary hedge.

Making his way through the tiny maze of sculptured shrubbery, he found a concealed corner flanked on all sides by the tall hedge. His immediate thought was one of relief—until he noticed the statue of Hercules standing in the middle.

It wasn't the statue that caught his attention, but rather the six-foot plinth upon which it stood. Tall and wide enough to conceal a man, flat enough to lean back against, he knew exactly why Lady Colebrook had placed that particular statue in such a secluded corner. While various lanterns and braziers illuminated the garden, this area relied on nothing more than the soft muted light filtering through the windows of the house.

Desperate to find a place of sanctuary, he swung round and barged straight into—well, he was not sure who he had bumped into. The only thought that entered his head was he'd stumbled upon a delightful little wood nymph. He had seen a picture of one once, in a book entitled *Classical Mythology*, but he had never seen one in the flesh.

The nymph jumped back, her eyes wide with surprise. There were roses and leaves in her hair, and the silken sleeves on her dress flapped like faerie wings in the moonlight.

He was shocked to find that, for once, he was pleased with the lady who'd chosen to seek him out and rather liked the idea of frolicking with a forest dweller. "Were you looking for someone?" he asked in a neutral tone as he did not wish to appear presumptuous.

"Mr. Dempsey," she replied breathlessly, her dainty fingers fluttering up to her chest.

Good. She *was* looking for him.

The thought caused a familiar stirring in his loins. Perhaps the evening would not be as tedious as he first imagined. The corners of his mouth curled upwards, but he suppressed a salacious grin. It would not do to frighten off this fragile fawn.

"How may I be of service?" He offered his most respectable bow, confident she would be more than pleased with all he had to offer.

"Well, you can begin by telling me what you've done with her." Her tone resembled the shriek of a harpy rather than the soft song of a wood nymph, and he winced in response. "What have you done with Amelia?"

The illusion instantly shattered, he took a step back and replaced his mask of indifference. "I believe you are in the wrong corner of the garden," he said, disguising his disappointment. When she thrust her hands on her hips by way of a challenge, he threw his hands up and added, "There's no one else here with me."

"Where is she?" she persisted, grabbing the sleeve of his coat and pulling him to one side to check nobody was hiding behind him.

His mouth fell open, and he feared he might stumble over his bottom lip. "I have already told you. I am alone."

He tugged at the end of his sleeves to straighten them and flicked some imagined dust from his lapels. This was not the sort of attention he usually received from young ladies. Typically, they were either too frightened to look at him or were fawning over him like a pet monkey.

"I am not a fool, Mr. Dempsey," she said, looking directly at him without as much as a blush.

Feeling an overwhelming desire to intimidate, a desperate need to unsettle her steely composure, he stepped into the moonlight and bestowed his most dazzling, most self-assured smile.

Nothing.

No gasp, no languid sigh, no fluttering of the lashes, not even the unwitting wetting of the lips.

Nothing.

It was as though she had seen his face a million times before and remained equally unimpressed.

He frowned as he peered into her eyes, convinced she must have some sort of sight impairment. The more he stared, the more his mind played tricks. One minute he was studying the delicate green hues, noting how they embodied the whole theme of nature. Then she blinked, and they looked silver as though reflecting the light of the moon.

Gripped by an invisible force, his gaze dropped to her mouth, and he found himself drawn towards the tiny peachy bow, ready to taste a little piece of heaven.

"Step away, Mr. Dempsey," she said, slapping her gloved fingers against his mouth to halt his advance. She did not wait for his response but pushed his head back by way of a warning.

Lucas gasped at her audacity.

"It's as I said," he barked as she moved past him to search behind the large plinth. Failing in his amorous pursuit, he decided to flash his wolf's teeth. "I'm alone. Or at least I was alone, but now I have you to keep me company." When she ignored him and continued to search along the line of the hedge, he practically growled. "Do you know the danger you're putting yourself in by being out here with me? Are you aware of my reputation?"

His nymph stopped foraging in the bushes and turned to face him, tilting her head to one side as she narrowed her gaze.

"You do not frighten me, Mr. Dempsey." Her voice held a hint of amusement, and she took a few confident steps towards him. She stood rigid, her chin held high as though she was equal in stature to the muscular figure of Hercules and he was a mere insignificant mortal. "Fear is an irrational emotion brought about by the thought of impending danger. While I'm sure there are plenty of demons chained to your soul, I do not believe they are about to leap out and devour me whole." Her eyes widened as she gave a little smirk. "I think that rhymes, Mr. Dempsey."

Lucas had no idea how to respond to that, and while he stood in silence, desperate to conjure a witty retort, he heard the faint sound of someone calling his name.

With lightning speed, he moved towards his little sprite, grabbed her by the elbow and pulled her towards the plinth.

"Someone is coming. Now, unless you want to find yourself wed," he glanced back over his shoulder and then continued, "to some doddery old clergyman with the breath of an otter, I suggest you stay behind this plinth." By way of reinforcing his point, he quickly added, "No inducement in the world would ever persuade me to marry. So it's the plinth or the otter, your choice."

CHAPTER 3

Upon hearing the dulcet tones of a feminine voice calling out to Mr. Dempsey, Helena pressed her back against the stone slab and took a deep breath. She would whip Amelia with a birch for putting her in such a predicament.

"Lucas? Lucas? Where are you?"

Mr. Dempsey exhaled and muttered a string of incoherent curses. "I'm over here, Lady Colebrook."

"Oh, Lucas, there you are." Lady Colebrook entered the concealed area and stood on the other side of the statue. "What are you doing out here?" she asked, failing to disguise her accusatory tone, and Helena imagined that her thoughts were occupied by jealousy and suspicion.

"I was waiting for you, of course," Mr. Dempsey replied with just a mild hint of affection.

Lady Colebrook giggled playfully. It was the sound of someone skilled in the art of seduction, someone who knew how to play the game and play it well. "So, now I'm here, what do you intend to do with me?"

Mr. Dempsey snorted. "Fifteen minutes ago, I imagined all sorts of delicious things. Now, I'm afraid you will have to be content with an escort back to the ballroom."

"Oh, Lucas, you're such a tease," Lady Colebrook replied. Helena had a vision of her thrusting out her well-endowed cleavage by way of offering an inducement. "Do you like to see me beg, is that it?"

There was a moment of silence, followed by the soft rustling of silk, a sigh and the smacking of lips. Helena blushed, her face tingling from the sudden rush of blood. Surely, she was not going to have to stand there and listen to them copulate.

Were there no depths to the gentleman's depravity?

"Miranda, please, we can't stay here," he said with a frustrated sigh. "If only you'd found me sooner—we don't have time to—"

Lady Colebrook gave a low, pleasurable hum, the noise conjuring a vision of a cat preening itself and licking its paws. "Oh, Lucas, you do not have to be shy about asking for what you want. You know I would do anything for you."

"No ... Miranda ... I did not mean that."

Struggling to suppress her curiosity, Helena peeked around the plinth to find Lady Colebrook on her knees, her gown gathered up to her waist, as Lucas Dempsey slapped her hand away from the fall of his breeches.

"Get up, Miranda. I said not here." He took hold of her arm and pulled her to her feet. "Good God, woman, you're losing your fruit."

What looked like an over-ripe cherry bounced past the plinth and landed somewhere in the hedge.

"Who cares about a bit of old fruit," Lady Colebrook said as she pressed her hands to her hair. "What's wrong with you? You were not so reticent last night." She brushed the front of her gown, hitting out at the crimson silk for some imagined *faux pas*. "I am beginning to believe you were not waiting for me at all. Perhaps another lady has taken your fancy this evening."

She glanced left and right, up and down, scouring the gigantic hedge for hidden clues like a hawk locating its next victim. When she took a step towards the statue, Helena thought she looked ready to swoop and so sucked in a breath, hoping it would somehow render her invisible.

Lucas Dempsey put his arm out to prevent her from taking another step and pulled her into an embrace.

"Don't be so dramatic." He tapped her playfully on the nose. "What I have in mind cannot be accomplished out here." His eyes scanned hers with a predatory hunger. "I want to lavish you with attention. I want to make you sing with pleasure." While his words lacked sincerity, his voice was smooth and rich and caused the hairs on Helena's nape to tingle. "Come. Let us return to the ball and relish in anticipation of what the night will most surely bring."

She watched him place an arm around a placated Lady Colebrook, splay his hand against her back as they moved to depart.

"I suppose it is a little cold," Lady Colebrook muttered. "I should be grateful that we have managed to steal a moment alone."

"Indeed." He glanced back over his shoulder and offered Helena an arrogant, self-assured smile. "The night has been full of surprises."

Five minutes would be long enough, Helena thought, as she contemplated how long she should wait behind the plinth before attempting to return to the ballroom. All eyes would be on Lucas Dempsey so she doubted anyone would notice her creeping back inside. Those five lonely minutes felt more like an hour and in her boredom she found herself contemplating the character of Mr. Lucas Dempsey.

Contrary to their most recent exchange, Helena would bet a hundred guineas that he didn't even like Lady Colebrook. Of course, there was evidence to support her theory. Both his tone and his stance conveyed a level of disdain he tried his best to hide beneath a veil of arrogance. Other than the most obvious reason, Helena wondered why he chose to entertain Lady Cole-brook at all. When he spoke to his mistress, his words suggested a degree of affection, a degree of unbridled passion. But the emotion behind such words was seriously lacking.

There were moments in *her* brief exchange with him where he unwittingly revealed something of his character, where arrogance gave way to uncertainty and confidence gave way to doubt. Helena did not see it as a flaw. For some strange reason, she saw it as a sign of hope, like a fissure of light in a dark cave; hope there was something brighter and better beyond the cold wall.

Though why she should feel concern for the salvation of Mr. Dempsey's character was a mystery.

While contemplating that conundrum, she heard the pad of footsteps along the path, followed by raised voices. The thought that she may have to listen to another amorous interlude caused her to groan, albeit silently. The argument, however, involved two gentlemen, who were trying to whisper but were possessed by such a level of anger and frustration it was impossible.

"Look. I never said Dempsey would stay in Boston permanently. When I persuaded Harwood to send him away, there was always going to be a chance he would return."

The other man sighed. "I know, I know, but I had convinced myself the matter was dealt with. What if Margaret should say something and it arouses his suspicions? You know how mindless she can be."

"Margaret has not been about in Society for weeks."

"I know. I called around yesterday. Sedgwick informed me she was still in bed with a migraine. But migraines do not last forever. She will soon be up and about and then what will I do?"

"Look, I will deal with Margaret," the other gentleman said with some impatience. "You know she always listens to me." After a brief moment, he added, "But I'll need another five hundred for her silence."

There was a sharp intake of breath. "Five hundred! Look here … you … you cannot blackmail me for the rest of my life. No, you've had all you're going to get out of me."

Helena heard a sinister chuckle, a sound that sent an ice-cold shiver down her spine.

"If that's the way you want to play it. Remember, suffocating your own brother is deemed far more serious a crime than killing a man with a punch. It would not take much to rouse Dempsey's suspicions, and I guarantee the magistrate would be interested to hear my theory as to how Lord Banbury died."

Helena plastered her hand over her mouth to suppress a gasp. Fear coursed through her veins. If they even suspected she was listening, the outcome would be rather more severe than being forced to marry a clergyman with bad breath.

"K-kill Lucas Dempsey and I will pay you a thousand."

His counterpart gave a sly chuckle. "I am not the killer here. But for such an incentive perhaps I could arrange for a small accident, nothing too obvious. Meet me for supper tomorrow, the usual place, and I'll see what can be done."

"And you promise you will talk to Margaret?"

"Yes, yes. You have nothing to fear. As I said, I will deal with Margaret."

When Helena heard their retreating steps, she breathed a sigh of relief.

For fear of stumbling upon another illicit encounter, she decided she should return to the ballroom as quickly as possible and so crept around the plinth and tiptoed towards the path. With a quick peek around the corner, she made her way back to the ballroom sneaking in behind a couple who had just taken a turn about the terrace.

Once safely inside, and her breathing had slowed to a more regulated pace, she acknowledged the severity of the information she had just overheard.

Someone wanted Lucas Dempsey dead and had offered an extortionate amount of money to achieve his goal.

Her wide eyes flitted about the crowd. The men were probably in the ballroom concealed somewhere amongst the guests, smiling and laughing as they devised their devilish plot. They were probably dancing, playing cards, or eating supper with their unsuspecting peers.

Then a thought struck right between the eyes, forcing her to come to an abrupt halt.

She would have to do something. She could not let a murder take place and just stand by idly, even if the intended victim was a disreputable rogue.

Besides, what was the purpose of salvation if not for sinners?

Moving slowly through the crowd, she spotted Amelia gliding around the floor with graceful ease in the company of Lord Claredge. Her face beamed with contentment and showed not the slightest sign of concern for what she had put Helena through.

When the last notes of the longways waltz played themselves out, Lord Claredge gave a rapturous applause, as he regularly forgot he was in town and not at a provincial assembly, much to the embarrassment of his dancing partner. While some looked at him with a frown, others accepted the mishap with joviality and patted Claredge on the back, as though he was feeble-minded and somewhat different from normal people.

In a desperate bid to rid herself of him, Amelia bobbed a quick curtsy and scurried back through the crush towards Helena.

"Mother is looking for you, and she is not happy," Amelia informed with some satisfaction in an attempt to detract from her own feelings of mortification. "She is wearing a permanent pout, as though she's accidentally eaten a slice of lemon and is too polite to spit it out." With a demanding tilt of the chin, she added, "Where on earth have you been?"

Helena wanted to say she had been in a secluded corner of the garden with Lucas Dempsey; that would soon wipe the smirk off her sister's face. Perhaps she could say she had listened to him cavort with his mistress while men plotted his murder.

"I have been looking for you," Helena replied, deciding it was best not to reveal such information to a consummate gossip.

"Mother insisted we impress ourselves upon all the eligible gentlemen, but I can see you do not need my help. After your dance with Lord Claredge, there's not a man in the room who doesn't know who you are."

Amelia huffed, but as she searched the crowd her countenance changed. "Perhaps I should be thanking Lord Claredge," she countered haughtily, "as it is not only the eligible gentlemen whose attention I've captured."

Helena followed her sister's gaze across the ballroom to the ominous figure of Lucas Dempsey. Standing with his arms folded across his broad chest and one hand supporting his sculptured jaw, he studied them with a level of focus and intensity Helena found a little disconcerting.

"Perhaps it's not wise to let him know he has an effect on you," Helena said, struggling to understand why her own face burned. "It is always best to be subtle about such matters, even if the recipient is a notorious rake."

"You're right," Amelia replied, affecting an exaggerated laugh and extending her neck majestically like a swan about to spread its wings.

Helena sighed. There was no hope for her sister. Not when character was at the bottom of the list of attributes she sought in a gentleman.

"Tell me, Helena, is he still staring?"

Someone could have placed a hood over Helena's head, and still she would have known that the answer was yes. Perhaps her awareness of him was heightened by the threat of impending danger.

"Yes, he is still staring. Talking of Mr. Dempsey, I wonder if he finds it difficult living with Viscount Harwood after having been away for so long?" Helena asked and then waited for the wheels of the gossip cart to start turning.

Amelia laughed and gave her sister a little tap on the arm with her fan. "I doubt it," she replied, "Mr. Dempsey refused to stay with the viscount. It has something to do with him vowing never to step foot in the house again."

Feigning surprise, Helena added, "Don't tell me he has taken a house next door to Lady Colebrook?"

"Of course not," Amelia replied indignantly. "Millicent says he has taken a house on Mount Street."

Helena gave a dismissive wave of the hand. "You can't believe everything Millicent tells you," she sneered and waited for her sister to nibble the bait with all the naivety of a brown trout.

Desperate to prove her point, for when one has the reputation of a gossip integrity is everything, Amelia said, "He has taken the house next to Lord Marshbrook if you must know. Number fifty-eight to be precise. You can ask Lady Marshbrook if you don't believe me."

Helena smiled and patted herself on the back for a job well done. "No, no, I believe you," she consented as she wondered when would be the best time to call on Lucas Dempsey.

CHAPTER 4

As a man who rarely declined the offer of warm arms and cushioned thighs, Lucas Dempsey stood at the foot of Miranda Colebrook's bed, his fingers entangled in the folds of his cravat, and froze.

The sight of his mistress swathed in a silk sheet, her eager eyes fixated on his every movement, her golden hair splayed with careless abandon across the pillow, should have caused a rush of desire. He should have been tearing at his clothes in a desperate bid to satisfy his throbbing manhood, instead of untying every knot and fold with the vitality of a man in his dotage.

"Oh, Lucas. You will insist on teasing me," Miranda said with a soft purr as she stretched her limbs to expose the curve of her breasts. "I believe you enjoy making me wait."

The creamy-white flesh failed to whet his appetite, and he wondered if he was suffering from some strange malady. His stomach felt empty and hollow, and an icy chill had penetrated his bones. Even the most vital part of his anatomy seemed detached and unresponsive.

There had been no problem earlier in the evening when he'd dallied with his dainty woodland creature. On the contrary, the sight of her heated his blood until he feared he might cook from the inside out. He'd spent the rest of the evening wondering if the lips of a faerie tasted as sweet as honey and if her hands had a magical touch that could soothe his soul.

"Oh, Lucas, do stop dithering."

Lucas massaged his face with the palm of his hand to clear his head, but the thought of burying himself in Miranda Colebrook's vacuous body brought on a bout of nausea.

"I do not feel well," he said, rubbing his eyes with the pads of his fingers before bending down to pick up his crumpled coat.

Miranda sat bolt upright and, disregarding all modesty, scrambled to the end of the bed. "You're not leaving?" she said, reaching out to touch him.

He stepped back, leaving her hand hanging limply in the air. "I'm afraid that I must."

"Perhaps if you were to lie down for a moment," Miranda suggested. There was a sense of panic evident in her tone, and she wiggled forward to grab his hand. "I'm sure I know just the thing to soothe your ailments."

"No." Lucas recoiled. "That would not be wise."

With pursed lips and a raised brow, Miranda slumped back down onto the bed. "If you don't want me then just say so. There is nothing more pathetic than a man who cannot speak his mind." She snatched the sheet and wrapped it around her naked body in protest. "Just because you have a face women swoon over, doesn't give you the right to treat me in such a manner. There *are* other handsome men, you know."

Miranda Colebrook could not have said anything more damning.

Lucas sneered as he shrugged into his coat. "How foolish of me. I thought it was my character you held in such high regard." He marched over to the door. "We have used each other, Miranda, but I'm done with it."

"If you leave, I won't have you back." She rushed to the top of the landing and shouted down the stairs. "Do you hear me? If you walk out of that door, don't come back."

Some hours later, roused by a constant tapping on his bedchamber door, Lucas raised his head in an attempt to ascertain the time. He could not have been asleep for more than a few hours, but when the rhythmical beating failed to cease, he shouted, "For goodness sake, Jenson, come in."

His valet opened the door and peered round before creeping in on the balls of his feet, as though the movement conveyed his remorse. "Forgive me, sir. I know you do not like to be disturbed but—"

"Then why are you knocking on my door?"

Jenson shuffled, shifting his weight from one foot to the other. "It's the lady, sir. Gregson tried to stop her, but she just barged right past him."

Lucas sat up, clenched his jaw and raised a brow to show his disappointment. "What's the point of having rules when no one can seem to follow them?" His tone conveyed his frustration. "Ladies are not to be permitted without prior arrangement." From experience, he knew it would be one lady today and three tomorrow, all intent on dabbling in the delights of cardinal sin. "Who is she?"

Jenson shrugged, which was not considered an appropriate gesture for a valet. "She refused to say. She just insisted she had something important to discuss, and it couldn't wait."

The art of conversation was usually the last thing on the minds of the ladies who were at liberty to call on him. "You can tell Gregson I am not pleased. I am not pleased at all. We shall most certainly be having words." Lucas dragged his hand down his face. "What does this lady look like?"

Jenson scratched his head. "Well, I don't rightly know."

Anyone would have thought he'd been asked to name the books of the Bible and recite them backwards. "You have eyes, Jenson," Lucas groaned. "Is she fair or dark, plump or slim? It is not a difficult question."

Jenson thought for a moment. "Her hair is fair, like straw."

"Straw!" Lucas suppressed a grin. "One is supposed to say it's golden like the sun or something of a similar vein." He doubted Miranda would be pleased with his valet's assessment. "You must tell her I am not at home, that I had an important meeting at eleven and won't be back for hours. Can you do that?"

Jenson bit down on his lower lip. "But it's only nine, sir."

"Nine o'clock! In the morning?" Obviously, Miranda couldn't wait to berate him for leaving her alone and unsatisfied. "Then just tell her the meeting was at ten and I have already left."

"She won't believe me, sir," Jenson implored looking a little terrified. "When Gregson called me to see if you were available, the lady said ... well, I should not really repeat it."

"Just tell me what she said, Jenson."

Jenson took a step back, his stance rigid as though he was expecting Lucas to throw a boot at him or some other equally hard object. "The lady said she has found Amelia and that ... that unless your demons have chained you to the bedpost, she expects to see you downstairs in ten minutes."

Jenson was nearly blown over by the sudden gust of wind as Lucas threw back the coverlet with lightning speed and bounded over to the window. "Quick, hand me my clothes," he snapped as he pulled the curtains aside and looked down at the street below.

It was a dull, dreary day. The buildings, the horses, and the people were all like faint shadows obscured by a blanket of thick fog. A man would be lucky to see his hand in front of his face, let alone an unaccompanied woman wandering the streets. While he admired such an ingenious plan to avoid recognition, a feeling of irritation surfaced, which simmered into annoyance, bubbled into anger.

What if a scout from the rookeries was out looking for an easy target? She could have been abducted. She could have disappeared from the street never to be seen or heard from again.

It was while he was fastening his coat, for he had dismissed Jenson for being far too slow, that he felt his heart racing, the hard thud of anger replaced with a sort of light-hearted skipping. For the majority of people, such an event would hardly cause notice. But for a man who had locked the vulnerable organ in an iron chest, spent years strapping it tightly with chains, securing it with the sturdiest of locks, it was something of an awakening. Even as he made his way downstairs, the playful beats continued to cause a rather odd tickling sensation in his stomach.

After taking a deep breath, he entered the parlour to find the lady in question sitting in the wingback chair next to the fireplace, her gloved hands resting demurely in her lap. Having removed her pink bonnet, she attempted to straighten the golden curls of what was obviously a wig.

"Mr. Dempsey," she said by way of a greeting but did not offer her name. "I see you've managed to break free from your shackles at long last. I have been waiting for fifteen minutes."

Lucas bowed and suppressed a grin, for he admired directness in all things. "Forgive me. I find that I am not so nimble in the mornings. Have you been offered some refreshment?"

"When I declined the offer of tea and asked for a nip of sherry, your man nearly expired on the spot." She put her hand to her mouth and chuckled. "He is probably swooning in the hallway as we speak."

Lucas raised a curious brow. "Sherry? At nine o'clock in the morning?" he said, and then it occurred to him one should expect faerie folk to be unconventional.

"It is so cold out," she said, looking at him directly, "and a lady needs courage when entering the lair of a dragon."

"The lair of a dragon," he repeated, curious as to her choice of words. He wanted to say that the touch of his lips would sear her skin. That one lash of his tongue would cause a fire in a far more intriguing place. "Well, I have been known to bite."

He stood there gaping, his hands clasped firmly behind his back. What on earth was she doing visiting the home of an unmarried gentleman? While pondering the question, his mind scrambled to classify the character of the lady in front of him.

Even though she enjoyed teasing him, there was nothing coquettish about her manner. It was as though she assumed he could not possibly be interested in her, which in itself was a highly attractive quality.

He considered her pink dress, embroidered with pretty poppies; the jade-green walking boots that encased the tiniest feet and the matching Spencer jacket whose hues enhanced the vibrancy of her eyes to perfection. She appeared as dainty and as delicate as a doll. Yet her character posed an intriguing contradiction, for she was strong-willed, determined and not the least bit superficial.

There was something ethereal about her, something earthy, something bewitching.

"You appear to have an obsession with mythical creatures," he found himself saying with amusement. "One's obsessions can often reveal much of one's character."

She sat back in the chair, her gaze challenging. "And what, pray, does such an obsession reveal about mine?"

It was rare to meet a woman who was interested in his opinion.

"May I?" he asked gesturing to the sofa. With her permission, he sat down and draped his arm along the back in a languid motion. "In our brief association, you have mentioned both demons and dragons as a point of reference. It tells me that you feel the need to speak your mind and use such analogies so as not to offend. By suggesting I share a similarity with devilish creatures, you convey a preoccupation with morality, a disdain for shallowness and frivolity. It may surprise you to hear that I believe you also yearn for adventure. You yearn to experience all the world has to offer—as one does not align their thoughts with the imaginary unless one secretly dreams of breaking free from constraint."

She gasped. "How observant of you," she said, her face

alight with pleasure. "I believe you have impressed me, Mr. Dempsey."

"Oh, I always aim to please," he drawled, his voice heavy with promise.

"Indeed," she replied, showing not the slightest sign his words had any effect on her. "It is my preoccupation with morality that has brought me here this morning."

Lucas laughed. "You have obviously put yourself at great risk in coming here," he said, casting a questionable look over her straw-like wig. "But I'm afraid there is no hope for me. I am beyond saving, Miss—?"

"Miss Ecclestone," she informed with a nod. "Miss Helena Ecclestone."

Oh, God, Helena!

He imagined panting those words in the throes of passion, imagined his little nymph writhing beneath him, clutching at his shoulders screaming *to hell with morality*.

Shifting in his seat to alleviate his aching manhood, he mentally chastised himself for having such lurid thoughts. He was not about to ruin an innocent—well, not unless she begged and somehow he could not imagine Miss Ecclestone begging for anything.

"As difficult as it may be," she began in a solemn tone. "You must listen carefully to what I am about to say. Whether you choose to accept it or not, I am here to save you, Mr. Dempsey."

The thought that she was one of those preacher types dampened his desire considerably, but when he opened his mouth to speak, she raised her hand to silence him.

"Last night, after you left the garden with Lady Colebrook, I waited there for a while just to be sure I would not be noticed. It was then, while hiding behind the hedge, I overheard two gentlemen arguing about you."

Lucas sat up and shuffled to the edge of his seat, his intense gaze focused on Miss Ecclestone. "Go on," he said, his tone conveying the point that he was suddenly more than interested in what she had to say. He sensed that behind her calm facade, she was grinning with smug satisfaction.

"One of the gentlemen, I'm afraid I don't know their names, said that *he* had persuaded Harwood to send you to Boston, and there was always a possibility you would return."

A hard lump formed in Lucas' throat and pulsated against his skin desperate to burst free. "Go on," he snapped, but then modified his tone. "Please continue, Miss Ecclestone."

"The other gentleman was worried someone named Margaret might say something that would arouse your suspicions."

"My suspicions about what?" Lucas interrupted, exhaling deeply as he brushed his hand through his hair.

Miss Ecclestone pursed her lips and threw her hands up. "I don't know. One gentleman has been paying the other large sums of money and has refused to pay any more. It became quite heated. The man responded by suggesting that suffocating one's brother was a far more serious crime than killing someone with a punch. He said the magistrate would be interested to hear his theory as to how Lord Banbury died."

Lucas sank back into the sofa and rubbed his face with his hands, his mind frantically trying to piece together the fragments of information. Someone had persuaded his father to send him away to Boston, and Margaret knew the gentlemen involved.

"Thank you for bringing this to my attention, Miss Ecclestone." He sighed. "Please, allow me to instruct my coachman to see you safely home."

There was a brief look of pity on her face, a look rarely expressed in his company. "That is not the end of the conversation, Mr. Dempsey." She took a deep breath. "I'm … I'm afraid they want to kill you and plan to devise some sort of accident in order to accomplish the task."

Lucas shot to his feet.

"Bloody hell! I knew I should have stayed in Boston." He paced the floor, unsure what to do, back and forth, back and forth, his mind too jumbled to think coherently. "Forgive me. I did not mean to curse." He pressed the side of his temple in an attempt to stop the pounding. He should never have come back. He should have known it would bring nothing but trouble.

"Is everything all right, Mr. Dempsey? Is there anything I can do to help?" Miss Ecclestone's melodic tone seemed to penetrate the chaos, the sweet sound like a lover's soft caress. As he turned around she was standing in front of him, her face marred with concern. "I did not mean to cause you any distress."

"You're not the one causing distress, Miss Ecclestone," he said, attempting to gain some clarity. She placed her hand lightly on his arm: an innocent gesture that expressed a level of sympathy, but he felt desire shoot through him like a bolt through the heart. "I find your presence calms the soul," he added. Well, the words tumbled out of his mouth, yet he had no recollection of forming them.

With bright eyes and a peachy pout she looked up at him, and he saw honesty, purity, and divinity. And he wanted to feel it, wanted to taste it, wanted to lose himself in all that goodness —just once.

In a movement as sudden as it was swift, he pulled Miss Ecclestone to his chest, knowing that in doing so he was committing himself to the fiery pits of hell for all eternity.

"Mr. Dempsey," she gasped.

"My dear, Miss Ecclestone," he whispered as he lowered his mouth to hers. "When you enter the lair of a dragon you must expect to get a little burnt."

CHAPTER 5

The feel of her soft, innocent lips proved everything he hoped it would be and more, much more.

Surprisingly, she offered little resistance, letting him plunder her hot, wet mouth, letting him coax and tease until her tiny hands fluttered up to grasp the lapels of his coat. Spurred on by an urgency he could not control, he delved deeper, his hands cupping her face, his thumbs stroking her cheekbones with a level of tenderness that usually played no part in such a lascivious act.

With her sweet body pressed against his, he felt her nervous shiver and somewhere in a dark and dusty corner of his mind he knew he should stop. Yet the sweet taste of innocence surged through his veins like a powerful tonic, healing, strengthening and restoring. When he heard her enchanting little sigh, he felt as though he could conquer the world.

With a loud gasp, Miss Ecclestone tore her lips from his. "I believe that is quite enough, Mr. Dempsey," she said, placing a gloved hand on her chest as she took a few deep breaths.

With his body still racked with desire, he lowered his head once more, his lips drawn to hers by a mysterious force. "I have only just begun."

She took a step back, forcing him to straighten. "I have allowed you a certain degree of liberty, sir," she said, her gaze meeting his as she regained her composure, "on account that you have received some very distressing news and, as such, your actions may be excused as irrational."

As Lucas tried to form a response, he was aware that the movement of his mouth resembled that of a fish gasping for air.

What was she saying?

That she'd not enjoyed the feel of his lips, that she didn't appreciate the skill and mastery required to entice such an eager response? Did she not feel the same level of arousal, the same burning desire thrumming through her veins?

It was most peculiar, most odd.

"If that's the sort of sacrifice one makes to ease an irrational mind," he mocked, feeling a strange sense of rejection. "What would you be prepared to do if you thought me deranged?"

Miss Ecclestone shook her head as though looking at a spoilt child throwing a tantrum. "Do not be so downcast, sir. I merely said I understand the reason behind the act. I never said I did not enjoy the experience. On the contrary, I find your approach far superior," she said, showing no sign of embarrassment as she cast him a satisfied smile.

With his masculine pride restored, he found himself wondering how she had come to that conclusion. Not that he was superior, he knew that to be true, but what other experiences had she drawn on to make the comparison?

An odd feeling rose up from his stomach and settled in the middle of his chest, leaving him desperate to know how many other men she'd kissed. Who were they? What were their names and what were their intentions?

Her voice woke him from his reverie. "I do not know what you intend to do about the matter," she began. Then noticing his wide-eyed expression, clarified, "I am referring to the subject of murder, Mr. Dempsey, not of our kiss. But I would appreciate it if you do not mention I was the one who informed you of the plot." Moving to the side table, she picked up her bonnet and placed it on her head.

"You're not leaving?" he mumbled, not knowing why he found the thought so distressing. "You said you'd come here to save me."

Looking a little confused, she said, "Have I not just told you that someone wants to kill you? Surely, you don't expect me to grab a bayonet and stand guard at your door."

What he did next was probably the rudest, most inappropriate thing he had ever done to a respectable young lady.

He walked over to Miss Ecclestone and placing both hands on her shoulders pushed her towards the sofa and forced her to sit down. Then he yanked her bonnet from her head, and in the process of being heavy-handed managed to pull her wig off, too.

"Mr. Dempsey!" she cried, tidying and patting down the brown locks he found much more comely. "I find your manner highly offensive."

With a small stab of guilt, he brushed the comment aside. "Forgive me, Miss Ecclestone. I am irrational, remember, bordering on deranged." He walked over to the chair and threw himself down. "You cannot come here and tell me my father was coerced into sending me away. Tell me men want to kill me, tell me I have been living under a misconception for the past four years, one that has dramatically altered the course of my life. You cannot expect to walk out as though you've said nothing other than divulge the recipe for shortbread biscuits."

He threw his arms open asking her to defy his logic.

She sat there gaping at him and then narrowed her gaze and asked, "What misconception?"

Lucas sighed and raked his hand through his hair. "Margaret was Lord Banbury's wife. The wife of the man I killed with a single punch." He waited for a reaction, for a gasp or a look of horror, but when she held the same inquisitive expression, he knew she was already aware of the fact. "Lord Banbury accused me of being on intimate terms with her and felt the need to reclaim his dignity."

Lucas had not spoken of the event since that fateful day. There were times when he was alone, and the house was silent, that he could still hear the jeers of the crowd ringing in his ears. To be considered handsome was to be considered conceited. It had taken nothing more than a glance at his face for the crowd to deem him guilty.

"When I accepted the challenge," he continued, "I did not know it would be a fight to the death."

"So you were merely defending yourself?"

"Of course! I avoided numerous punches before throwing the blow that rendered him unconscious."

Miss Ecclestone brought her finger to her lips and began patting in silent contemplation. "The consensus must have been that you were innocent, as you have never been charged with a crime."

"Not in the legal sense. Society played judge and jury, Miss Ecclestone. My father donned his black cap and delivered the sentence himself." He could not suppress the bitter edge to his tone, and he gave a disdainful snort. "I shall never forget his ice-cold stare when he called me into his study to inform me that Banbury had died in his bed, to inform me I was a murderer."

Miss Ecclestone's eyes widened. "You mean to say Lord Banbury was at home when he died?" There was a moment of silence while he waited for her to piece together the relevant bits of information. "I am sure you have already come to the same conclusion," she said with a serious expression. "But considering the conversation I overheard in the garden, I do not believe you killed Lord Banbury. Someone else must have murdered him in his bed that night."

Hearing her say the words caused a warm feeling to rise from his stomach and flood his chest. "I'm inclined to agree with you," he replied, his mood growing melancholic as he wondered what he'd done to deserve such condemnation from men he barely knew. He was staring into his lap, contemplating past events when he heard Miss Ecclestone clear her throat.

"I have decided I will help you, Mr. Dempsey, though I do not know what use I can be."

Oh, he could think of a million and one ways she could be of use to him, none of them respectable, of course.

"Thank you, Miss Ecclestone," he said, aware that the warmth in his chest was now migrating in a southerly direction. "The first thing we must do is discover the identity of the gentlemen you heard in Lady Colebrook's garden. It's fair to assume one of them is the current Lord Banbury, his predecessor's brother. Only then can we begin to devise some sort of plan to gain an admission of guilt."

And a plan to ruin all those concerned, he added silently.

"Perhaps we could persuade Margaret to make a statement with the magistrate," she said with a level of optimism.

"We must do nothing to alert their attention," he replied, beginning to feel apprehensive about involving Miss Ecclestone. It seemed the overwhelming desire to spend more time in her company overrode all reasoning. "Perhaps it would be best if I dealt with the matter myself," he said reluctantly. "If these men have a mind to murder, then I do not wish to put you in any danger."

She scoffed. "I'm afraid it is too late, Mr. Dempsey. I am already committed to your cause. The defamation of one's character is an unforgivable crime that must be punished." There was a slight hesitation, the first sign of self-doubt and she added, "Unless you think me incapable of helping you."

His gaze drifted slowly over her lithe form, settling on her soft lips and his mouth curved into a half grin. "I believe you capable of anything you put your mind to, Miss Ecclestone."

"Good." She gave a confidant nod. "Should Lord Banbury make an appearance at Lady Mendleson's ball tonight, I shall watch him carefully to see if I can ascertain the name of his counterpart."

Forming a frown, he said, "Should Lord Banbury ask you to dance, you must not say anything to arouse his suspicion."

Miss Ecclestone laughed; the melodic sound was as soothing as a gentle breeze on a hot summer's day. "Gentlemen do not ask me to dance, Mr. Dempsey. Or if they do, they rarely ask a second time." She gave a little shrug, suggesting she was not the least bit concerned by it.

"Why ever not?" he said with a look of bewilderment. He could think of nothing he would rather do than hold her in his arms and feel the warmth radiate from her body, feel the brush of silk against his legs as he led her around the floor. "Is there something about you I have failed to notice?"

Her gaze suddenly sharpened, and she considered him with keen interest. She strummed her fingers on her mouth, her brows drawn together as if contemplating a complex mathematical puzzle. Lucas was so absorbed in watching her that when she spoke he almost jumped from the chair.

"I shall make a deal with you, Mr. Dempsey," she said suddenly, placing her hands in her lap as her mouth curved into a mischievous grin.

It was not wise to make a deal with the Devil.

"I shall answer your question honestly and completely," she continued. "However, in return, you must allow me to ask one of my own and consequently afford me the same courtesy."

Intrigued by her proposal, he found he could not refuse. After all, what could she possibly want to ask him that he wouldn't be happy to answer? "Very well," he began, but she raised her hand by way of a caution.

"Before you accept, you must understand something," she said, her disposition suddenly rather stern. "Honesty is extremely important to me. Without honesty, there can be no trust. Everyone makes mistakes, Mr. Dempsey, and more often than not they are easily rectified. However, once the bonds of trust are broken they are beyond repair."

Feeling a slight sense of trepidation, he immediately shook it off.

What could she possibly want to know about him that he was not willing to divulge? Did he prefer fencing or boxing? Strawberries or blackberries? Perhaps she was interested in something a little more topical and wondered what he thought about the Missouri Compromise, or if he felt it was wrong not to hang all the Cato Street conspirators.

"I understand, Miss Ecclestone," he said, overcome with an eagerness to use their deal to ask his own probing questions. "I agree to your terms."

She nodded respectfully but looked thoroughly pleased with herself. He wondered if *she* was a devil in disguise and he was the one who had just pledged his soul.

"All this talking has left me a little parched," she said, putting a hand to her throat.

Lucas shot to his feet. "Forgive me. I am not accustomed to entertaining at home," he said, looking for a drinks tray. It was the first time he'd been in the room since moving in. Spotting it on the far wall, he walked over to the side table and examined the silver labels before pulling the stopper from a decanter. "No sherry, I'm afraid. Will port do?"

She nodded, and he poured two glasses, wondering if thirst was the motive or rather nerves. He offered one to Miss Ecclestone and watched with keen interest as she took a small sip. It was barely enough to wet her lips.

Taking two large sips himself, he sat back in the chair. "You were about to tell me the reason gentlemen do not ask you to dance," he reminded her.

"Oh, yes," she said, holding the glass in her lap. "There's more than one reason. Would you care to hear them all?" When he inclined his head, she continued, "First of all, it could not have escaped your notice that I am extremely direct in my observations. Gentlemen do not like to be corrected on their deportment or have a lady disagree with them. Even regarding such trivial matters as the weather." When he looked at her with some curiosity, she added, "Fog and mist are not at all the same thing, Mr. Dempsey."

Lucas nodded. "I believe mist reduces visibility by a lesser degree," he replied, for he was equally pedantic about such things.

"Precisely," she beamed with a sigh of relief. "Also, my mother is fond of forcing the hand, so to speak, and often says the most inappropriate things to encourage a prospective suitor." Again observing his expression, she added with a raised brow, "She once informed a gentleman that, with a little more meat on my bones, I would be fit for rearing."

Lucas coughed into his fist to hide his amusement. "I agree. That is highly inappropriate." It was a good thing he didn't give a fig for what her parents thought of him. "Is there any other reason?" he asked, hoping there were five hundred as he was enjoying himself immensely. So much so, he had almost forgotten men were plotting to murder him.

"There is another reason," she said. Again he saw a flicker of self-doubt, sensed a nervous edge to her tone. "I do not stand a chance of attracting attention when in the company of my sister, Amelia." She breathed a sigh as though it had been a difficult thing to say and he decided he admired her a little more for it. "She is extremely beautiful, and well, I'm sure you understand."

Lucas moved to the edge of his seat as he had a personal interest in the answer to his next question. "Do you wish you looked like her? Do you wish you turned heads wherever you went?"

She smiled; a sweet springtime sort of smile that lit up her eyes and gave one hope for new beginnings.

"That is another question, Mr. Dempsey," she teased. "But I'm happy to answer if you're prepared to acknowledge I now have two questions to ask." When he nodded, she asked, "Are you sure you want me to answer?" He nodded again, and her gaze skimmed over his face, lingered on his mouth and dimpled chin. "Everyone wants to be loved and admired, Mr. Dempsey, but the simple answer is no. There are things I value more. I value strength of character, integrity, loyalty, intelligence. So, no, I do not wish I looked like Amelia."

He had a sudden urge to tell her she was beautiful, that she had a natural warmth he had never encountered before. That she was intelligent and honest and amusing and bewitching and a whole host of other attributes he could name. He wanted to tell her no other woman had ever roused his interest. He wanted to tell her she was a shining light in a world full of hopeless cynics.

"So, Mr. Dempsey, we come back to the original point. I doubt Lord Banbury will ask me to dance."

Struggling with a range of unnerving feelings and having a desperate need to prolong her visit, he said, "Would you care to ask me a question?"

She stood, and he followed. Patting down her hair, she picked up the wig and arranged it on her head before putting on her bonnet and tying the ribbons. "I think I will save my questions for another time. But thank you, Mr. Dempsey, for an enlightening morning." Pushing her fingers securely into her gloves, she added, "I will do everything I can to help you clear your name."

If only she would have walked into his life four years ago. How different things could have been.

"I cannot allow you to walk home, Miss Ecclestone. Gregson will escort you to the mews, and my coachman will take you wherever you need to go."

She accepted his offer with a smile and an inclination of the head.

Having given Gregson instructions, he followed her out into the hall. "Perhaps I may see you this evening at the Mendlesons." He suppressed his enthusiasm and kept his tone neutral.

"I am sure you will," she replied, "but I doubt we'll have a chance to speak. We have not been formally introduced. If I discover anything of any importance, I shall send you a note. Good day, Mr. Dempsey."

He bowed. "Good day, Miss Ecclestone," he said as she walked away from him without the customary glance back he was used to.

He would move heaven and earth to speak to her tonight, and woe betide anyone who tried to stop him.

CHAPTER 6

"What an unusual headband." Amelia stared down her nose at the golden laurel wreath threaded through Helena's hair. "I do not recall seeing it before."

"I bought it this morning," Helena replied as they made their way into the Mendlesons' ballroom. "It's from the new haberdashery in the Burlington Arcade."

Mr. Dempsey's coachman had dropped her at the Piccadilly entrance, and she walked back to her parents' house on Grafton Street.

"You look different," Amelia said, examining Helena's stylish coiffure. "You look more radiant. Like you're actually pleased to be here."

Helena *had* taken more care with her appearance, believing it the best way to attract Lord Banbury's attention in the hope of him asking her to dance. "I'm never pleased to be paraded around the room like a lamb on market day."

"Well, you seem intent on catching someone's eye." Amelia made a weird snort and nodded towards the sea of crushed bodies. "Although I expect your cheerful mood is about to turn sour."

"My girls, my girls," their mother chirped, her gloved hands clasped to her bosom as she greeted them with a smile that had taken hours to sculpt. "You shall be the toast of the ball this evening," she continued, looking with admiration at Amelia's perfect pout and dazzling blue eyes. She turned to Helena, her gaze flitting to the new headband. "Is that what you bought this morning?" she asked with a grim expression. "The style is so last Season, Helena. But it's too late to do anything about it now. It is my fault for not being at home to help you dress."

"How is Aunt Augusta?" Helena asked, ignoring her mother's fussing. Aunt Augusta recently discovered that her husband had fathered an illegitimate child, some twenty years earlier.

"Downright miserable," her mother moaned. "I do not know why she makes such a fuss. Half the men with titles are probably the sons of grooms and footmen. She should be grateful that Henry is a respected member of Society, instead of mithering him about silly things such as trust and fidelity." She gave a look that suggested the world had gone mad, and she was the only sane person in it.

"I think I could tolerate anything as long as my husband was handsome," Amelia added dreamily, oblivious to their mother's disapproving glare. "And I believe I have the perfect gentleman in mind."

Helena followed her sister's hungry gaze to the striking figure of Lucas Dempsey, who stood at the top of the stairs with his brother, Viscount Harwood. It crossed her mind to offer Amelia a handkerchief as excessive salivating was not considered an attractive quality.

As he scanned the crowd, Mr. Dempsey smiled when he noticed them, and for some unfathomable reason, Helena's heart skipped a beat.

"Did you see that?" Amelia cried, pulling down her bodice to reveal another inch of bare flesh. "Mr. Dempsey looked directly at me. Oh, I should be thanking Lord Claredge for his mishap. I may even applaud the orchestra myself this evening." She patted her hands together as though rehearsing for the event.

Their mother interrupted Amelia's musing. "Mr. Dempsey is not a respectable gentleman, Amelia. You must stay away from him." Her nose was stuck so high in the air she was in danger of catching her nostril on the chandelier.

Amelia gave a sulky pout. "It's not fair. Practically all the respectable gentlemen are either bald or portly." She sighed before glancing back to Mr. Dempsey. "Does that mean we must also stay away from Viscount Harwood?"

"Of course not, you silly goose. He is a viscount and a respected gentleman. He cannot be held accountable for the sins of his brother. If that were the case, we'd all be locked up in Newgate."

"Good," Amelia said, flapping her hands as she struggled to keep her feet on the floor, "because the crowd has parted, and they are both heading this way."

Helena watched Lucas Dempsey approach.

There was something different about his manner, something so opposed to the relaxed attitude he demonstrated in the privacy of his home. There, he had been amusing, unpretentious and had responded to her with a level of intelligence she had not expected. Yet under the scrutiny of Society's upper circles, he exuded an insolent arrogance, his predatory expression suggesting he would take a bite out of anyone who dared to step in his way.

"Mrs. Ecclestone, what a pleasure it is to see you again," Viscount Harwood said as both gentlemen offered a graceful bow.

Forced to swallow her irritation, her mother did what most people in Society did when faced with an awkward situation: she hid her true feelings and demonstrated impeccable manners cultivated from a life of highborn breeding. "Viscount Harwood. It is always a pleasure to see you."

Helena looked past the viscount's soft features straight into the discerning gaze of Mr. Dempsey. Convinced he must be staring at something specific, she pushed an imagined tendril behind her ear and brushed her cheek with the back of her hand.

"You know my brother, of course, Mr. Lucas Dempsey," Viscount Harwood said. "He was just reminding me that he has not seen you since the Radley soiree, some four years ago." When her mother raised a curious brow, the viscount added, "When Lord Radley discovered his wife had secretly substituted his brandy for tea."

Faced with no choice other than to acknowledge Mr. Dempsey for fear of offending the viscount, her mother smiled. "Mr. Dempsey," she said with skilled artifice. "How nice it is to see you again." There was a long pause, and when both gentlemen glanced at the matron's companions she was obliged to ask, "Have either of you gentlemen met my daughters?"

Helena took a peek at Mr. Dempsey, and while his face remained expressionless, there was a glint of amusement in his piercing blue eyes.

Their mother swallowed visibly, and as they curtsied, she informed, "This is my eldest, Miss Helena Ecclestone and her darling sister, Amelia."

Both gentlemen inclined their heads respectfully, and as the orchestra played the first few strains of a waltz, Lucas Dempsey was the first to step forward.

In an attempt to disguise her distress their mother blinked rapidly, accompanied by the tell-tale trembling lip that always preceded a disapproving reprimand. Before giving him an opportunity to open his mouth, she blurted, "I'm afraid Amelia will not be dancing this evening, Mr. Dempsey, as she has hurt her foot. A silly little accident on the stairs as we arrived."

Amelia let out a muffled screech in protest, the sound similar to a kitten mewling.

"It is terribly painful, as you can hear."

Mr. Dempsey shook his head. "That is a shame," he declared. "My brother will be so disappointed. I, on the other hand, hope Miss Helena Ecclestone will be happy to accompany *me*."

"I would be delighted, Mr. Dempsey," Helena said, offering her hand before her mother could snatch it back. She even took a moment to peek at Amelia's thunderous expression, suppressing the need to gloat.

Fifty pairs of eyes followed them as they walked out onto the floor. Helena's cheeks flushed as she usually had to stamp on people's toes to get their attention. Then she felt his hand settle on her waist. A shiver of awareness fluttered through her body as he flexed his fingers.

His mouth curved into a satisfied grin. "You will get used to it," he said, and for a moment she thought he meant the feel of his hot palm. "No doubt they are all wondering why you have decided to dance with a murderer."

"We both know you're not a murderer," she said. "Besides, I won't need to get used to it. As I told you, gentlemen rarely ask me to dance a second time."

He looked down at her, his blue eyes drifting over her hair, her face, lingering on the low-cut neckline of her gown. "I have never been considered conventional, Miss Ecclestone. My tastes are different from those of other men, at least, they are now."

It was odd how the richness of his voice caused the hairs on her nape to tingle, but she pushed the thought aside. "I suppose you *will* have to dance with me a second time as I've not had a chance to observe Lord Banbury."

"If I am not mistaken, Lord Banbury is standing to the left of the alcove, scowling at my back. Do let me know if you see a dagger flying my way."

"I cannot see past your broad shoulders," Helena complained, unable to stretch too far for fear of falling out of step.

"Is that a compliment, Miss Ecclestone?" he asked, twirling her around with such ease that her feet came clean off the floor, leaving her somewhat giddy. "Or is it the fact you're wearing slippers?"

"It's the slippers," she groaned. "But you do have excessively broad shoulders." She caught his amused grin and felt a sudden urge to offer a real compliment, a compliment about something other than the way he looked. "And you are an exceptional dancer. I feel as if I am floating."

With an arrogant curve of the lip, he warned, "Dancing is a prelude to seduction, Miss Ecclestone. Naturally, I'm exceptional."

Her stomach performed a little somersault forcing her to suck in a breath.

Being inquisitive by nature, she observed how easily he commanded the floor. Yet the steps were predictable, rehearsed. They claimed he had seduced many women although she doubted it involved any real sentiment.

"And will you attempt to seduce *me*, Mr. Dempsey?" Helena asked, not the least bit embarrassed as she knew the only feeling she roused in men was irritation.

Lucas Dempsey laughed loudly, much to the annoyance of the couple on their right, as the distraction caused the gentleman to miscalculate his timing. "Is that to be one of your questions, Miss Ecclestone?" he replied, his tone rich and inviting. His gaze fell to the neckline of her gown, loitered on the curve of her breasts and the room began to feel a little warmer. "Are you sure you're ready for the answer?"

In some faraway place, deep down in the depths of her stomach, the first flicker of desire ignited. The sensation being somewhat foreign, a feeling she did not understand, she dragged her thoughts back to Mr. Dempsey. He was as skilled in seductive repartee as he was dancing, and if she ever hoped to learn the true nature of his character, she needed to avoid such artifice.

"No, that's not my question," she replied confidently. "But the question I wish to ask does relate to seduction."

Now she had his undivided attention.

"I can hardly contain myself," he replied. "Please ask away, Miss Ecclestone."

She took a deep breath and looked at him directly. "Why do you feel the need to have intimate relations with Lady Colebrook, when you obviously do not even like her?"

Stunned, was the only way to describe his expression as his eyes grew wide and his mouth fell open. With a shake of the head, he regained his composure, yet she felt him drawing away from her, retreating to the inner sanctum of his keep and barring the door to all intruders. "That is not an appropriate topic of conversation," he said coldly.

"I did warn you I have a tendency to be direct." She doubted he'd ever speak to her again, let alone ask her to dance a second time. "The only rules pertain to telling the truth, Mr. Dempsey," she persisted, determined to hear his confession. "If you break your oath then it means I cannot trust you and I cannot be friends with someone I do not trust." After a brief pause, she added, "Friends do not judge."

The heavy silence drew on, the lines on his brow growing deeper, more prominent. "Very well," he eventually said, his tone suggesting she only had herself to blame if she did not like the answer. "If you value directness, then I shall give it to you. Like most men, I find the act pleasurable. I find it necessary. There is no emotional attachment involved. And I have never been overly concerned about who I perform it with."

Helena was not offended by his bluntness but rather saddened by his lack of sentiment. "What about character or physical attributes, do they not concern you?" she asked in so neutral a tone they could have been discussing the merits of his new horse. "That is not another question," she quickly clarified. "I am just determining your meaning."

He clenched his jaw, and the muscles in his cheek twitched. "How a woman looks does concern me. I am not ... I was not," he corrected, "particularly interested in a lady's character."

Well, she could not complain about his honesty. Perhaps she

should give Mr. Dempsey something to contemplate. "You mean you judge the worth of your mistress as others judge you—on physical appearance."

He stared at her, his eyes darkening.

For a moment, she wondered if his demons were about to leap out and avenge their master. Sliding his hand around her back, he pulled her close; so close she could feel the power in his muscular thighs as she brushed against them.

"I find my tastes have changed, and I have suddenly developed a particular weakness for wood nymphs. A weakness that encompasses certain elements of character such as honesty, wit, and intelligence, all of which I now find strangely alluring and highly arousing."

She could feel his warm breath against her cheek; she could feel the tips of his fingers pulsating. An unexplainable heat radiated from his palm and rippled through her body, and she stared at his mouth with a strange sense of longing.

"Therefore," he continued, easing her away to a more respectable distance, "Lady Colebrook and I are no longer compatible in that regard."

"I see," she said, wondering why the thought pleased her. "Have you informed Lady Colebrook of that fact?" When he nodded, she added, "That would explain why she is standing at the edge of the floor, staring at me like a wildcat about to pounce on its next victim."

Lucas Dempsey glanced over Helena's shoulder, his mouth taking a downward turn. "Ignore Lady Colebrook," he said with an exasperated sigh and as the dance ended he placed Helena's hand in the crook of his arm and escorted her from the floor. "Despite your probing questions, Miss Ecclestone, I shall return to claim another dance," he whispered as he returned her to the safety of her family.

With a graceful bow, he turned to leave and could not have been more than a few feet away when her mother pulled her by the arm. "What on earth possessed you to dance with Mr.

Dempsey?" she snarled. "Do you honestly think that any respectable gentleman will even dare approach you after that debacle? You let him ravish you with those sinful eyes of his. I must have been talking to myself all these years, as you have not paid any attention to a word I have said."

"We were just dancing," Helena groaned, waving her hand in the air to express her irritation. "And he was not ravishing me with his eyes."

"You've certainly made a fool of yourself," Amelia snapped. "And he *was* looking at you rather strangely. You must have flirted outrageously, as he threw his head back and laughed."

Before Helena could think of a witty retort, they were interrupted by the sound of a gentleman clearing his throat. As they all swung around to inspect the unwelcome intrusion, they gave a collective gasp.

"Lord Banbury," her mother croaked in a voice an octave higher than usual. "How nice to see you."

Lord Banbury bowed, and Helena examined him with keen interest. After her dance with Lucas Dempsey, it could not be a coincidence that he chose this moment to introduce himself. Helena had seen him once before, but only from a distance. He was older than Mr. Dempsey, yet there was something childlike, something simple about his countenance. His pastel-blue eyes were framed with long feminine lashes, and they held a look of innocence and wonder. They were not the eyes of a man capable of plotting murder, Helena thought. Indeed, it must have taken an enormous amount of effort just to form a scowl. Eager to confirm her theory, Helena had to wait until the introductions were over before attempting to make conversation.

It was while she was determining how best to approach the subject of Mr. Dempsey, that Lord Banbury, compelled by the need to offer caution, blurted, "Forgive me for intruding, Mrs. Ecclestone. I do not wish to ruin such a delightful evening, but I feel at liberty to warn you of the inadequacy of Mr. Dempsey's character. He is a dangerous fellow and not deemed fitting company for respectable young ladies."

Helena frowned. There was something amiss. "Why is that, Lord Banbury? What makes him such a dangerous fellow?" she asked desperate to hear him speak again.

"Helena!" her mother cried with a hand to her breast as though mortally wounded. "You should not ask such impertinent questions."

Lord Banbury gave a dismissive shake of the head. "No need to chastise the girl, madam," he said calmly. He turned his head and focused a concerned gaze on Helena. "You must know Mr. Dempsey killed my brother and to avoid punishment fled to Boston."

Sensing her mother's eyes boring into her like a hot poker, Helena chose to ignore it. Someone needed to oppose Lord Banbury's biased opinion. "I know your brother challenged Mr. Dempsey to a fight and threw the first punch. I know Mr. Dempsey was forced to defend himself, know his father sent him to Boston against his will."

No doubt her mother's sharp intake of breath was heard as far afield as Norfolk. "Thank you, Lord Banbury. Your concern is duly noted," she interrupted, flapping her arms about like a bird gathering in her chicks. "However, I am afraid we must be going. Amelia has hurt her foot, and I can feel one of my migraines coming on."

"We have only just arrived," Amelia groaned as they pushed their way through the crowd, leaving Lord Banbury standing there, gaping at their backs.

"Blame your sister. I shall have plenty to say on the matter when we return home. Now, wait in the hall while I make our apologies to Lady Mendleson."

While her mother fretted and fussed and her sister groaned and grumbled, Helena could think of only one thing: Lord Banbury was not the man she heard talking in Lady Colebrook's garden.

CHAPTER 7

Lucas dashed out of the Mendlesons' townhouse at the pace of a racehorse on Derby day. Scouring the line of carriages, he could find no sign of Helena Ecclestone or her sour-faced mother.

He punched the air, furious that Miranda's whimpering and bitter comments had captured his attention.

In a jealous rage, Miranda had stormed after him, laughing that he'd terrified Miss Ecclestone with his amorous ogling, and so she'd scurried off home in a bid to protect her virginity. Only when he returned to claim another dance, did he discover that his nymph actually had left the ball. At that moment, he felt the blood surge through his veins at far too rapid a rate, felt the disappointment of missing her enchanting company like a hard blow to the stomach.

What was it about her that intrigued him?

What was it he found so alluring?

Deciding to walk the short distance home in the hope the exercise would improve his mood, he made his way down Davies Street, revisiting his conversation with Miss Ecclestone to pass the time. The memory of her probing question caused the same tightening sensation in his throat: a feeling of shock and then disgust for his blunt, rather crude response.

Was that what had brought her to her senses?

Did she now think him too shallow to save?

As he turned the corner to cut through Mount Row, he heard the gruff whispers of masculine voices trailing behind him, the dull thud of heavy footsteps getting closer as he quickened his pace.

Someone wanted him dead.

It would only take a blow to the back of the head and a ripped pocket to make a murder look like a mugging.

O'Brien, a bare-knuckle fighter from Cork, taught him that the element of surprise always proved to be the best weapon, as long as your fist was as hard as a mallet.

In their haste to catch up with him, his pursuers were as noisy as a gaggle of migrating geese.

Lucas waited until they were just a few steps behind before turning swiftly, using all his weight to launch his fist directly into the face of one of the men. The man crumpled to the ground with a yelp, his hands shielding a bloody nose. His accomplice darted forward, flashing the sharp edge of a blade, slashing at the air between them. He snarled like a rabid dog as he spat a string of curses.

Lucas stood in a defensive position and nodded his head to a point beyond the lout's shoulder. "You know, if you're going to attack someone, you should at least make sure they're alone."

As predicted, his quarry glanced back over his shoulder and Lucas used the mistake to his advantage, kicking the knife from his hand and lunging forward, taking him down to the ground and pounding him with punches.

While the man hovered on the brink of consciousness, his friend took to his heels and fled. Lucas stepped back, wiped his mouth with the back of his hand and glanced at the flailing figure in the distance. Fearing the possibility he could return with reinforcements, Lucas rifled through the bruised man's pockets, finding nothing other than a stained handkerchief and a few loose coins.

What was he expecting to find, Banbury's blasted calling card?

A groan escaped from the swollen mouth of the man writhing on the ground. Lucas took a few steps back, surveying the scene as he made a hasty retreat.

On his return home, Gregson's greeting did little to improve his irate mood. "You have a visitor, sir," his butler announced, quick to add it was not a lady. Lucas suppressed his disappointment. The desire to talk to Miss Ecclestone and to seek her opinion on the events of the evening was overwhelming.

"Oh, it's you," Lucas said as he entered the study to find Anthony sitting in front of the fire, cradling a glass of port. "Isn't it rather late to make a house call?" Lucas shrugged out of his coat and threw it over the back of the chair before walking over to the drinks tray. "I thought you were still at the ball."

"I left early and decided to wait for you here. I want to speak with you about the Mendleson ball," Anthony said, sounding rather like an overbearing parent.

"Chastise me more like." Lucas drained his glass and refilled it, flexing his fingers when he noticed his grazed knuckles. "Lucky for you I chose to come home, else you'd be stuck in that chair until morning."

Anthony sighed. "I want to talk to you about your relationship with Miss Ecclestone."

"My relationship with Miss Ecclestone? There is nothing to discuss. I merely asked the lady to dance, so you can cease with the lecture."

Shooting out of his chair, Anthony slammed his glass on the mantelpiece and strode over to Lucas. Taking him by the arm, he pulled him round to face him. "There is more to it than that, and you damn well know it. That was not the first time you've met. You did not stop talking through the whole dance. I saw the way you looked at her, the way you held her."

Lucas yanked his arm free. "I don't know what you mean," he said, his tone conveying indifference. He brushed past his brother, sauntered over to the fireplace and dropped into the other chair.

Anthony followed him and threw himself back down. "You want her. It was blatantly obvious. If I noticed it, then you can be sure others did, too. Come tomorrow it will be the topic of conversation in all the best drawing rooms." When that failed to rouse his ire, Anthony added, "It's one thing to seduce a string of experienced women, but to ruin an innocent."

Lucas shrugged with indifference. "I've done nothing wrong."

"I have to say I am a little surprised, I mean she's not to your usual taste," Anthony said with a smirk. "She's such a timid little thing."

"Timid!" That was the last word he would use to describe her. Miss Ecclestone was the most courageous person he had ever met, and he owed her a debt of gratitude. "You don't even know her."

"Are you saying you do?" When Lucas made no attempt to answer, Anthony added, "I mean, when you compare her to Lady Colebrook she lacks a certain …"

Lucas thrust himself forward, his elbow resting on his knee and said through gritted teeth, "Do not dare compare Miss Ecclestone to Miranda Colebrook."

"I knew it," Anthony cried, punching his fist in the air. "I allowed you to use me to make the introduction because I thought you were trying to make a good impression," Anthony said. "I thought it would be good for you to be seen in the company of respectable people. I did not expect you to use Miss Ecclestone to embarrass Lord Banbury."

With his brows drawn together, Lucas shook his head. "What the hell are you talking about?"

"Look, I'm sorry for what Father put you through," Anthony said with a hint of compassion. "It must have been difficult being away from home and the experience has obviously hardened your heart."

"Difficult!" Lucas cried, holding back a curse foul enough to frighten the devil. "Which would you deem as being the most difficult? Being forced from your home and disowned by your family? Being sent thousands of miles away to a foreign land, or having your funds cut off because everyone believes you're a murderer?"

Anthony's face flushed, and he swallowed deeply. "And I'm sorry for that, but it still doesn't give you the right to use an innocent woman. You must have known Banbury would approach her."

A sudden wave of panic took hold.

He had assumed she'd gone home. "What the hell did Banbury do to her?" Lucas cried, his heart beating so fast he thought it might burst from his chest. "I should have been there. I should have been watching her, but I was accosted by Miranda Colebrook. When I looked for Miss Ecclestone, she was gone. If he has harmed a hair on her head—"

"Why on earth would Lord Banbury want to do anything to Miss Ecclestone?" Anthony's eyes widened as his gaze dropped to Lucas' bruised knuckles wrapped around his glass. He lurched forward, grabbed his brother's wrist and nodded to his hand. "What the hell have you done? Lucas, you had better tell me what is going on."

There was a long pause while Lucas contemplated his relationship with his brother. He had always been able to trust him in the past. Perhaps he needed someone to confide in now, someone other than Miss Ecclestone.

"Can I trust you, Anthony?" he asked looking his brother straight in the eye, as he knew insincerity when he saw it.

Anthony jerked his head back as though reeling from an invisible punch. "Of course you can trust me," he announced without hesitation. "Why do you think I am here? I only want what's best for you, Lucas."

Lucas took their empty glasses and refilled them, then returned to his seat by the fire. "I did not kill Lord Banbury," he said, handing the glass to Anthony. "I believe that someone else murdered him in his bed that night and used the fight to cover it up. Miss Ecclestone overheard a conversation between two gentlemen who more or less confessed to the crime. They agreed it would be best if I suffered a fatal injury before I discovered the truth." He studied his brother's shocked expression then added, "Miss Ecclestone came here to warn me."

There was a brief silence while Anthony absorbed the information.

"And you think the current Lord Banbury is the one responsible for his brother's murder?" he said, shaking his head numerous times by way of conveying his disbelief. "Are you sure? Are you sure you can trust Miss Ecclestone, that this is not some story she concocted just to—" He waved his hand at Lucas' impeccable features. "Are you sure she's not just trying to get your attention? Not all ladies are as direct as Lady Colebrook."

Lucas laughed. "Miss Ecclestone is the only woman I have ever met who is not the least bit interested in my face." Sadly, she did not seem that interested in the rest of him either—other than in the redemption of his soul. He wondered what he could do to change her mind. "Besides, I believe whoever killed Lord Banbury took the trouble to hire two thugs, who have just tried to murder me in the street."

Anthony sat bolt upright, his gaze focused on Lucas' battered knuckles before scanning the rest of his body as if searching for some reassurance no harm had befallen him. "You were attacked in the street?"

"I'm fine," Lucas reassured, "which is more than can be said for them. On the crossing to Boston, I was fortunate enough to meet a boxer by the name of O'Brien and discovered that I'm rather partial to the art of pugilism. O'Brien has worked for me ever since."

Anthony sat back in the chair, gaping at him as if he were a stranger. "Sounds like an interesting fellow," he said. "So, what do you intend to do about Banbury? I assume he has no idea Miss Ecclestone was listening to his conversation?"

Lucas shook his head. "Miss Ecclestone was hiding behind a hedge and didn't see either of them."

"Well, that's a relief." Anthony sighed. "For Miss Ecclestone, I mean." He brushed his hand through his hair and exhaled slowly. "Lucas, I do not think it is wise to involve Miss Ecclestone in all of this. She is young and innocent and does not deserve to be embroiled in a scandal."

Lucas felt a stab of guilt as he acknowledged the logic in his brother's words, but the thought left him feeling strangely bereft. "Miss Ecclestone is the only person who can identify the gentlemen involved, even if it's only by their voices," he said, challenging his brother to argue with his reasoning.

Anthony threw him a look of caution, a look that suggested Lucas would be unwise to ignore his counsel. To add weight to his warning, he remarked, "Miss Ecclestone defied her mother in public this evening, and practically accused Lord Banbury of concocting his own version of events relating to the death of his brother. In a crowded room, she defended you, Lucas."

The news caused a rush of conflicting emotions: an odd mixture of fear and pride.

The thought that Miss Ecclestone had put herself in danger by confronting Banbury caused all the air to leave his body. But it took a strong woman to stand by her principles, to place integrity before her own safety and his chest felt full again at the thought.

"I did not hear the conversation myself," Anthony continued, "but you know how people like to gossip. It will not be long before assumptions are made as to the nature of your relationship. Everyone will think Miss Ecclestone's formed an attachment and will no doubt believe the worst. You, more than anyone, know how these things work."

In his four-year absence, nothing had changed. Anthony was

right. A whisper here and the odd word there was enough to ruin a reputation.

Lucas stood. He placed his empty glass on the mantelpiece and gazed at the flames as he tried to gain some perspective on the situation.

When it mattered most, when he truly needed him, his father had turned him away. Yet here was a woman he had known for just a few days, standing up to the elite of Society and defending him. A warm feeling encompassed him and settled in his chest. No one had ever spoken up for him before. No one had ever believed him worthy.

And how would he repay her loyalty? By throwing her into the path of a murderer, by ruining her reputation so that no true gentleman would look her way again.

Perhaps he had been right all along. Perhaps Helena Ecclestone had a magical faerie ability, a way of secretly weaving a morality spell to make him engage with his conscience. It was an odd feeling: the need to put someone else before himself, the need to be prudent.

With this new-found resolve, he could not disgrace the woman who had come to save him. He would meet with her one last time, explain the need for caution, and thank her for her help and support.

For the first time in years, he was going to have to push his needs aside and do something selfless. For her sake, he was going to have to put an end to his friendship with Helena Ecclestone.

CHAPTER 8

Two days he had wasted. Two days spent trailing from the Reinhardt's musical soiree to Miss Peabody's picnic, to scouring the length and breadth of Hyde Park. All in the hope of tracking down the elusive Miss Ecclestone. Either the lady had taken to her bed suffering from a serious malady, or she was doing her utmost to avoid him.

Lucas was not used to this sort of evasive treatment. He was not comfortable in the role of pursuer. It created a sense of instability, a mental imbalance that consequently affected his mood. Perhaps she wished she'd never spoken up for him. Perhaps she wanted to put some distance between them. If that were the case, surely he should be glad as it saved him the trouble of hurting her feelings.

So why did he feel so irritated, so frustrated, so downright miserable?

By the time he arrived at Lord Amberly's mansion house, his mood had still not improved. While others pushed and jostled to catch a glimpse of Madame Antolini: the famed opera singer who had been persuaded to travel to England to perform for her patron—he sulked in the corner.

When the call came to take their seats in the garden, he felt a prickling awareness, a feeling that caused the muscles in his shoulders to tense. "I didn't know you were an opera enthusiast," Lady Colebrook purred, appearing at his side and forcing her arm through his.

"Amberly assured me this would be the event of the Season," he replied, although his indifferent expression did little to support his statement.

Indeed, Lord Amberly had spared no expense. A makeshift stage had been erected on the lawn in front of an oriental pagoda and candles in glass lanterns illuminated the aisle between the rows of chairs.

"I hear Lord Amberly has been pestered day and night by people offering a boon to secure an invitation. Shall we sit here?" she asked, guiding him to a row of empty seats. "The view will be poor, but one does not have to see opera performed to feel its emotive qualities."

Lucas would have preferred to sit alone but had neither the desire nor the inclination to argue. "I'm afraid it would take more than a few ear-piercing notes to move me," he replied coldly. "I try to avoid sentiment whenever possible."

Miranda tittered. "Such a wise philosophy in a society such as ours. In the pursuit of pleasure, one does not need to be encumbered by emotion." Her hungry eyes roamed over his face, along his jaw, across the breadth of his chest. "You do not need to be so aloof, Lucas," she whispered, her voice revealing a more seductive quality. "After all that has passed between us, surely we can still be friends."

"Of course," he replied reluctantly. However, as they took their seats, Miranda took a moment to smooth out her gown, her fingers brushing idly against his thigh in the process. "Friends, Miranda, nothing more," Lucas clarified, jerking his leg in the opposite direction.

To fill the uncomfortable silence that ensued, Lucas scanned row upon row of heads, wondering if Miss Ecclestone was amongst them. He imagined she would like opera, imagined she would like the complexity of love and passion entwined with the tenacity of human nature. Would those powerful notes arouse some feeling within her, arouse hunger or desire? Or would she simply be able to provide a more theoretical analysis of the dramatic composition?

"If you are looking for your little friend," Miranda said icily, "you will find her on the left-hand side, in the second row. She's the one wearing the iron chastity belt."

She did not wait for a reply but turned away sharply and struck up a conversation with the gentleman to her left.

Feeling a strange churning sensation in the pit of his stomach, Lucas raised his chin and searched the crowd once more. Now that he knew where to look it was easy to spot her. Seated with her mother and sister, he could just make out her profile: the pert nose, the soft peachy lips formed into a thoughtful pout as she gazed meditatively upon the pagoda. He would have given everything he owned to know what she was thinking.

He was so captivated by the enchanting vision that he wasn't even aware the orchestra was playing, not until he heard the first few notes of the soprano.

Singing an aria from Rossini's *Tancredi*, Antolini gave a heartfelt performance as the condemned Amenaide, who, after refusing to marry a man she did not love, finds herself imprisoned for treason. As Antolini sang of her innocence, sang of her true love who she feared was lost to her, he watched Miss Ecclestone with keen interest.

Gripped by the powerful performance, she bit down on her bottom lip, blinked repeatedly and clasped her hands to her bosom as her breath came more rapidly.

Lost in the moment, his mind wandered so that he imagined himself above her, looking down at her naked body, her face revealing a passion reserved only for him. He would sit through a thousand performances, just to study her expressions, just to marvel at the depth of her emotion.

Such is the beauty of tragedy.

When the rapturous applause burst forth from the crowd, Lucas sat back in his chair and sighed. He would need to find some way to speak to Miss Ecclestone and inform her that it would be wise if she did not acknowledge him in public again.

The thought caused anger to flare, the muscles in his jaw growing firm, rigid.

He should tell the world to go to hell; he would see whomever he pleased. Why, when he had found one person who saw him as more than just a handsome face, should he feel forced to give up her friendship?

That feeling was still with him as he sat alone in the garden, still with him when he entered the ballroom to find Miss Ecclestone waltzing in the arms of a young gentleman.

He was of slender, yet athletic proportion, whose face portrayed the perfect picture of respectability, but whose eyes held a predatory hunger that was unmistakable. Miss Ecclestone said something and the gentleman laughed: a false demonstration of admiration to lure in his prey. Indeed, as Lucas prowled the perimeter of the floor, his gaze fell to the gentleman's hand, gripping Miss Ecclestone's waist like the talons of an eagle clinging to its next meal.

Lucas muttered a curse.

"Now you see why it is imperative you avoid any contact with Miss Ecclestone," Anthony said wearily, coming to stand at his shoulder. "You have opened the gates for a whole host of disreputable gentlemen to test their seductive skills."

"I do not see how," Lucas protested, aware that his body was primed and ready to pounce. "It's not as though I ravished her on the dance floor."

Anthony put his hand on Lucas' shoulder. "It was the way you looked at her, Lucas," he said with a sigh, "and the way she responded to you."

The way he looked at her! The way she responded!

They had done nothing other than talk, and laugh, and perhaps been a little flirtatious in their manner. So what if he'd been too friendly, he'd never had to concern himself with the reputation of an innocent before.

"Who is he?" Lucas asked curtly. "I do not recall having ever met him."

"Mr. Huntley-Fisher is the illegitimate son of the Marquess of Durham. Now that his father has publicly acknowledged him and settled on an allowance, the gentleman has been seen at many a ball and rout." In a grave tone, Anthony added, "It is said that he has a fondness for virgins. That he has already ruined one respectable lady this Season."

Lucas curled his fist into a ball at his side. He wanted to charge onto the floor and strangle the man with his cravat.

When Mr. Huntley-Fisher caught his reproachful stare, the gentleman smirked and raised a challenging brow. The pounding in Lucas' head drowned out every other sound. His heart was racing, and he reassessed his initial feeling of hostility—now he wanted to rip the man's heart out with his bare hands and serve it up for dinner.

"You are not helping matters," Anthony claimed. "Standing here glaring at him will only add weight to the theory that you have claimed her for yourself."

Lucas was tired of people telling him what to do, of people judging and interfering. "I need a drink," he said, knocking shoulders with his brother as he barged past him and stormed off in search of something to dull his newly awakened sensibilities.

The waltz with Mr. Huntley-Fisher had been interesting.

Why he had chosen to ask her in the first place was baffling enough. However, when he complimented her beauty, when he laughed at her remark about untitled gentlemen having to try harder, when he suggested they partake in a further examination of Lord Amberly's pagoda—then the reason became abundantly clear.

Did he think her some pea-brained, gullible little fool?

She would have had more respect for the man if he had just propositioned her directly. Although she had to give him some credit, for he was nothing if not persistent.

Sending him off in the direction of the refreshment table, Helena used the opportunity to visit the ladies retiring room, in the hope that Mr. Huntley-Fisher would have found some other distraction by the time she returned.

As she made her way along the hallway, she spotted Mr. Dempsey, propped up against the wall, emanating a level of hostility that was highly intimidating.

"Mr. Dempsey," she said as she approached him, unperturbed by his menacing scowl. She wondered what he had made of her note. What reason he had for not responding. "Is everything all right? Are you well?"

He stared at her beneath hooded lids. "No, Miss Ecclestone, I am not well. I am suffering from some indefinable malaise." His eyes swept over her with a look that made her question the decency of her clothing. "It is not wise to be seen talking to me," he said, looking past her shoulder, "not out here. I do not wish to be held accountable for tainting your reputation."

What on earth was wrong with him?

Fearing he had succumbed to some sort of disorder of the mind, which would hardly be surprising given people were hatching a murderous plot against him, she glanced over her shoulder. Relieved to find the corridor empty, she grabbed him by the sleeve of his coat and pulled him towards a door.

Opening the door and glancing inside, she said, "Then quickly, we will talk in here."

Without any protest, he pushed himself away from the wall and followed her.

She shut the door gently and turned to face him. The room was dark, and it took a moment for her eyes to become accustomed. Perhaps suffering from the same problem he stepped closer, and she shuffled back only to find herself against the door.

A faint whiff of brandy wafted through the air.

"What is it that troubles you?" Helena asked, looking into eyes that, even in this light, were remarkably blue. "If it is this business with Lord Banbury, then why did you not reply to my note?"

"I am ill, Miss Ecclestone," he whispered, his head bent so low it almost touched her forehead.

"You're ill?"

"I appear to have lost all logical function of mind and body."

She could feel the heat radiating from him, could feel his breath like a soft caress against her ear. "What can I do?" she asked, overwhelmed with the need to help him.

"What can you do," he repeated as he glanced down at her bosom and then slowly raised his gaze to meet hers. "I could tell you, but you will not like the answer."

She smiled. "Did we not make a pact to be honest, Mr. Dempsey? I will not judge you for that." Intrigued to discover what plagued him and by way of an inducement, she added, "You may take comfort in the knowledge that this will be regarded as my second question."

"Very well," he drawled and with a little shrug, confessed, "what have I to lose?" Bracing his hands against the door, he pressed closer until the material of his coat brushed her gown. "I want you, Miss Ecclestone," he said with a degree of passion she had never heard spoken before. "I want you more than I have ever wanted anything." His breath came more rapidly as his eyes fell to her mouth. "I want to marvel in the softness of your lips, want to taste you, want to plunder your sweet mouth until you groan with pleasure."

Helena swallowed.

He made it sound so tempting, so appealing that her body stirred in response. Trying to dismiss the throbbing sensation that pulsed through her, she attempted to inhibit her feelings. "Mr. Dempsey, I do not think—"

"I want to run my hands over your naked body," he interrupted.

Using his knee, he found the narrow gap between her legs and forced them apart, his hard body pressing her back against the door. "I want to know what it's like to be inside you." The words sounded more like a growl as he ran his hands down her back. He clutched her hips as he pulled her closer, and she could feel the evidence of his arousal.

A soft moan left her lips as a jolt of pleasure burst through her body. She grabbed the lapels of his coat, feeling light and dizzy, dragging his mouth down to meet hers in the process.

Needing no further inducement, he claimed her mouth with an urgency that was as desperate as it was dangerous.

It involved no gentle persuasion, no tender coaxing or slow tutoring. Wild and unbridled, hot and wet, he delved deep into her mouth until she could no longer rouse any rational thoughts. Again, he wedged his muscular thigh between her legs, pressing against her as his breath came short and quick.

When her hands came up to cup his neck she pulled him closer, her tongue meeting his with equal enthusiasm. His groan of appreciation gave her a boost of confidence and she could hear herself moaning into his mouth.

She felt as if she was floating, flying free. A cool summer breeze drifted over her thighs, the feeling so real that she failed to notice he had hiked up her gown and his fingers were tracing circles on her bare skin.

"Mr. Dempsey," she panted, suddenly frightened that things were progressing at too rapid a rate. "Please … I cannot …"

He froze, stood motionless for a moment before dropping his hands and smoothing down her gown. Like a passing storm, the atmosphere changed. He wrapped his arms around her, pulled her close like she was the most fragile, most precious thing in the world.

He kissed her slowly, more gently and she felt strangely connected to him, as though he had opened the window to his soul and allowed her to peek inside. Buried beneath his raging passion, she could feel his sadness. She could feel his pain.

As their lips parted and their breathing slowed, he stepped away from her. It did not take long for him to regain his composure. "Forgive me, Miss Ecclestone," he said, sounding surprisingly sincere. "I was not aware that honesty could be so arousing. But I believe I overstepped the bounds of propriety."

"There's no need to offer an apology, Mr. Dempsey," she replied, still feeling the blood pulsing through her veins, still feeling so desperately drawn to him. Indeed, she had never felt so alive, so delightfully sinful and all she could think to say was, "It was a rather enlightening experience."

He smiled, her comment pleasing him, but then his lips thinned. "It will not happen again," he said, nodding respectfully.

Helena smiled too but felt the sharp stab of rejection. "Perhaps that would be wise," she replied, knowing she'd lied, knowing she would respond to him with the same level of unbridled passion should he touch her again. The thought that it had taken very little effort to rouse a response caused her to blush.

Feeling a sudden wave of panic that he should notice her embarrassment, coupled with the thought that she had been absent from the ballroom for far too long, she quickly said, "My sister will be looking for me, but I am sure you wish to discuss the contents of my note."

"What note?"

Turning swiftly, she grasped the door handle. "Meet me tomorrow at two, at Miss Linwood's Egyptian museum in Coventry Street."

As she pulled open the door and stepped out into the hallway, she was vaguely aware of his protestation, of him calling for her to wait.

In the hallway, Mr. Huntley-Fisher and her sister, Amelia,

were involved in a heated discussion with Viscount Harwood. Hearing the door open, all heads turned to face her.

"There you are," Amelia cried, stomping over. "We have been looking for you everywhere. There's a toast for Madame Antolini, and Mother sent me to find you."

Three pairs of eyes swept over her, starting with her hair and ending at the upturned hem of her gown. Amelia looked shocked; Mr. Huntley-Fisher looked annoyed, and Viscount Harwood looked embarrassed.

"Where have you been?" Amelia asked suspiciously, her brows drawn together in a frown. "What were you doing in that room? Who was in there with you?"

Hearing the confident stride of Lucas Dempsey exit the room to stand at her side, she said in as confident a manner as possible, "I have been talking to Mr. Dempsey."

Amelia gasped and put her hand to her head in a feigned swoon. "You were alone in that room with Mr. Dempsey? Look at the state of you. What were you thinking?"

Mr. Huntley-Fisher smiled deviously. "I am sure Mr. Dempsey is aware that such a declaration may have devastating consequences," he mocked. "Perhaps he should consider what he can do in order to silence the witnesses." The gentleman raised a challenging brow and his mouth curved into a sardonic grin.

"Perhaps you should go back to the pond you hopped out of and keep your nose out of matters that do not concern you," Lucas said through gritted teeth.

"I am not the one dragging ladies into secret rooms to ravish them."

"Mr. Dempsey has done nothing wrong," Helena barked, stepping to the left to prevent him from lunging forward and grabbing Mr. Huntley-Fisher by the ends of his cravat.

"No?" the gentleman replied, looking at her hair with an amused expression. "Perhaps that is because you do not seem to have offered any objection."

A low growl emanated from the back of Mr. Dempsey's

throat, and he looked ready to beat the gentleman to a pulp. "I'm going to knock those crooked teeth right down—"

"Enough!" Viscount Harwood yelled much to Helena's relief. "If we all calm down, I'm sure there is a reasonable explanation."

Mr. Dempsey's disdainful gaze flitted between the three of them. With a huff of contempt, he grabbed Helena's hand and thrust it in the crook of his arm.

"No," Helena whispered as she glanced up into eyes that were determined and focused, knowing what he was about to do. "Don't."

He reached out to her and tucked the loose strands of hair behind her ear, before turning to the group. "Miss Ecclestone has just accepted a proposal of marriage," he declared arrogantly. Turning his hard gaze on Mr. Huntley-Fisher, he added, "And if you ever talk to my betrothed like that again, I shall string you up outside Newgate and leave you to rot with all the other reprobates."

CHAPTER 9

The reception they received at the Ecclestones' townhouse the next morning was hostile at best.

Mrs. Ecclestone refused to leave her bedchamber, while Mr. Ecclestone escorted both Lucas and Anthony into the study, insisting he be convinced of Mr. Dempsey's worth. Even the cat sounded distressed as a high-pitched whimpering could be heard coming from somewhere upstairs.

The news of their betrothal had spread through the ballroom like a fire in a hay barn. Lucas ignored the contemptuous stares and the sucked cheeks of disapproval, but anger pumped through his veins, hot and volatile, at the disrespectful glances cast Miss Ecclestone's way. Indeed, anger still simmered beneath the surface—for the way Anthony assumed he would want to break his vow, for his own recklessness in compromising an innocent.

But what if he decided he did want to marry Miss Ecclestone?

For some bizarre reason, the thought of any other man bedding his wood nymph was incomprehensible. With her witty banter and honest mouth, she aroused him in ways he'd not thought possible. The knowledge that he might get to taste the forbidden fruit had also cured his malaise.

As Lucas recited an extensive list of his assets, including three properties in Boston, a share in a cotton textile company, three trade vessels that shipped cargo from Madras and Calcutta and a yearly income from leasing warehouses, Anthony leaned closer. "I see you have kept yourself busy, Lucas," he whispered, radiating brotherly pride.

Lucas raised an arrogant brow. "What did you expect me to do, spend my days in a drunken stupor?"

Whether out of pride, vanity or as a matter of principle, Anthony saw fit to bolster Lucas' suit. "My brother also inherited a substantial property in Shropshire and an income of five thousand a year."

Lucas swallowed his irritation. This was not the time to challenge his father's will or inform Anthony that he would rather live in a hovel and feed on scraps than accept their charity.

As though reading his brother's mind and just to rub salt in the wound, Anthony added, "As my brother had no need to draw on his income, all unclaimed amounts have been placed in trust for any future children."

Mr. Ecclestone made a strange chomping sound as he nodded with satisfaction and offering no further objection to the match, suggested that the gentlemen take tea before departing. Under the guise of being called away on another matter, he directed them to a room across the hall and, after whispering in Anthony's ear, excused himself.

"I am instructed to see that you maintain a respectable distance," Anthony informed with some amusement as they entered the room. "Although I think it is a little too late for that."

Miss Ecclestone stood at the window, her arms folded across her chest as she stared at the street in thoughtful contemplation. Her hair was swept up in a simple style, the odd stray tendril tickling her neck. The bodice of her pale green dress was embroidered with ferns and orange flowers, evoking thoughts of wild woodland walks.

Hearing their footsteps she turned to greet them, and Lucas

heard her deep intake of breath. "Lord Harwood," she said, pausing to curtsy. "And Mr. Dempsey," she continued, her eyes brightening as she straightened.

Remembering how soft and warm she felt in his arms, his gaze drifted down to those luscious lips and her mouth curved into a mischievous grin in response. "Miss Ecclestone," he said, offering a graceful bow.

He brought her bare hand to his lips, aware that even in such a short greeting, in such a simple gesture, he conveyed the depth of his desire.

"W-would you care for some tea?" she asked, her face flushing crimson as her hand came up to rest just below her throat. With a quick shake of the head, she regained her composure and anticipating their answer, rang the bell.

She gestured to the chairs, and they all sat down, the room suddenly swamped by an uncomfortable silence. "Well, this is awkward," she complained, much to Anthony's surprise.

Lucas chuckled. "You should know that Miss Ecclestone likes to voice her opinion, whether appropriate or not." Then he decided that in itself was not a sufficient explanation, so added, "Honesty is important to her."

"I see," Anthony replied somewhat bemused.

When the tea tray arrived silence ensued once again, and while Miss Ecclestone poured she turned to Anthony and asked, "You do not approve of our betrothal, my lord?"

With a smile, Lucas took his cup and sat back in the chair ready to be entertained.

Anthony raised a stunned brow. "No."

"Come now. You can do better than that," she mocked as though talking to her maid and not a peer of the realm. "Your brother does not love me, and I do not love him. Therefore, you do not approve."

Lucas shuffled uncomfortably. Although he knew she spoke the truth, there was something about the words that irritated him. He brushed the feeling aside and continued to watch the show.

"If you do not love him why place yourself in such a compromising position?" Anthony asked honestly, but his tone held a hint of remorse, as though he had not intended to ask such an impertinent question. In an attempt to hide his embarrassment, he sipped his tea.

"Of all the stupid questions." Lucas sighed.

Miss Ecclestone offered a demure smile. "I think what Mr. Dempsey is trying to say is that there is some indefinable attraction between us and in my eagerness to save his soul, I inadvertently got a little over-excited."

Lucas felt a familiar tightening in his abdomen as he remembered her delightful pants and moans, her willing hands grabbing at his coat, the way her tongue danced with his. He agreed with her assessment: there was some ineffable attraction between them, and he was pleased she felt it, too.

"However," she continued. "Mr. Dempsey does not want to marry me, and I do not want to marry him. So, we will need to find a way to put an end to our betrothal."

The sudden pounding in his chest made him sit upright, causing the teacup to rattle on the saucer. How was he supposed to bed his wood nymph if she refused to be his wife? Perhaps he should offer an incentive. After the wedding night, she could keep the house in Shropshire while he returned to Boston. Though he doubted that would appeal to Miss Ecclestone, as she was not the sort to be interested in financial gain.

It occurred to him that perhaps one night might not be enough to sate his desperate hunger. He imagined a week of debauched antics, and his teacup rattled again at the prospect.

"You see. Just the mere mention of marriage has unsettled his nerves," Miss Ecclestone said in the tone of a physician. She looked directly at Lucas and tapping her finger on her chin, said reflectively, "However, a feigned betrothal would provide the perfect opportunity for us to resolve our problem."

While Anthony choked on his tea, Lucas felt his stomach

grow warm as he tried to ascertain her meaning. Surely, she was not suggesting they conduct an illicit liaison.

"I assume you *have* told him?" Miss Ecclestone asked anxiously, jerking her head towards Anthony.

What was he supposed to have told his brother? That he dreamed about bedding a woodland creature? That, for the first time in his life, he found conversation highly stimulating? That he did have demons chained to his soul and they were busy conjuring all sorts of wicked things?

"Told him what?" Lucas shrugged.

Anthony suddenly breathed a sigh of relief. "I think Miss Ecclestone wants to know if you have told me about Lord Banbury."

"What else would I be talking about?"

With a stab of disappointment, Lucas glanced at Anthony, whose mouth curved into an amused grin. "Yes, Miss Ecclestone. I have told him about the conversation you overheard in Lady Colebrook's garden."

Miss Ecclestone gave a satisfied nod, shuffled to the edge of her seat and placed her teacup back on the tray. "Good," she said, "and I assume you have also told him about what I wrote in my note."

Lucas cleared his throat. "I'm afraid my butler thought it was … well, a different sort of note and failed to alert me of its arrival. It has since been misplaced." He had searched the house looking for it, wondering if the scent of her skin lingered on the paper, hoping the sweet smell would evoke a memory of their passionate encounter.

"Oh, I see," she said. "That explains why you failed to reply. Well, in that case, I have something extremely important to tell you."

They both placed their cups on the tray in order to give Miss Ecclestone their full attention and shuffled forward in their seats as they waited for her to speak.

"There is no easy way to say this," she continued, "but Lord Banbury was not the man I heard talking in the garden."

"What?" Lucas cried in disbelief as he gripped the arms of the chair, ready to jump out. "But he must be. You heard him say that he suffocated his brother."

"Then Lord Banbury must have another brother," she said, throwing her hands in the air, "because the current lord was not the person I heard. I spoke to him at the Mendlesons' ball, and I do not believe he is capable of murder."

"I must say I was a little surprised when Lucas informed me of Banbury's involvement," Anthony said. "He always appears so affable."

Banbury could not be that affable, Lucas thought. He had obviously made some damning remarks about Lucas, forcing Miss Ecclestone to jump in and defend him. He was suddenly curious to know why she had done that, knowing it would cause tongues to wag.

"I heard that you challenged Lord Banbury's account of what happened to his brother," Lucas said languidly, his gaze focused on her green eyes. Like the varying hues of the forest, they caressed him with a serene, soothing quality. "Why would you do that?"

She raised a brow, her lips parting ever so slightly and he knew he had piqued her interest, knew her mind was excitely engaged in delivering a response.

"Is that a question, Mr. Dempsey?" she asked in such a provocative tone he felt his manhood stir and swell.

"I believe it is, Miss Ecclestone," he replied, the pleasure of anticipation thrumming through his veins. "It is a question that requires an honest answer."

"Very well," she countered, using his phrase to suggest the answer might be classed as an inappropriate form of conversation. "Would you care to hear my answer now?" she continued, her eyes flitting in the direction of his brother.

Entranced by her playful teasing, Lucas had almost forgotten

Anthony was still sitting there, but he didn't care. "I would, Miss Ecclestone," he replied, inadvertently wetting his lips. "I'm sure my brother is just as interested."

With a nod of compliance, she said, "You have a tortured look about you, Mr. Dempsey. Your eyes are the brightest blue, ethereal and angelic in quality. Yet behind them, there is darkness and pain."

Lucas stared at her, his head hanging forward as he absorbed every word. He noticed Anthony doing the same.

"I believe I have done you an injustice, sir," she continued, "for my initial assessment of your character was that you were, indeed, a man capable of murder. Like everyone else, I based my opinion on what I saw, not what I have come to know and so I felt compelled to speak up for you and would certainly do so again."

Lucas held his breath, his chest swimming with an unnamed emotion. If they were married, he would carry her upstairs and show her the depth of his gratitude in the only way he knew how.

"Wait a minute," Anthony suddenly interjected. Miss Ecclestone looked a little startled as though she, too, had forgotten he was there. "Lord Banbury had a brother-in-law, his wife Margaret's brother. A Mr. Henry Weston."

Lucas dragged his attention away from Miss Ecclestone. "Was this Mr. Weston a guest at Lady Colebrook's ball?" he asked, grateful for the distraction. All these strange sensations made his head hurt.

"Yes, I believe so, but you will have to check with Lady Colebrook."

The mere mention of his former mistress made Lucas squirm in his seat, and he glanced at Miss Ecclestone, who showed not the slightest irritation at the mention of her name. Of course, there was no reason why she should. After all, theirs was to be a feigned betrothal. But he had witnessed the uneasiness gleaned from suspicion and fear many times. He had observed how the jealous resentment of a rival inspired nothing but hatred and loathing.

"Weston was in the crowd on the night you fought Banbury," Anthony said, interrupting Lucas' musing. "He helped carry Banbury back to his carriage and could easily have gone home with him."

"I would only need to hear his voice to confirm his identity," Miss Ecclestone added. "If confirmed, we will need to find out what possible motive Mr. Weston had for killing Lord Banbury."

Anthony's lips thinned, and he said rather gravely, "You understand that your betrothal to Lucas, feigned or not, puts you in danger, Miss Ecclestone. If these men are truly trying to kill my brother, there is a chance you may get hurt in the process."

With a little shrug, she said, "What sort of person would I be, my lord, if I withdrew my support out of concern for my own interests. I could slip on wet steps, could catch my foot in the counterpane and break my neck. If I am to meet my demise, I would prefer to do so doing something I feel passionate about."

If only that passion extended to someone and not something, Lucas thought.

Anthony inclined his head respectfully.

"Will you be staying at home this evening, Miss Ecclestone?" Lucas asked sounding like a young buck and not a seasoned seducer. "As my brother said, we do not know what these men are capable of. I would feel more comfortable if we attended the same engagements." It was also a plausible reason for him to spend more time in her company. How else was he supposed to ignite the fire of passion that he knew lay hidden within?

Her gaze swept over him leisurely, as though she had just heard his thoughts and was assessing his ability to perform the task. "I believe that's what betrothed couples do, Mr. Dempsey."

Lucas wanted to say he hoped they did a lot more than just attend the same functions but refrained from making any comment.

"I'll be at home this evening," she continued. "But I would like to visit Miss Linwood's museum tomorrow afternoon." She gave Lucas a coy smile. "That is if you have no prior engagement."

If he did, he would cancel it. "I shall call for you at two," he confirmed.

"Splendid," she replied, her pleasure evident.

As the gentlemen moved to leave, Anthony said, "I shall see what I can find out about Mr. Weston, and with any luck, my brother will have some news for you tomorrow."

Miss Ecclestone thanked them and bid them a good day, and as they made their way along Grafton Street, Anthony turned to Lucas. "Miss Ecclestone is a remarkable woman, a true original. She has a tremendous amount of faith in you, considering she has only known you for a few days."

"Which is why I could not let her suffer the shame of being found in such a compromising position," Lucas replied, sounding rather magnanimous.

"And I thought your heart had withered away," Anthony grinned. "It's a shame you're not serious about your betrothal."

"Oh, and why is that?"

Anthony placed his hand on Lucas' arm, and they stopped walking. "Because I believe she is the only woman who can save you."

CHAPTER 10

Having escorted Mr. Dempsey and Viscount Harwood to the door, Helena decided to go to her room and rest.

She had spent the best part of the morning arguing with her mother, and if that wasn't exhausting enough, Amelia had decided to join them so that she could have her say.

Amelia had taken great delight in explaining that with such plain features, Helena would struggle to maintain the attention of a man like Lucas Dempsey. As an expert in human nature, Amelia felt that whatever novelty Helena had employed to catch the eye of a man with such a voracious appetite, he would soon tire of it.

Although their opinions were as useful as a wet charcloth in a tinderbox, Helena did wonder what he found so appealing.

When he stared at her with those ravenous eyes of his, as though suffering from a serious lack of sustenance, she thought he might leap from the chair and devour her. What was baffling was she had no idea why. There were many beautiful women willing to throw themselves over a puddle so that he could step over them. So what did he see in *her* that he could not find more conveniently elsewhere?

Her thoughts drifted to her own feelings.

In just a few short days, she had grown to admire Mr. Dempsey. She admired the way he stuck to their pact and told the truth, even though it left him vulnerable and exposed. She admired his resilience. Having suffered a great injustice, he'd not crumbled in despair but had rebelled against his aggressors. He was witty and intelligent. When he kissed her, the whole world seemed to tilt on its axis—her mind plunging into a place new and undiscovered, a place where logic gave way to lust and prudence gave way to pleasure.

In that respect, he was the most dangerous, most exciting man she had ever met.

The following morning a note arrived from Mr. Dempsey stating there had been a sudden development, and consequently, Viscount Harwood would accompany her to the museum. Pushing through her initial feeling of disappointment she read on, relieved to discover that Mr. Dempsey would be meeting them there. He also suggested she invite her sister to act as chaperone and to show that their families were supportive, which would add a degree of credence to their betrothal.

Amelia was delighted to be asked. And their mother spent almost an hour enlightening her on the best ways to impress a viscount. No mention was made of Mr. Dempsey. Her mother had already expressed her disappointment in Helena's choice and thought once the horse had bolted there was little point dirtying one's skirt trying to chase after it.

"What a lovely afternoon," Amelia beamed, glancing out of the carriage window so she could feign ignorance when her knees knocked against Viscount Harwood's for the fifth time. Viscount Harwood shuffled to the left, and Amelia turned to him and said, "Forgive me, my lord, the road does seem rather bumpy today."

Helena rolled her eyes, wishing Amelia would be a little more subtle.

"You look tired, my lord," Helena remarked as she glanced

across the carriage, observing his drooping lids and the faint shadows beneath his eyes. "Are you well?"

Ignoring Amelia's noticeable intake of breath, he smiled, as though he'd been expecting the question. "My brother said you would notice," he replied. "I was out late last night, at my club. I'm afraid I played a little too deep at the card table and lost a substantial sum to Mr. Weston." He gave a covert wink, alerting Helena of the new development Mr. Dempsey had mentioned in his note.

"Mr. Weston must have been delighted," Helena replied in an attempt to glean more information.

Amelia turned to Helena and raised her chin. "I'm sure Lord Harwood does not care to be reminded, Helena."

"On the contrary," he replied with a carefree wave of the hand. "One must accept one's losses with good grace. Besides, Mr. Weston must be in desperate need of funds as he has requested settlement today." He pulled out his pocket watch and checked the time. "Good, it's a little after two. My brother should be waiting for us at the museum."

The carriage drew to a halt at the end of Coventry Street, and they alighted. While Amelia fussed with her dress and straightened her bonnet, Helena glanced up at the impressive building.

It was rather grand. Four tall Doric columns flanked the doorway, supporting a balcony fenced with elaborate iron scrollwork. The rent on such a place must be exorbitant. Had Miss Linwood deliberately created the mystery surrounding her identity to attract more custom?

As they hovered near the entrance, a gentleman approached. He was short and painfully thin, with a nose so long that it seemed to begin at his forehead and end at his chin. "Lord Harwood, I say, Lord Harwood," he called out with a wave as he tottered up to meet them.

"Mr. Weston," the viscount said with some surprise. "What can I do for you?"

Mr. Weston's gaze flicked between Helena and Amelia and

then he said with some embarrassment, "I thought we were to meet this afternoon, to complete our business."

Viscount Harwood looked puzzled. "Did I not say we would meet at my club at four?"

"I'm confident you said two," Mr. Weston replied, looking equally as puzzled. "Yes, two, outside Miss Linwood's museum." He turned to look up at the building and then gave a satisfied nod.

Helena pursed her lips to suppress a gasp. Mr. Weston was definitely one of the men she had heard in Lady Colebrook's garden.

Viscount Harwood bowed to Helena and Amelia. "Forgive me. This is highly inappropriate, but I must deal with this matter." He reached into the inside pocket of his coat and removed some folded notes. "All three hundred," he said, handing it to Mr. Weston. "Perhaps you will give me an opportunity to win it back."

Mr. Weston's body jolted, as though someone had prodded him with a hot poker. "The tables are not always kind, my lord, and so I have decided to find another less crippling pastime."

"A wise decision, Mr. Weston. Perhaps you should try investment. Thanks to my association with Mr. Thorpe, my investments are proving to be a much less risky venture." Viscount Harwood stepped closer and, handing Mr. Weston a card, whispered, "I have tripled my stake in less than a week. I'm sure you'll agree. It's a much better return than the tables."

Mr. Weston stared at the card in his hand like a starving man would look upon a fat piece of gooseberry pie. With a mumbled response and a tip of his hat, he hurried away down the street, only looking up from the prize in his hand when some man shouted for him to move out of the way.

With a sly smile, Viscount Harwood watched Mr. Weston scurry away and gave a satisfied sigh before suggesting, "Shall we go inside and see what delights Miss Linwood has prepared for us?"

Amelia barged past Helena, sidled up to the viscount and placed her hand on his sleeve. "I hear she has procured a painting of Napoléon perched upon a white charger, although there are those who are quick to testify against the likeness." She bestowed her most coquettish smile and arched a brow. "I trust you will be able to enlighten me, my lord."

Attempting to conceal a look of trepidation, Viscount Harwood simply nodded and then escorted them into the entrance hall and paid the six shillings admission.

Mr. Dempsey was waiting for them inside, gazing thoughtfully at a white marble figure of Minerva, the goddess of wisdom. Upon hearing voices, he turned to face them and strolled over, wearing his usual arrogant smile. He was immaculately dressed in a dark blue coat and a pair of pale suede buckskins, whose job it was to restrain his muscular thighs.

Helena recalled the feel of those powerful legs pressed against hers, and her heart thumped against her chest as she struggled to catch her breath.

"So you have found a friend at last, Mr. Dempsey," she said, nodding to the statue.

Mr. Dempsey glanced briefly over his shoulder. "She is a little too quiet for my liking," he replied, taking Helena's hand and bringing it to his lips. He held it there for a few seconds longer than was deemed appropriate. "Although there is no denying wisdom is a beautiful thing."

Helena looked up into eyes that were breathtakingly blue, like a cornflower in the height of summer. "Beauty can be found in many things, Mr. Dempsey, if one knows where to look," she replied, trying to calm the nervous flutter in her stomach. And while introductions were made to the rest of the party, Helena took the opportunity to take a few deep breaths.

Amelia sighed, her brows drawn together in concentration. "There are paintings on the ground floor," she informed as she studied the pamphlet, "while the upper floor houses the Egyptian antiquities. Shall we start down here and work our way up?" she asked, hooking her arm around Viscount Harwood's and leading him through the door on the left before he could protest.

Falling in behind them, Mr. Dempsey whispered in Helena's ear. "Personally, I prefer to start at the top and work my way slowly down."

His tone was deep and rich and sent a small shiver down her spine. His masculine scent caressed and stroked her senses: a mix of bergamot, cedarwood and some other undefinable undertone specific to him.

"My methods are a little more spontaneous, Mr. Dempsey," she admitted in a far more flirtatious tone than she intended. "I prefer to go wherever my heart leads me, as I find it makes for a more pleasurable experience."

Lucas Dempsey's mouth curved into a salacious grin and he laughed, much to Amelia's disgust, who turned to offer Helena a look of reproach. Viscount Harwood's sullen expression conjured an image of a man being held against his will, desperately wanting to shout for help, but too afraid to open his mouth.

"Miss Ecclestone, remind me never to put a sword in your hand for your parrying skills are more than a match for mine," Mr. Dempsey replied with a hint of admiration.

Helena couldn't help but smile, as it was perhaps the finest compliment she had ever received. "I'm sure there are things you could teach me," she replied innocently, but when Mr. Dempsey's eyes widened she felt her cheeks flush.

Swiftly changing the subject, Helena asked, "I wonder why there are nautical paintings in an Egyptian museum?"

"Perhaps they're on loan, or the artists have paid to display their wares. No doubt, Miss Linwood needs the funds."

"Like Mr. Weston," Helena chuckled. "Am I right in thinking that our encounter with Mr. Weston was deliberate, and you planned for me to meet him?" she said as they stopped to admire a landscape by Francisco Mila. "You want me to tell you if he was the gentleman I heard in the garden."

"Was he?"

Feigning interest in Mila's depiction of an ancient seaport, Helena could feel his penetrating gaze. "Yes, I'm convinced he is."

He inhaled sharply and then moved to stand at her side, their arms touching as he studied the painting. "It seems that Mr. Weston has a weakness for faro and has a long line of creditors awaiting payment." He turned his head to face her, his gaze falling to her mouth. "Personally, I can think of far more pleasurable ways to spend my time, but such is the way of men."

"You do your sex a disservice, Mr. Dempsey," Helena disputed. "I'm sure not all men are possessed of a mind for overindulgence. Are there not women who are equally as negligent when it comes to scruples?"

"Like the ones who find themselves forcibly betrothed to a scoundrel," he teased offering her a guilty grin.

"Contrary to popular belief, Mr. Dempsey, you are not a scoundrel."

He narrowed his gaze. His expression grew dark—a look as cold as it was severe—and the air whirled ominously around them. "That is where you err, Miss Ecclestone. I am not the man you think I am. You would be wise to remember that."

So, his demons had finally decided to make an appearance.

As she looked up into his stony face, she could imagine them, like mischievous little gargoyles pressing down on his shoulders, dragging at the corners of his mouth, reminding him he was not worthy of anyone's good opinion.

Helena smiled as she refused to be intimidated. "We are all entitled to our own opinions, whether others believe in them or not."

He gave a mocking snort. "Miss Ecclestone, the truth is before your eyes if you would only care to look." He lowered his head and whispered, "I have disrespected you on more than one occasion. And would gladly do so again should the opportunity arise. Remember, I am a man conceived from hostile opinion, a man delivered from a womb of immorality."

She wanted to tell him he was wrong. She knew the truth, she had seen it, felt it and heard it.

In her opinion, he had acted more respectfully than any other man she had known. He had saved her from a scandal in Lady Colebrook's garden. He had challenged Mr. Huntley-Fisher for his disrespectful comment. He had offered himself up as the sacrificial lamb to protect her reputation.

Yes, he had made improper advances. Advances she had encouraged. And, like him, would probably do so again if the opportunity presented itself. In her eyes, he was not a scoundrel. Circumstance had made him believe so. There was no point trying to persuade him otherwise. She had to prove to him that he was a better man.

"It can take just one good opinion to change a man," she said, stepping closer to the painting to examine the brush strokes. "As long as it is based on friendship and trust. Any other opinion does not deserve such notice."

"Do you believe love can change a man?" he suddenly asked, and when she glanced at him with surprise, he looked shocked that the words had left his lips.

To prevent any awkwardness, she acknowledged his comment. "Yes, Mr. Dempsey. I believe love can change a man. I believe love can heal most wounds."

He tilted his head and looked at her through narrowed eyes. "I think I have a better chance of finding a dragon in my drawing room than of finding love," he replied, his dark mood lifting.

She was suddenly overcome with the need to place her hand on his cheek, to run her fingers through his tousled black locks, to put her head on his chest and listen to his heartbeat, to kiss him deeply until he forgot all of his woes.

"I trust you will succeed on at least one of those counts," she mused, attempting to dampen the feeling of need that shook her to her core. "I have heard there is an exceptionally good sculptor of mythical statues living in Hertford Street."

He laughed as his eyes found hers and settled there for longer than was customary. "Then I must pay him a visit."

Something passed between them, a look that suggested they were allies fighting together against the rest of the world, a feeling that they each had something the other desperately needed and could not live without.

"You must come and look at this," Amelia cried, barging in between them to break the spell. "I am convinced it is not Napoléon at all, but Lord Byron, trekking through the mountains on his way to Italy."

CHAPTER 11

The portrait was definitely of Napoléon, Lucas explained, as Lord Byron was much taller with wavy hair and full lips, as opposed to the thin, weak mouth depicted in the painting. And after bringing the animated discussion to an end, the party moved upstairs to examine the Egyptian antiquities.

As they entered the long gallery, Anthony struck up a conversation with Miss Ecclestone, and they stopped at the first display cabinet to admire a bronze figure. While Lucas, out of politeness, strolled on with her sister, Amelia.

"Well, I can certainly see why some argue against the likeness," Amelia complained, still struggling to accept that she'd been wrong in her assessment of the painting. Wearing a sulky pout, she ambled over to a mahogany display case. "These items once belonged to the daughter of a pharaoh," she said, pointing to a comb and a hairpin, her tone conveying her petulant mood. "Somehow, I expected something more elaborate. If I were the daughter of a pharaoh, everything would be encrusted with jewels and …"

Distracted by the sound of laughter, Lucas glanced over his shoulder and observed his brother and Miss Ecclestone examining an alabaster figure with a grotesque head. Lucas sighed, as he would much rather be bantering with Miss Ecclestone than looking at combs with her impudent sister.

"What do you think that was used for?" Amelia asked nodding to a piece of bone carved into a sharp point.

Lucas shrugged and stifled a yawn. "To pick meat from one's teeth," he guessed as his concentration was waning.

His brother and Miss Ecclestone were talking quietly now, almost whispering, and through the constant hum generated by the other visitors, he was struggling to hear what they were saying.

Sensing his disinterest, Amelia turned and peered over his shoulder. "You must forgive my sister, Mr. Dempsey," she said with some disappointment, and he followed her gaze to find that Miss Ecclestone had placed her hand over her mouth to suppress a giggle. "I'm afraid she often refuses to obey modes of proper conduct when out in public."

Lucas gazed longingly at the scene and had a sudden urge to use his pugilistic skills on his brother. "In that, we are alike," he replied bluntly, feeling compelled to defend his betrothed.

Amelia gave a weak smile. "Well, it was very good of you to make her an offer. Although I am sure we could have saved you the trouble and persuaded Mr. Huntley-Fisher to look the other way." With a censorious shake of the head, Amelia tutted, "Never mind, I'm sure you'll be able to find some way to relieve yourself of the burden."

If Amelia Ecclestone were a man, he would have grabbed her by the lapels of her coat, thrust her up against the glass cabinet and shoved the toothpick up her nose. Instead, Lucas looked her directly in the eye. "I have no intention of ending our betrothal," he replied fiercely. "Your sister is the most fascinating woman I have ever met. And it is certainly no burden to have her name associated with mine."

Amelia's bottom lip quivered, and her cheeks flushed a deep shade of scarlet. "I'm sorry, I did not mean to suggest … it's just that …" Her gaze flitted across his face and lingered on his dimpled chin. "It's just that you're so, well, you're so …" She shook her head, exhaled and then said, "Let's go and join the others."

Lucas gave a curt nod. "You go. I shall be along in a moment."

He turned his back to her and peered into the display case. The rustling of her dress indicated she had walked away.

As he stared through the glass at the array of objects, he did not know which feeling to address first. His head was aching, his body throbbing, his heart pining. He had never known jealousy, not until Miss Ecclestone breezed her way into his life. He had never experienced that feeling of mental unease, that gut-wrenching agony that makes one feel inadequate and unworthy. He knew his thoughts were irrational, yet he could not seem to rein them in.

"Have you always found old combs interesting?" Miss Ecclestone whispered, coming to stand at his shoulder. Her soft silky voice caressed his senses, easing his frustration almost immediately. What he would give to lie her down and show her a more satisfying way to ease his torment.

He turned to face her, suppressing the hunger that writhed through his body. "It is the past that informs the future," he said, aware that his tainted past could not be shaped into a future worthy of her. "Even insignificant items such as these have some part to play in history."

Her eyes brightened. "I didn't know you were so philosophical, either."

"Neither did I," he replied, his tone a little melancholic and as her eyes searched his face, there was a trace of pity in them. "Don't look at me like that," he protested, as that was the last feeling he wanted to evoke.

"Look at you like what?"

"Like I'm a bird with a broken wing in need of tending."

Miss Ecclestone laughed. "Mr. Dempsey, even with a broken wing I'm sure you would find some way to fly."

Lucas drank in the compliment, and it lifted his spirits. He glanced over at Anthony whose foot tapping and wandering gaze suggested he was suffering from the loss of his amusing companion. "I didn't know my brother could be so entertaining."

The words held a trace of resentment; after all, a viscount was considered a much more respectable companion than a man with a scandalous past.

"There is a statue with an overly large head," she chuckled, pointing to the cabinet. "We were saying that it bears some resemblance to Rowlandson's caricatures." Looking up at the corner of the ceiling, she mused, "I wonder if that is where he got his inspiration." Her focus continued to drift away and then as if suddenly aware of her surroundings, she said, "Your brother is quite funny and utterly charming. I'm surprised he's not wed."

The words were not said to entice jealousy or cause hostility but were an honest appraisal of his brother's character. "He takes his responsibilities very seriously, so I'm sure he has some sort of plan in that regard."

"Perhaps it would be best if neither of us mentions that to Amelia."

With a quick glance over her shoulder, she shuffled closer, as though she had some information to impart and his nostrils were filled with the sweet smell of strawberries.

Aware that he'd inhaled deeply, she said with a dismissive wave of the hand, "It's the face cream. I was rather liberal in my application. It smells so delicious I have to stop myself licking it off my finger."

Heaven help him! He'd happily lick it off every inch of her given the chance. He would find out where she bought it and send her a crate full of the stuff. "It smells divine," he said, hungry to taste her once more.

"Why, thank you," she replied, appearing happy with the compliment.

They simply stared at each other for a moment, the air about them charged with some strange force that made the hairs on his nape tingle.

Miss Ecclestone put her hands to her cheeks and patted them gently. "Your brother mentioned your plan, your plan to trap Mr. Weston."

"It's my brother's plan. Mine was much simpler and involved nothing more than a hard fist." However, Anthony insisted a more covert approach was needed and had reminded Lucas that a scandal would also tarnish Miss Ecclestone's name.

Aware that someone was waiting to examine the antiquities, Lucas placed Miss Ecclestone's hand in the crook of his arm, and they strolled to a display of stone tablets.

"He said that you have hired a gentleman to act as the owner of an investment company," she whispered.

"Mr. Thorpe," Lucas confirmed, feeling the pads of her fingers moving gently back and forth on his arm as she explored the point where bone met with hard muscle. "Apparently, he is renowned for helping members of the nobility who find themselves in unfortunate situations."

"It has all come together rather quickly," she said with some surprise.

Lucas nodded. "Anthony interviewed an associate of Mr. Thorpe's at his club and hired his services. Indeed, Mr. Thorpe sent a note within hours informing us of Mr. Weston's predilection for gambling and instructing Anthony to lose at the faro table."

Miss Ecclestone's luscious lips thinned to express her admiration.

"Further instructions were received this morning, along with a card that Anthony was to pass to Mr. Weston. We are only to contact Thorpe if Mr. Weston was not the man you heard in the garden. If we're wrong, I told Anthony to deduct the money from my inheritance."

Enjoying the feel of her hand on his arm, Lucas led her around the perimeter, only stopping to scan the objects.

"How do you know you are not being duped? How do you know you can trust this Mr. Thorpe?" she asked as her hand moved fractionally higher up his arm.

Lucas stiffened as the old feelings of hostility resurfaced. "I do not trust anyone, Miss Ecclestone. If it were a simple case of righting an injustice, then I would not waste my time. But Mr. Weston wants to do me harm, and so I am left with little choice, other than throttling the man myself."

A week ago, he would have beaten Weston within an inch of his life; it would not take much for him to squeal like a pig. Now, out of concern for Miss Ecclestone, he was forced to partake in a complicated charade. When his attention was drawn back to the lady in question, she gave him that look again, the one that suggested he had unwittingly revealed something else of his character.

His assessment proved accurate when she turned to him and beamed, "Oh, I believe it is time for a question, Mr. Dempsey."

"What, so soon?" he asked, failing to lighten his mood.

She tightened her grip on his arm and led him out into the hallway, to stand next to the balustrade between a bust of Nefertiti and Ramesses the second. "You said a moment ago that you do not trust anyone. Was it your experiences with your father that led you to feel that way?"

Lucas felt his chest tighten as he recalled the moment he stood before his father to answer for his crimes. He remembered the hollow void in the pit of his stomach feeding on the uncomfortable silence, remembered his father's bloated face when he called him a lying savage.

Why did people assume that being deemed handsome meant you were somehow impervious to pain? His father's actions had reinforced the point that if he could not trust those closest to him, who could he trust?

"I was once naive and wildly optimistic about life," he said, resentment woven through every word as there was a part of him that still grieved for the loss of that man. "Every person I have ever met has tried to carve out a small piece of me to keep and use for their amusement."

"Not everyone," she said a little too haughtily.

But the old feelings of distrust and suspicion had woken from their slumber, reminding him he was a fool if he believed she was any different from all the others. That if he took a moment to look closely, he would see that even she was using him for her own enjoyment.

He stepped closer so that he towered over her, anger and pain brimming beneath the surface. "Everyone!" he exclaimed, his voice dark and oppressive. "Even you, Miss Ecclestone, with your prying questions." Yes, he thought, even she wanted something from him. Mentally, he tightened the chain around his heart and secured the lock. "You coerce, and you intimidate until you get whatever it is you want. You're no different," he scowled with contempt. "I have seen the pleasure you glean when you have manipulated and extracted the information you desire."

Miss Ecclestone met his sinister gaze, and he saw sadness and pain reflected back at him. She placed the palm of her hand on his chest and pushed, forcing him to straighten.

"Thank you for making me aware of your true feelings." Her voice sounded strained as she took a step back. "I bid you a good day, sir."

Without another word, she turned her back to him and walked towards the stairs.

A hard lump formed in his throat, his stomach flipping over as his heart pounded and thumped against its shackles. For the first time in years, he felt an inner turmoil as he struggled to decide what to do.

From experience, he believed it best to detach himself from feelings of sentimentality, to avoid complicated entanglements, to refrain from making protestations he had no intention of keeping. Miss Ecclestone had changed all of that, and he knew if he let her leave, their friendship, like all good things, would be lost to him forever.

"Miss Ecclestone," he called out to her, acting on impulse. "Miss Ecclestone, please wait."

She continued down the curved staircase and did not look up.

He raced down the stairs, stepping past her, turning to block her path, to prevent her from taking another step. A few people had congregated in the hallway and were peering over the balustrade, keen to observe the spectacle.

"Helena, please," he begged, the use of her given name causing her to inhale sharply.

"I … I believe you have said all there is to say, Mr. Dempsey."

Suddenly, he was aware of a deep rumbling sound coming from above, followed by someone shouting, "Look out!"

He glanced up to see the bust of Nefertiti tipping back off its plinth. Desperate hands clutched at the carved stone as it tumbled over the balustrade.

Grabbing Miss Ecclestone around the waist, he pulled her into his chest and threw himself against the wall, using his body to shield her as the bust hit the steps.

Lucas heard the heavy thud, heard the gasps of disbelief and said a silent prayer as he looked over his shoulder at the lumps of stone scattered over the stairs.

He looked back at Miss Ecclestone's ashen face. "Are you all right?" he asked, gasping for air as he blocked out the noise of footsteps racing down the stairs, of a high-pitched scream and someone shouting their names.

When she nodded, all the muscles in his body went limp. His shoulders sagged as he wrapped his arms around her and drew her back to his chest.

Despite all the shouts and protestations, he refused to let her go. Yet he knew that this world of danger and sin was not the place for her. With an ache in his heart, he let Anthony pull him away, knowing she was better off without him.

CHAPTER 12

Henry Weston hurried down New Bond Street in search of the offices of Thorpe & Jones.

Standing on the street outside number twenty-five, he glanced down at the card in his hand and then examined the row of small signs fixed to the wall. With his gaze drawn instantly to the buffed brass rectangle, his eyes widened with delight at the company's polished plate, which shone like a glittering jewel amongst dirty pebbles.

First impressions were everything when it came to business, and he felt a sudden burst of optimism, for he could not afford to make another mistake, not at this stage.

His thoughts turned to Viscount Harwood, and he chuckled to himself at the irony of it all. Would the viscount have been so forthcoming with his money and his advice if he'd known the truth? Would he have been as eager to help the man who had ruined his brother's reputation?

Henry opened the door, stepped into the hall and mounted the stairs to the second floor. Perhaps fate had already altered its course and was now working with him rather than against him, he thought, believing he was due a run of good luck. However, it would not pay to be too confident. He still had two problems that required his attention before he could feel safe and secure again.

It was no easy feat turning three hundred pounds into a thousand; he just hoped that Thorpe & Jones were as competent as Viscount Harwood had suggested. He chuckled again knowing that the viscount had helped him to find the funds that would eventually lead to the death of his brother.

Henry had no real gripe with Mr. Dempsey. In truth, it would have been far easier to do away with Margaret, as she was the only witness. However, Margaret received an allowance from her late husband's estate and was always willing to pay the odd tailor's bill or provide food and lodgings when he was on a losing streak.

As he reached the landing, he noticed that the door opposite was ajar, yet he could see nothing more than a thick forearm resting on the desk.

He crept closer, tried to peer around for a better view, but to no avail. He gave a few light raps on the door. "Excuse me," he called politely. "I am looking for the office of Thorpe & Jones."

There was a rustling of paper, the sound of a chair scraping against the wooden floor and the door suddenly flew open. Henry Weston could do nothing other than gape at the mountain of a man filling the doorway, his eyes falling on the man's coat where the material stretched and strained against bulging muscles.

"Do you have an appointment?" the man asked sharply as though he was used to people calling without one and had no difficulty in removing them physically if necessary.

Henry swallowed and could feel cool beads of perspiration forming on his brow.

Without waiting for an answer, the beast barked, "Mr. Thorpe will not see you without an appointment."

Henry's tongue felt heavy and thick in his mouth. "My name … my name is Henry Weston," he stuttered. "Viscount Harwood gave me your card and well ..." He held out his hand almost dropping the card as it shook and quivered.

Chunky fingers ripped the card from his hand and examined it closely, turning it over a few times as he cast Mr. Weston a curious glance. "Wait here a moment," he instructed, squeezing past and stomping towards another door further down the hallway.

Mr. Weston waited. Minutes rolled by and he pulled out his watch to examine the time, replacing it quickly when the door finally opened.

"Mr. Thorpe will see you now," the giant bellowed, standing back against the open door to allow Henry room to shuffle past.

Sucking in his stomach so that his ribs protruded, Henry edged past, breathing a sigh of relief when he heard the door close behind him and the thud of heavy footsteps retreating down the hallway.

Thorpe sat behind his desk, his fingers steepled as he assessed the man standing before him.

Over the years, he had met many gentlemen like Mr. Weston: frail and feeble men who craved power to mask their inferiority. Men who believed money commanded respect.

"Take a seat, Mr. Weston," he said, waving his hand to the chair, placed just far enough away from the desk so as not to appear rude.

His disguise had been professionally applied to make him look older—white lead and flour for his face and Indian ink to create a few wrinkles and folds. The effect appeared natural from a distance. Although somewhat outdated, the powdered wig served a specific purpose: it disguised his ebony hair and gave an impression of authority and respectability.

"Thank you," Weston replied, his countenance brightening as he relaxed into the chair.

"I believe Viscount Harwood gave you my card," he said with a degree of admiration, as it served to let Weston know that he'd been granted a privilege.

Raising his chin, Weston replied, "Yes, yes that is correct. We were together at his club when he mentioned his ... investment."

"He should have spoken to me first," Thorpe said sharply, showing his irritation. Mr. Weston needed to be clear as to who was in charge of this game and to feel that Thorpe & Jones were particular about their choice of clientele. "Do you wish to invest?"

Mr. Weston's mouth opened and closed a few times. "Well, I should like t-to know a little more about it."

Thorpe steepled his fingers once more and let his gaze roam over the gentleman opposite. "At Thorpe & Jones, we invest in many things, Mr. Weston." He shrugged. "Are you interested in long or short-term gain? Obviously, you receive a greater percentage the longer you invest."

"I was thinking of something short term," Weston answered, "just to begin with."

"That is perhaps the wisest choice. May I also suggest that your first deposit is a small one, somewhere between twenty and fifty pounds?"

A look of panic flashed across Mr. Weston's face. "I ... I was thinking of investing a little more," he replied nervously.

Thorpe pursed his lips, giving the impression he was thinking as opposed to suppressing a grin. "What figure did you have in mind, Mr. Weston?"

"I was thinking more in the region of three hundred."

Showing that he was impressed that the man had access to such an exorbitant sum, Thorpe shuffled through a few papers on the desk and then handed one to Mr. Weston, who looked a little confused. "It is an investment opportunity that I have received only this morning, an opportunity for a serious investor," he clarified. "You may keep that copy should you need to verify its authenticity."

"There's no need," Mr. Weston replied, trying to hand back the paper, albeit unsuccessfully. "Viscount Harwood has assured me of your credentials."

"Very well," Thorpe nodded. "With that particular investment, you could double your money by tomorrow."

Mr. Weston looked astounded and ecstatic. "Tomorrow!"

"Later this afternoon, The London Dock Company are auctioning off all crates and casks where the owners have been unable to pay the company's storage fees. Once we've won the auction and have the contents confirmed, I have an array of merchants willing to purchase them. All business should be settled this evening, and so you would have your return in the morning."

Mr. Weston struggled to keep his backside on the seat. "That would be wonderful, Mr. Thorpe," he beamed.

"Excellent. I shall leave it for you to decide how much you wish to invest," he replied, knowing that Weston would invest the whole three hundred. Dipping his nib in the inkwell, he began scrawling and said without looking up, "Bostock will see to the paperwork. His office is at the end of the hall."

Mr. Weston stood to leave. "Thank you, Mr. Thorpe. A good day to you."

"Just a few things before you go," he said, looking up from his desk. "Do not encourage any other investors without speaking to me first." When Weston nodded, he added, "I have another investment should you be interested, a shipment of silk that has been damaged in a wreckage. A similar venture saw a yield of seventy percent." Thorpe waved his hand in the air. "It's something to consider, but I shall need to move quickly."

"Would tomorrow be too late to consider another investment?" Weston asked eagerly.

"No, no. Tomorrow will be fine."

CHAPTER 13

Lucas lounged back in the copper bath and tried to blot out the image of the stone bust crashing down on top of Miss Eccle-stone. He had not slept a wink: his thoughts jumbled and chaotic as he played out every devastating scenario. At the first sign of sunrise he'd groaned, tossed and turned for a few hours before finding the strength to crawl out of bed.

"This one's warmer than the last," Jenson said as he came into the room carrying a bucket.

"Pour some of it over my head," Lucas instructed, hoping the sensation would ease his troubled mind.

As the water ran down his face he imagined blood trickling down Helena's cheek, her eyes wide and lifeless as she lay buried amongst the chalky rubble. Flicking back his hair, he grabbed the glass from the wooden stool, tipping it up and shaking out the last drop of brandy as though the motion would somehow make it magically refill.

Jenson glanced up at the clock on the mantel and raised a curious brow. "Shall I go and get the decanter?"

"Only if there's brandy in it," Lucas replied, hoping he'd feel better after another glass or two.

Lucas sighed. It was all his fault.

He should never have come back. His head didn't throb when he was in Boston, and his heart didn't beat against his chest like a battering ram determined to find a breach in the stone wall.

He had spent the last four years believing he'd killed a man, the rotten feeling in his core always there as a constant reminder. Though he would choose to suffer that feeling for all eternity rather than have Helena Ecclestone's death on his conscience.

The thought made him shudder.

Lucas had examined the scene, spoken to the curator, Mr. Pearce, and to the witnesses. There had been a number of people on the upstairs landing; none of them could remember seeing anything untoward. He knew that someone had deliberately pushed the plinth with the intention of causing them harm. The curator seemed unperturbed by the event, commenting that people often tended to gravitate towards the macabre and as such expected to see an increase in visitors. Lucas contemplated hanging the man from the balustrade, confident the chilling spectacle would draw an even bigger crowd.

In truth, Helena *had* received a hurtful blow. One he had delivered.

He recalled the pain and sadness in her eyes when he unleashed the tirade of abuse. Something inside him had snapped. Doubt and fear had surfaced, warning him not to trust her, telling him that she was a traitor and using him for her own pleasure, her own gain.

His thoughts drifted to the note he had sent her, a note that should have clearly forbidden any further association with him. Yet he'd not been able to scrawl the words, his numb fingers refusing to acknowledge the truth. Instead, he sent a few feeble poetic lines: a cryptic message alluding to the possibility that they did not belong together.

"Th-there's a lady waiting for you downstairs," Jenson blurted, the crystal top on the decanter clinking in his trembling hand. "I told Gregson you wouldn't be happy, but he couldn't stop her."

Lucas felt a rush of exhilaration lifting him from his languid mood. Perhaps Helena had understood his message and had come to challenge him. "Never mind, Jenson, just hand me my robe," he said, water cascading over the floor as he stepped out of the tub.

In his haste to help his master, Jenson fumbled about with the garment. "What will you wear, sir?"

"They'll do," Lucas said, pointing to the breeches hanging over the chair, "and just get me any shirt." He was certain Helena would not object to his casual attire.

Thrusting his arm into the shirt, he descended the stairs two at a time, brushing his hand through his damp locks as he strode into the parlour.

"This is becoming quite a habit," he said playfully as he entered the room.

Miranda Colebrook stood to greet him, aware of the look of disappointment etched on his face. Her eyes roamed over the loose shirt, lingering at the dusting of hair below his throat with the same eagerness one would look upon an oasis in a dusty desert.

"Lucas," she chirped with outstretched hands, which she dropped when he made no move towards her. "Were you expecting someone else?"

Honesty being his new faithful friend he saw no point in lying. But then he hesitated. It would not do for people to know that Helena had visited him in his home, not when one considered the relaxed manner of his dress.

"Jenson mentioned I had a visitor, but he did not say it was a lady. I came down expecting to find my brother."

"I see," she replied dubiously. "Forgive the intrusion, but I heard about the accident at the museum and simply had to come. I trust you were not harmed in any way?"

He waved his hand down the length of his body. "As you can

see, I'm perfectly fine. But I thank you for your concern, Lady Colebrook."

"Oh, Lucas," she said, taking a few steps towards him. "You do not have to call me Lady Colebrook. It sounds so … so formal after what has passed between us."

Lucas stifled a groan as he did not care to be reminded. "I believe it is for the best now that I'm betrothed."

"Oh, I heard about your silly little charade. Mr. Huntley-Fisher was very forthcoming. Tell me you're not going to go ahead with it. I know you find the chit entertaining, but marriage!" She waved her hand in the air to show the absurdity of it all. "I just don't see it. You would die of boredom within the month. All that simpering and bashful modesty. If you'd wanted to play knight and virgin, you only had to ask." Moistening her lips with the tip of her tongue, she stared at the opening of his shirt and then her gaze dropped to the fall of his breeches. "Poor Miss Ecclestone, how on earth will she manage you?"

Lucas gave her a satisfied smile. "You underestimate her capabilities on all counts," he said, hoping his expression revealed the pleasure he received from Helena's company, from her witty banter, from her wet mouth. "I only hope that I am able to meet her expectations."

Recovering quickly from a momentary lapse of confidence, Lady Colebrook came to stand in front of him, placed her hands on his chest and let her long fingers glide slowly up to his shoulders.

"It is not the same, Lucas, and you know it. She will not be able to satisfy you as I can."

It crossed his mind to tell her that she'd never truly satisfied him. But then she lunged at him, pressed her lips to his and thrust her tongue into his mouth before he had a chance to speak. Every muscle in his body fought against the intrusion, and he jumped back, breaking all contact. "I think it's time you left," he growled, wiping his mouth with the back of his hand to show his disdain.

"You don't mean that."

Ignoring the look of shock and embarrassment on her face, he strode towards the door and held it open. "Gregson will see you out. And I must insist that you never come here again."

$\sim$

Helena moved away from the window and flopped down onto the bed, flicking through a book of poems in the hope of stumbling across something exciting enough to distract her thoughts away from Lucas Dempsey.

It was no use.

She had spent a restless night recalling the feel of his strong arms around her, hearing the beat of his heart when he'd cradled her head to his chest. His words of comfort still drifted through her mind in a bid to heal the wound he had inflicted. The cruel comments still pained her; his lack of trust had cut deep.

She sighed as she had no right to dwell on it. Not when he had suffered four years of injustice and betrayal. The thought brought a tear to her eye, and she felt a deeper ache: a burning desire to touch him, to ease his pain, to help him heal until no sign of a scar remained.

When she asked her little questions, when she prodded him for the truth, she was only trying to help him.

Surely he knew that.

Walking away from him at the museum had caused a disturbing reaction: a hollow ache in her stomach that grew bigger with every step until it felt like an empty cavern. The sense of loneliness was the most shocking. It crept upon her unawares, shrouding her in a cloak of vulnerability, evoking a deep sadness she couldn't shake.

Yet all those desolate feelings had disappeared when she snuggled against his hard body. Viscount Harwood had pulled them apart, gesturing to the crowd when Mr. Dempsey initially refused. It was the viscount who brought her and Amelia home, who explained the accident to her parents while Mr. Dempsey waited at the scene to talk to the attendants.

Helena walked over to the flower arrangement on her dressing table, a bouquet sent by Lucas. The varying green hues of laurel and ivy swamped the assortment of white flowers, and they made her think of the forest. She glanced down at the note and read it again:

Darkness and Light,
Day and Night,
An impossible existence.

She had spent hours studying those lines, wondering what thoughts prompted the combination. She imagined him sitting down to write them, scrunching up piece after piece of paper desperate to find the right words to convey his emotion.

A tap on the door disturbed her reverie.

"I thought I'd come and see if you needed anything," Amelia said, stepping into the room and closing the door.

She had come to snoop.

"No." Helena sighed. "I'm fine."

Undeterred, Amelia wandered over to the flower display and inhaled the aroma. "The flowers are beautiful. They're a little wild and untamed, but beautiful all the same."

She glanced down at the note but said nothing.

"Wild and untamed," Helena repeated feeling a sudden urge to talk to someone. "Do you suppose Mr. Dempsey is trying to tell me something?"

"I think Mr. Dempsey believes you're an original. I think he likes the fact you're unconventional." Amelia walked over to the bed and sat on the end. "Although I have no idea why," she added honestly, her tone sad and melancholic. "You're not exactly beautiful. You laugh loudly in public, say the most inappropriate things, find yourself in compromising situations. Still, the most handsome man in all of England falls at your feet."

Amelia found it hard to accept that there was a man in the world who wasn't interested in her.

"Mr. Dempsey does not fall at my feet. We are friends, Amelia, friends who happen to find themselves temporarily betrothed."

"You do not think Mr. Dempsey is sincere in his declaration?"

"Under the circumstances, he did the only thing he could. I am confident he will find a plausible reason to put an end to our arrangement."

"That's not what *he* said." Amelia walked over to the dressing table and sat down on the stool. "Do you think I should do something different with my hair?" she asked, turning her head from left to right and examining her profile, bouncing the golden ringlets in the palm of her hand.

Helena ignored the last question. "What do you mean, that's not what he said?" She hurried over to stand behind her sister. "Has Mr. Dempsey said something?"

"He may have, but perhaps I can't remember now."

When faced with one of Amelia's stubborn moods, Helena had two choices. Beat it out of her, which she'd wanted to do many times, or pander to her whims until she forgot she was in a mood at all.

"You could try braids instead of curls and dress them around your crown," Helena suggested, holding her hand like a claw above her sister's head to demonstrate. "I think the height will accentuate your cheekbones."

Amelia stared thoughtfully at her own reflection. "I don't want you to marry Mr. Dempsey," she said with a feigned sniff. "I don't know what I would do without you here for support."

It was impossible to follow her sister's fluctuating emotions, but Helena knew better than to be touched by a remark brought about for selfish reasons.

"I am not going to marry Mr. Dempsey," Helena said though the words caused her stomach to churn.

Rather than appear placated, Amelia looked forlorn. "When I implied the marriage would not take place, Mr. Dempsey got very angry with me. He said he does not intend to end your betrothal. He said you're the most fascinating woman he has ever met."

Helena could only stare at her sister's reflection as a whirlwind of emotions tore through her body. All sense and reason escaped her as she found herself swept up and carried along by a profound passion, a desperate craving to be held, cared for and loved by Lucas Dempsey. She wanted to feel his warm lips on hers. She wanted to wrap her arms around his neck, trace her fingers through his tousled hair, and hear him call her name as he'd done on the stairs at the museum.

"Are you sure that's what he said?" Helena asked, trying to focus on a rational thought. She picked up the note and handed it to Amelia. "I believe this implies otherwise."

Amelia took a moment to read it, looked up at Helena and then read it a few more times. "I think he means he is not worthy of you, Helena. Darkness and night imply danger, decadence, and dissipation. While light represents innocence and purity. The assumption would be that darkness can corrupt light as it is not possible to purify that which is already tainted."

To say that Helena was amazed by her sister's insightful response was an understatement. "I had not really thought of it like that," Helena replied, a little annoyed as she was usually the first to see the logical in any situation. "So, is he saying we're unsuited?"

"I think he is saying you do not belong in his world, and he has no place in yours."

Lucas was wrong. He didn't belong in a tainted world, either. "I didn't know you were so adept at deciphering symbolism?"

"It is a hobby of mine," Amelia whispered, putting her finger to her lips, "but don't tell anyone. Mother would not approve."

Feeling a genuine wave of affection, Helena placed a kiss on her sister's head. "Thank you," she said softly, "my head was throbbing just thinking about the note."

"Of course, he is wrong in all that he implies. There is a time and place where you may meet him, a time where you may experience his world."

Amelia fell silent for a moment while she contemplated her profile in the mirror.

"Are you going to enlighten me or are you waiting for me to compliment your eyes?"

Amelia smiled. "Oh, there's no need. I've been told that my eyes are like the ocean—intensely blue and serene. Besides, I rather like being the knowledgeable one for a change. There is a time when day and night merge, when it is neither one nor the other, like at dusk. You could also explain to Mr. Dempsey that there are elements of day and night within all of us, to some degree."

With a sudden burst of excitement, that was highly uncharacteristic, Helena said, "I should send a reply, something poetic like—dusk, a time where day meets night for a forbidden liaison."

Amelia pondered the words and then scrunched up her nose. "Poetry is not your forte, Helena. I think you should just be yourself. Mr. Dempsey obviously admires the weird and unusual." She took a moment to inspect her fingernails, and then added, "We would never have suited. I have to say I find his manner rather coarse. But you seem to know what you want."

"I don't know what I want. For the first time in my life, logic has escaped me. My head feels as though it's stuffed with feathers and periodically they float down and tickle my heart to make it flutter."

Amelia laughed. "Well, for someone who is usually so intelligent, you *are* acting like a goose. Write your note, and I will see to it that Mr. Dempsey receives it."

"You would do that?" Helena asked with some suspicion.

Amelia arched a mischievous brow. "Of course. And in return, you will promise to arrange another outing with Viscount Harwood."

CHAPTER 14

Lying on his bed with his hands clasped behind his head, Lucas contemplated how a small insignificant incident could change the course of one's life. What if Helena hadn't bumped into him in the garden? What if he'd not decided to seek sanctuary from the crowded ballroom?

They would never have met.

The thought caused a sudden pang of sadness.

Aware of Jenson's pacing outside his door, Lucas called for him to enter, his abrupt tone conveying his frustration. Not with his staff. He was too busy thinking about Helena's reaction to his note, too busy wishing he had the gift of invisibility so he could ride over to Grafton Street and observe for himself.

"There's a letter for you," Jenson informed, stepping around the bed to hold out the salver. "I wasn't sure if you were expecting it, so thought it best not to wait," he continued, swallowing deeply.

Lucas stared at the small rectangle lying in the middle of the silver tray. "Thank you, Jenson. At least this one has not been mislaid."

Instinct told him it was from Helena, and he wondered if the contents would aggravate his melancholic mood. With his hand suspended in the air, as though the note lay nestled amongst a pit of spitting vipers, he found the courage to pull it out.

The floral scent confirmed his suspicion and Lucas waited for Jenson to leave before breaking the seal.

She had not replied in verse. There were no poetic meanderings, no flowery prose, just a simple response delivered in her usual intriguing tone.

Can anything be so clearly defined, Mr. Dempsey? If you care to hear my view on the subject, I suggest you meet me later, at dusk. I shall wait for you in my garden.

Those simple words stimulated his senses, roused his desire like the caress of soft hands on his body. Just the thought of being alone with her in the garden caused his manhood to throb and ache with need. God, he had never wanted a woman as much as he wanted her and he imagined all sorts of lascivious scenarios involving long grass, the trunk of a tree and a naked wood nymph.

Reason and rationale fought heavily against his voracious appetite, against the burning need that consumed him. His mind told him not to go. His heart pleaded and his body begged him to.

Yet amongst all the confusion one thought dominated all others: when it came to Helena Ecclestone, doing the wrong thing felt so damn right.

Explaining that she still felt exhausted after the accident at the museum, Helena informed her family she wished to retire to her room for the rest of the evening.

In her excitement, she forgot that meant the maid helping her into a nightgown. She would have to throw on her cloak, the green velvet one with the ermine trim, as the air had grown cooler, the gentle breeze gathering momentum.

Having dressed her bed: plumping her pillows and shaping

them to look as though a body lay huddled beneath the sheets, Helena crept through the house and slipped out into the garden unnoticed.

There were two paths leading from the manicured lawn. One led to the fountain, attendant topiary and raised beds. Helena took the other, less tamed walk that curved past the rose garden, a rainbow of rhododendrons and through a willow tunnel that led to the gate in the boundary wall.

After unlocking the gate, she stepped back to the entrance of the tunnel and pressed her palm against her stomach in an attempt to calm the wild flutter.

If Lucas Dempsey actually believed what he'd written in his note, there was a chance he wouldn't come. Indeed, she found his emotions to be unpredictable, chaotic at times and it was difficult to know what he was thinking. One minute he announced that he had no intention of ending their betrothal, the next he sent cryptic notes suggesting they should never meet again.

Helena sighed, and her stomach flipped over.

How was she supposed to help him when she struggled to understand her own feelings?

Perhaps that was her problem. She over-thought everything. She dissected every word and nuance to be probed and examined before she could even begin to reach a conclusion. What if life was too complex to be defined by such a rigid set of rules? She should try to stop thinking, should start following her intuition, be guided more by her feelings.

The sound of the wooden gate scraping against the gravel broke her reverie, and her heart began to beat loudly in her chest.

Failing to notice her immediately, Lucas Dempsey closed the gate, using two hands to ease it back gently before turning to inspect his surroundings. He scanned the willow arch with some surprise before locating her.

His gaze raked boldly over her from head to toe as his mouth curled into a devilish grin. "Miss Ecclestone," he said, his tone deep and languid as he offered her a graceful bow. He looked every bit a rogue dressed in a fitted black coat and matching waistcoat, his breeches a pale, neutral grey, pulled taut across hard, toned muscle.

The sight of him caused heat to pool at the apex of her thighs as she remembered what it was like to be held against his chest, held tight by those strong muscular arms.

"I don't know whether to say good afternoon or good evening," she said, trying to maintain her composure though her breath came more quickly and her tongue felt thick and clumsy. "As you can see, it's dusk. It is a time where day and night conduct their daily liaison."

Lucas Dempsey raised a sinful brow, and she flushed under the heat of his gaze. "A liaison, Miss Ecclestone?" he murmured stroking his chin in a slow, rhythmical motion, his eyes falling to her mouth as he moistened his lips. "You mean it is a time where a dragon may leave his lair and roam freely in the garden of a wood nymph." His words dripped with desire, and when she inhaled deeply, he added, "It is said that dragons possess a venomous bite that once inflicted renders the recipient helpless."

It was as though the words floated from his mouth, carried on a soft breeze to tempt, to entice. She scoured the deserted recesses of her mind, a place long vacated by logic, to think of a witty retort that would equal his, something to arouse the same feeling of shameless abandon.

"They say nymphs possess an amorous freedom that sets them apart from their chaste sisters." She took a few slow steps towards him, drawn by an overwhelming feeling she could not define, an overwhelming need to feel the warmth of his body next to hers. "They say a dalliance with such a creature may render the man besotted, infatuated to the point of madness."

He opened his arms wide and beckoned her to come forward. "Then chain me up and drag me to Bedlam."

Released from the ropes of restraint, she ran the few remaining steps towards him. He wrapped his arms around her, devouring her mouth with a desperate urgency that almost knocked them both off their feet. Within seconds, their wandering hands conveyed their frustration, the breathless pants and guttural groans audible amongst the birds' bedtime song.

A craving for fulfilment swamped her as he ravished her mouth with fiery possession. Her hands clutched his broad shoulders, her fingers finding their way to the wavy locks at his nape, tugging at the hair as his tongue thrust rhythmically with hers.

"Mr. Dempsey," she panted as his hot mouth moved to the sensitive skin just below her jaw.

"Lucas," he growled, kissing her again, tugging at her cloak, his hands stealing inside and coming to rest on her hips.

The sensation of his warm palms penetrating the thin fabric of her nightgown was almost her undoing. But when he stopped abruptly, tearing his lips from hers with a gasp, she wanted to cry out in grief for the loss.

"Your dress. I was not expecting—" His hands froze on the curve of her hips, the cultivated mask of a seducer replaced by the tense, timid expression of a schoolboy.

At that moment, he looked more handsome than she had ever seen him, his blue eyes sparkling with a vulnerability that fed her need to soothe him.

"I am supposed to be in bed," she replied innocently, her thoughts flashing briefly to the mound of pillows, to her maid peeking around the door and nodding with satisfaction at the sight.

"Indeed," he drawled, the dragon stirring once more, batting the boy away to take the stage. "I think that could still be arranged."

Helena felt the pads of his fingers begin to move on her hips in slow circular motions. The subtle gesture caused a surprisingly intense reaction as desire pulsed through her body in waves rather than ripples, and she felt herself rocking back and forth as he deepened the stroke. She looked up at him, her lips parting with each breath, with each undulation, as she gave herself over to the sensation. His wicked grin suggested confidence in his ability to please.

When he lowered his head and took her mouth, the pace was gentle, more measured. The soft brushing of his lips caused a tingling that raced through her body to the tips of her toes. She raised a trembling hand, caressed his jaw, the skin smooth where he'd shaved.

When her fingers snaked up around his neck into his tousled locks, grasping at his hair to prolong the contact, she felt a surge of passion rush through him, and he deepened the kiss in response. A soft humming sound resonated from somewhere deep in his throat as their tongues met in a fiery dance and she pressed herself into him in a desperate bid to intensify the feeling.

Within seconds, the tempo changed again as he plundered her mouth, delving deeper, pressing himself against her so she could feel the thick, hard evidence of his arousal. The low groan revealed how the sensation increased his pleasure. His actions became wilder, rougher as he clawed at the fabric of her nightgown. As he bunched the garment in his fists and tugged it up around her waist, the cool air breezed over her bare thighs, heightening her desire.

"Lucas" she breathed, as his hands caressed the hollow of her back, skin to skin, moving around to touch her in a far more intimate place. "Lucas, no, not here," she whispered, a hint of fear evident as the words tumbled from her lips unconsciously.

He stopped, ripped his mouth from hers and cursed under his breath, reacting to her words as though they had rendered him helpless, as though they had robbed the dragon of his ability to breathe fire.

With another curse, he lowered her nightgown and stepped away. "Forgive me," he said, his voice strained. "I seem to make a habit of becoming overexcited in your company." He pushed his hands through his hair in frustration, turned and paced back and forth. "I don't know how to do this," he suddenly confessed, as he waved his hand down the length of her body.

"Do what?" she asked with some confusion. So far, he'd been magnificent.

He sighed and shook his head. "You must understand. My experiences, they have been … the ladies were … I don't want you to feel that I'm not mindful of your situation." He turned away from her again, the gravel crunching under his feet in protest. "I should leave," he blurted.

Leave!

He seemed lost, tortured, his countenance revealing an inner turmoil that influenced his reasoning. She thought she knew what he was trying to say. He'd never deflowered a virgin and didn't know how. Perhaps he thought his crude approach exposed the licentious side of his character; the side he felt was so opposed to hers.

"I must leave," he reaffirmed, straightening his back and puffing out his chest to show that he was determined in his course of action. Yet his eyes told a different story, as they begged and pleaded for her to ease his suffering.

"Then I am coming with you," she said, somewhat amazed the words had left her lips. The idea was irrational, irresponsible and highly immoral, but she was determined to drag him out from the darkness.

What was the worst that could happen?

Either they would be forced to marry, or she would be left in disgrace to live the rest of her days idling away in the country.

The first option was much more appealing to her than it had been a few days earlier; the second option, minus the disgrace, was the future she had always intended for herself. Besides, she doubted there was another man in existence that could make her feel the way Lucas Dempsey did.

"Take me with you," she persisted, eager for an opportunity to show that he could trust her, to show she didn't care about their differences. All she wanted was to be with him, in his world, in her world, in any world.

In that brief moment of reflection, everything suddenly became clear. It was as though her eyes had been bound with the thickest cloth and he'd untied it and let it fall. Now, she could see all the wonders the world had to offer, could see what was so blatantly obvious—she had fallen in love with Lucas Dempsey.

CHAPTER 15

"Take me with you."

The words echoed in his ears like a blissful melody, weakening his resolve. "You do not know what you're asking," he mocked. She was asking him to lead her down the road to ruin and past the stone pillar that said there was but one mile to disgrace.

He made the mistake of lifting his gaze, and she gave him a flirtatious smile. The look suggested he was wrong. She knew exactly what she was asking. The thought caused his manhood to pulse, urging him to reconsider and to give her everything she wanted, everything he had.

"Take me," she whispered, moving a step closer towards him. The sexual implication of her words conjured an image of her lying naked beneath him, of him settling between her sweet thighs.

With a heavy sigh, he looked to the heavens waiting for the Divine to respond to his predicament and give him the strength to decline such a delicious invitation.

But he was too late.

Darkness descended.

The voice of sin sounded so tempting. It forced him to

acknowledge the pleasure that stood a mere arm's length away, told him that the climax of their joining would satisfy on a much deeper level than he had ever experienced before. Fear gripped him as he considered the possibility he may never placate the craving that consumed him. He would always want her as desperately as he did at that moment.

As doubt crept in once more, the voice in the darkness quashed his concerns. They were betrothed. In giving her virginity she would be more inclined to give her hand and then he would be free to experience her delights as often as he liked.

"Are you sure this is what you want?" he asked weakly, praying that she'd not had a change of heart.

She took the last anxious step towards him, stood on the tips of her toes and brushed her lips against his. "I'm sure," she whispered softly, and his body rejoiced in anticipation of all that awaited him. As he drew the edges of her cloak together to protect her modesty, she said, "You're going to tell me you walked here, aren't you?"

Lucas shook his head. "No, my carriage is waiting outside the tobacconist. But I suggest you pull up your hood."

She did as he asked, linked her arm with his and they walked through the mews as if setting out for a leisurely stroll and not preparing to indulge in an illicit affair.

When they passed the groom, the man kept his head low and continued with his work. "You'd be amazed at how much it costs to render a man mute," Lucas said, keeping his eyes fixed firmly ahead.

"Then for your sake, I hope it will be worth it," she countered playfully.

"I would pay a hundred times more just to gaze upon your face," he replied truthfully, and she laughed as if he was being dramatic purely to tease.

Once safely settled in the gloomy confines of the carriage, his head fell back against the seat as he tried to calm his wild, erratic thoughts. Beneath Helena's thick cloak, there was nothing other than the thinnest nightgown covering her naked body. Nothing was stopping him from sliding across the carriage, letting his hand slip under the velvet garment, up her soft thighs, up to—

"It probably would have been quicker to walk," she suddenly said, breaking the silence. And as he looked across at her, he noticed she was unconsciously drumming her fingers in her lap. "I mean for you. Obviously, it would not be a wise choice for me. I have never seen a lady wandering the streets in her nightgown."

He knew her attempt to make conversation was a ploy to distract her mind. "While there's a bounty on my head I thought it best not to tempt fate," he said, relaxing a little more in the seat in the hope of putting her at ease.

"I didn't even consider that." She appeared thoroughly annoyed with herself, and the thought made him smile. "What happened yesterday at Miss Linwood's museum, do you think it was deliberate?"

The memory sent a shiver down his spine. He *would* commit murder if he ever caught the culprit. "Undoubtedly," he answered gravely. "I'm only sorry that you find yourself embroiled in all of this."

"I'm not," she said without hesitation. "I'm not sorry."

He stared at her, bemused. "Why, when you could have been killed?"

Just saying the words made his stomach lurch, and he focused his gaze on the arousing little curl that had escaped the mass of warm-brown hair to brush against her jaw.

The corners of her mouth turned upwards into the rebellious smile he was so fond of, her confidence making a welcome return. "Are you asking a question, Mr. Dempsey? I do believe it's your turn."

"It was more of an observation," he admitted, grateful she had reminded him he could ask any question he liked and would receive an honest answer in return. "But I do have a question to ask." Although he hoped her answer would not dampen his desire.

Lucas was used to women propositioning him. He understood their motives: lonely widows, jaded wives, rebellious daughters. There were those who saw him as a trophy; a symbol of their ability to attract the most coveted of his species.

Helena Ecclestone did not fit into any of those categories. If fate struck him down with some facial disfigurement, he doubted it would make a difference to her. That's what he admired about her, which was why he needed to understand her motives for coming with him. There was also an element of self-preservation. He needed confirmation that she was everything he believed her to be.

"I want to know why you're sitting here with me? Why are you considering sharing my bed?" he said, conveying the point that nothing was set in stone. He had no expectations.

There was a brief look of fear in her eyes as they widened. Perhaps she'd not expected his question to be so direct. Her gaze flicked to the window as she contemplated the row of houses: a ruse for her to regain her composure, knowing she had no other option other than to tell the truth.

"I have always been honest with you," he reminded her, "even when the words left me open to censure." For heaven's sake, he'd told her he bedded women just for the pleasure of it, yet he felt something profoundly more intense, more personal at the thought of joining with her.

Her gaze met his, and he was relieved to see that all her strength and inner confidence had returned. "I shall answer your question," she said, leaning forward, "because I trust you with the truth. But you will have to wait until we are inside, as we have just turned into Mount Street."

Lucas glanced out of the window, thankful he'd not moved to the opposite side of the carriage, as he would have barely had time to raise a sigh let alone anything more scandalous.

Number fifty-eight was on the end of the row, next to the

entrance to Reeves Mews and the carriage slowed to turn into the narrow lane before grinding to a halt. Without waiting for his coachman, Lucas threw open the door and jumped down, glancing left and right and then left again before offering his hand to Helena.

In light of his question, Lucas escorted her to his study. It would appear too presumptuous to move to his bedchamber. It would give the impression he did not truly care about her motives, an action that would undermine the foundation of their friendship. Besides, the evening had grown chilly, and as the study was his room of preference, the fire had already been lit.

Picking up the candle from the console table in the hall, he opened the door, stepping back so she could enter.

"Please, take a seat," he said, nodding to the chairs flanking the fire and he followed her inside and closed the door. He took his lonely candle and proceeded to light the ones on the mirrored wall sconces.

"Here, let me take that," he said, noticing she was opening the buttons on her cloak.

"It is rather warm in here," she acknowledged, watching him place the candlestick on the desk. She turned her back to him, and he stepped behind her, ready to catch it as she shrugged it off her shoulders.

He folded the garment and looked around the room for a suitable place to drape it, choosing the chair behind the desk as he hoped he'd have no need to sit in it tonight. After shrugging out of his coat, he turned to face her. She was standing in front of the fire, gazing up at the portrait of a gentleman wearing a long brown periwig that almost touched his waist.

Preoccupied with imagining all the possible answers she could give to his question, he'd forgotten she was wearing a nightgown. Against the orange glow of the fire, her soft womanly curves were detectable through the thin fabric. His gaze drifted slowly down to her bare ankles, clearly visible now that she had placed her hands on hips, and he observed the dainty silk dancing slippers that posed such an amusing contradiction.

"I take it he is no relation?" she asked, considering the portrait, unaware that he had been studying an entirely different work of art.

"No," he replied, his amusement evident in his tone. "I have no idea who he is, but he looks a little too pompous for my liking."

"It does seem as though he's pointing at you in a rather accusatory way," she agreed.

He walked to the side table, pulled the stopper from the decanter and poured two glasses of port before coming to stand beside her.

"I believe it is you he is pointing at," he challenged, handing her the glass. She thanked him, and he moved to stand on her left to study the viewpoint. "It's definitely you," he teased. "Perhaps he disapproves of your nightgown."

"What, too dowdy?" she asked scrunching up her nose as she ran her hands over the fabric.

As he followed the line of her fingers, he noticed the tips of her nipples pressing against the bodice. Good God, the lady had no idea how captivating she was, had no idea that even wearing the most modest of nightgowns she had an inherent sensual appeal that cried out to him. "Not at all. Cotton creates a particular silhouette that is quite arresting."

She looked up at him, looked down at her nightgown, confusion marring her brow. "I know you're probably used to seeing something ... something more ..." She paused and waved her hand in the air in a bid to recall the correct word. "I don't know, something more delicate, but there is no need to tease."

A flush warmed her cheeks, and she lifted her glass to her lips and sipped her port.

"I have no interest in the garment," he reassured her, "only what's inside it." Fearing his words could easily be misconstrued, he clarified, "I'm only interested in you, Helena."

She looked up at him, her eyes exhibiting a concoction of emotions: loneliness, longing, fear, desire, the fragments laid bare for him to see. It was like looking at the most resplendent stained glass window, each fragile piece contributing to its overall magnificence, to its awe-inspiring beauty.

He caressed her cheek, traced the line of her lips with his thumb, and she blinked slowly. "What is it that you seek here?" he whispered, prompting her to answer his question. "What is it that lures you into the lair of a dragon?"

She closed her eyes for a moment and inhaled deeply. When she opened them, her lips curved into the beginnings of a smile. "I'm in love with you, Lucas. That's what brings me here."

The words hit him squarely in the chest, as though he had opened a door only to be blown back by the force of a hurricane. The sweet declaration caused an overwhelming surge of desire, a desperate need to claim her, to ease himself inside her luscious body and relieve the physical ache that racked him.

Over the years, numerous women had professed their love. They loved his face, his voracious appetite, his wealth, his position. None of them were as honest as Helena Ecclestone. Indeed, the lady would not have made such a bold claim if she did not believe it to be true.

There was a part of him that refused to accept it, a part of him that thought her affections were misplaced, that she'd mistaken the all-consuming feelings of desire, mistaken them for love. The more he thought about it, the more convinced he became. In her innocence, she believed love had brought her here tonight; believed it was love, not desire that emboldened her to pursue this illicit liaison.

"Helena, desire is a powerful emotion. It is easy to mistake it for something else."

He blamed himself, of course. He was the one responsible for awakening her passion, for dragging her along this treacherous path. Under the circumstances, it was only right that he should decline the pleasure of her body, the very thing he so desperately wanted, so desperately needed.

"Perhaps we should wait," he continued. "Perhaps it would be best if I escorted you home."

As soon as the words left his mouth, he wished he could retract them.

When he caught her gaze, she was studying him with keen interest, and he could almost hear the tiny cogs whirring around as she attempted to gauge what had elicited his reaction. She looked down at his glass, which she took from his hand without protest, walked over to the side table and deposited both glasses on the silver tray. Rather than appear angry or hurt, she conveyed a level of determination he'd witnessed in her before.

Eager to know of her intentions, he asked, "Would you like me to take you home?"

As though oblivious to the fact he'd spoken, she moved behind the desk, picked up her cloak and walked casually over to the door.

When her hand settled on the handle, his stomach tightened and twisted into knots: his body's way of punishing him for his stupidity. She glanced back at him, before turning the key in the door. With a mischievous grin, she sauntered back towards the hearth, to the chairs that stood on either side of him and moved them a few feet further back.

He watched her, fascinated by the fluidity of her movements, by the sheer strength of will he could feel emanating from within.

Shaking out her cloak, she arranged it on the floor in front of him like a blanket as if preparing to sit down for a picnic. When she kicked off her dancing slippers, his gaze dropped to her perfect little toes, and he followed them as they padded the few steps across the floor before coming to a stop directly in front of him.

"I won't even begin to imagine what is going on in that thick head of yours," she said softly as she undid the three pearl buttons on the bodice of her nightgown. "Nor am I able to follow the erratic nature of your emotions." Her fingers moved to the buttons on his waistcoat and she began to undo them, albeit a little clumsily. "But you cannot tell me how I feel. I will not allow you to push me away." She forced the waistcoat off his shoulders until it fell to the floor, letting her fingers trail back down over the front of his shirt. The sensation caused him to suck in his breath. "I will not allow you to undermine whatever is happening here between us," she continued, the palms of her hands coming to rest on his narrow hips.

With a soft purr, she tugged his shirt out from his breeches; thrust her trembling hands underneath to caress the hard planes of his chest.

Lucas simply stood there and succumbed to his fate, thankful that every respectable thought had suddenly escaped him, leaving him to imagine a multitude of immoral things he wanted to do to his naughty little nymph.

CHAPTER 16

It had taken courage to let those words fall from her lips.

Pushing aside any reservations, she'd made the giant leap and convinced herself to trust him, hoping that he would learn to trust her in return. His reaction was to be expected. When one declared love to a man like Lucas Dempsey, one had to assume it would be met with a certain degree of cynicism. The man had openly stated that he didn't trust anyone; the look of utter disbelief in his eyes had confirmed as much.

Since making the declaration, she had already discovered something more of his character. Had Lucas Dempsey been the man everyone professed him to be, he would have used the opportunity to bed her. Instead, he had offered to escort her home.

Then he had made the comment about desire being a powerful emotion, revealing the crux of his dilemma—he did not believe she loved him.

She supposed it would take time to prove it to him. Lucas knew that she desired him and so that would have to be enough for now, which was why she was ripping his shirt from his breeches and letting her eager hands wander over his muscular chest.

As her nimble fingers skimmed over the dusting of dark hair, grazed over his erect nipples, his head fell back and he moaned softly. She didn't really know what to do after that. Was it even possible to seduce a seducer? But the sound of satisfaction was exciting and exhilarating, and she wanted to please him all the more. Sensing that his shirt was becoming an annoying restriction, she withdrew her hands and began working on the knot in his cravat.

"Here, allow me," he said, his eyes dark and heavy with desire. With swift efficiency he untied it and threw it to the floor. Crossing his arms over his chest, he yanked his shirt up over his head and discarded it in the same careless manner.

Helena couldn't help but stare in awe at the truly herculean specimen, a little ashamed that she finally understood the attraction of the male physical form. Her greedy eyes drifted over his broad shoulders, over honey-gold skin that seemed to radiate its own unique warmth. She drank in the sight: the muscled contours of his developed arms, the fine path of hair trailing down beyond the waistband of his breeches.

"Would you like me to remove them?" he asked as he followed her gaze, his face brimming with devilish charm.

Helena placed a trembling finger to her lips as she contemplated the question. "In a moment," she replied, somewhat surprised at the sound of her voice as it had a deeper, huskier tone.

Raising a curious brow, he nodded in acquiescence.

Heavens, if he removed his breeches now, she'd be too scared to touch him, and she so desperately wanted to experience the initial feeling of skin pressed against skin.

That left only one option.

Driven by her newfound courage, and before she could change her mind, Helena followed his lead. Gathering her nightgown, she pulled it over her head, hugging the bundle tight before finally feeling brave enough to let it fall to the floor, to join the ever-increasing pile of discarded garments.

Too embarrassed to meet his gaze, Helena heard his sharp intake of breath, sensed the tension in his muscles, felt his eyes caressing her naked body, scorching her skin.

"I don't deserve you," he whispered. There was a hint of sadness in his tone, a hint of self-loathing, which tugged at her heart and drew her towards him into his embrace.

Helena didn't give him an opportunity to kiss her. Instead, she put her head against his chest, just below the hollow of his throat, slipped her arms around his waist and inhaled his intoxicating scent, letting all her fears and doubts melt away. The potent masculine aroma warmed her blood, soothed her soul. Lucas pulled her closer, the palms of his hands coming to rest on the small of her back and she could not recall another moment in her entire life when she'd felt so safe, so protected.

"Helena," he murmured.

Threading her arms around his neck, she raised herself up on her tiptoes, desire ripping through her body as her breasts brushed against the hair on his chest. She offered him her mouth, which he took without hesitation.

She should have been used to the feel of his lips, to the soft, slow melding of mouths, but it felt vastly different without clothing. Now, she could feel the heat from his skin, hot and scorching. She could feel every flex of muscle, her body more sensitive to his touch.

With his mouth moving hungrily over hers, he fiddled with his breeches, stepping out of them as his tongue delved deeper. Naked and glorious he pulled her closer, thrusting the thick, hard length of his arousal against her stomach. The sensation caused a raging fire to flare between her thighs. A whimpering plea escaped from her lips as she clutched at his shoulders, at the bulging muscles in his arms, desperate to find a way to prolong the feeling.

Events progressed more rapidly then, as he lowered her to the floor and covered her with his hard body. He rained featherlight kisses down her neck, along her shoulder, down to her bare breast. When his wicked tongue circled slowly around her nipple, all the air seemed to dissipate from her lungs, and she began panting as his mouth coaxed it to peak. He rolled to lie at her side, propped himself up on his elbow and claimed her mouth while his fingers trailed down past her stomach to the intimate place that throbbed and ached for his touch.

"Lucas," she gasped, and he pulled his hungry mouth from hers and stared into her eyes.

"Trust me," he whispered, exuding an intensely masculine power, and on his word she relaxed back against the plush velvet and gave herself over to him.

Abandoning all inhibitions, she writhed and arched against the skilful strokes. She let him control the pace, her thoughts somewhat fragmented as his mouth devoured every inch of bare skin. She felt the invisible coil inside grow tighter, pulling her towards an unknown destination. And she cried out his name as her body suddenly exploded and convulsed, as she soared on the dizzying heights of ecstasy.

With the feeling of euphoria slowly ebbing, she had an over-whelming desire to please him in the same way. The inquisitive part of her brain longed to study the curious object brushing against her thigh. Unable to stop her eager hand in its quest for knowledge, her fingers curled around the thick shaft. His breath-less curse of approval was reward in itself. Hard, yet as soft as silk, she found the contradiction fascinating and was not the least bit embarrassed when Lucas covered her hand with his, moving it slowly and rhythmically until his breath grew ragged.

He stopped abruptly.

"Enough. Else it will be over before we've begun." He moved above her, settling between her legs so she could feel the hard length of him, probing and prodding. "You're sure about this?"

"Yes." She nodded, and he kissed her with a passion that was fierce in its delivery, his tongue teasing and coaxing until her mind was muddled and her desire for him like a fever.

"I'll try my best to be gentle," he growled, "but I have never wanted anything as much as I want you."

He moved slowly, his mouth moving to her breast, his tongue lightly sucking and flicking her nipple until she writhed against him, desperate for something more. His mouth claimed hers again. Wild and intense. Their breath became one. She was lost in him. When she felt him nudge against her, she tried to relax and welcome the intrusion.

Helena would never forget the moment he thrust past her virginity to bury himself deep inside her. Not because it was painful, as the sharp stinging soon subsided, but because she felt that they belonged together like this.

With him, she felt complete.

She clung to him as he quickened the pace. Each long thrust causing a wave of ecstasy that started in her core and surged through her body. One ripple flowed as another began, fusing into a tumultuous flood of bone-tingling pleasure. Meeting the undulating rhythm of his thrusts, her thighs clutching him and pulling him deeper, they found their glorious release together.

"Helena," he panted, as he collapsed across her, his heart beating so rapidly she could feel it against her chest. "Helena," he repeated, struggling to regulate his breathing.

She placed her hand on his back to soothe him, her fingers gliding smoothly across skin damp from over-exertion. Still buried inside her, Lucas shifted slightly, the movement causing another tiny tremor of pleasure to shoot through her.

She did not want this intimacy between them to end.

She wanted to lie there entwined with him until she was no longer able to draw breath. Her feelings confirmed what she already knew: she was so deeply in love with him it hurt.

Lying sprawled across her luscious body, Lucas closed his eyes and tried to regain some semblance of control. He'd always suspected that their coupling would be an enlightening experience, but he had not expected to feel such conflicting emotions.

It was all rather confounding.

On one hand, he'd never felt a level of bone-shattering satisfaction like it and could quite happily draw her to his side and sleep for eternity. Yet when he shifted his weight for fear of crushing her, he felt her body respond instantly, gripping him to draw him deeper. With his desire reawakened, all he could think of was driving into her again and again until she begged for release.

This obsession he had for her controlled his every thought and feeling.

He'd expected it to be eased by their joining, yet it had only served to intensify it.

He rolled onto his back and drew her to his side so that her head was resting in the crook of his arm. She wrapped her arms around him, her groan of discomfort causing guilt to flare. They should have been in a comfortable bed not sprawled across the hard floor. Were the depths of his depravity such that he'd not given a thought to her delicate situation?

"Come," he said, forcing himself to stand and he took her by the hand and brought her to her feet. "Let's go upstairs." He could not stop his greedy eyes from roaming over her naked form, over her perfectly shaped breasts, over the gentle flare of her hips. "You can wash, and you'll need something to eat," he added by way of convincing himself that he could not have her again tonight.

She looked up at him, searched his face and then simply nodded.

As he threw on his breeches, he could feel her assessing gaze, and he wondered if she approved of what she saw.

"Is it always like this?" she asked shaking out her cloak and wrapping it around her body.

Lucas scanned the floor in a bid to locate their clothing and then turned to face her. "I don't know what you mean."

Helena waved her hand back and forth between them. "Is it usual, this feeling of awkwardness? You seem distant, somewhat preoccupied."

He *was* preoccupied, with feelings of remorse, with guilty thoughts about the way he'd conducted himself. Her hair was mussed and bedraggled, her lips red and swollen. No doubt she would have a few bruises, and her whole appearance had an air of someone who had been ravished in a haystack.

"I am eager to move upstairs." He sighed and glanced down at the floor, but then honesty prevailed. "It cannot have been a very comfortable experience."

Helena snorted. "No, *comfortable* is not the word I would use to describe it."

Guilt lashed at his conscience, branding his soul with the word *profligate*.

"Transcendent or sublime, perhaps," she continued. "Certainly not something as mediocre as comfortable."

She was teasing him, her playful tone dispelling all melancholic thoughts like a powerful elixir. "Why you minx," he growled, picking her up and throwing her over his shoulder. Amidst shrieks of laughter, she kicked her legs in protest. "Keep still," Lucas instructed, climbing the stairs with effortless expediency.

When he entered his bedchamber, he walked over to the large mahogany bed and threw her down. He resisted the urge to follow her when her bare leg kicked out between the opening of her cloak, revealing a soft, creamy thigh.

"I'll be right back," he said, racing from the room to raid the kitchen, returning with a scone, some blackcurrant jam and her nightgown tucked under his arm. "This is all I could find at short notice."

She tucked into the scone as though she'd not eaten for a week. "Would you like some?" she asked wiping jam from the corner of her mouth, her greedy eyes suggesting he should refuse.

"No, I'm fine. There's clean water in the pitcher." He gestured to the washstand. "I shall leave you in peace."

She chuckled in surprise. "There is no need to leave, Lucas. After what's just occurred, you don't think it's appropriate to watch me clean my face? There is nothing to see that you've not already seen." Her tone conveyed the absurdity of it all. "You don't regret what happened between us?" she suddenly asked bluntly.

How could he regret all she had done for him, all she had given him? "My only concerns relate to your feelings on the subject."

She studied him for the longest time, and he wished he knew what she was thinking. "I have left half for you." She pushed the plate across the counterpane, and he sat down, popping a piece of scone into his mouth.

When he'd finished, he shuffled up the bed, leaning back against the mound of pillows as Helena wandered over to the washstand. She turned her back to him and stripped off her cape before draping it over the chair.

His mouth dropped open.

Lucas was familiar with many of the skills employed by women intent on seduction, but the pure innocence of Helena's actions affected him like nothing else before.

Did she know what she was doing to him?

He gaped as she poured the water into the bowl and soaked the linen square. Pushing her hair back to hang over one shoulder, she wiped her neck, her arms, across the front of her chest, bending slightly to wipe all traces of him from her legs.

A strange feeling rose up from somewhere deep in the pit of his stomach, a burning desire to leave his mark again so that everyone would know she was his.

"Could you hand me my gown," she said, turning her head and pointing at the garment he'd placed on the bed. It occurred to him that, naively, she didn't feel as exposed with her back to him.

Lucas didn't trust himself to walk over, so he tossed it to her. She thanked him, threw it over her head and was soon bounding towards the bed, jumping up to sit beside him. She could have been wearing a suit of steel, and still, he would have felt the instant tug of some magnetic force in the air between them.

"I should be going," she said, glancing around the room as if looking for some indication of the time.

"I'll escort you back to your garden."

The thought induced a melancholic mood. He wanted her to stay, to probe his mind with interesting questions, to probe his body with her soft hands, to eat with him, sleep with him, to do all the normal things he supposed one did when they were relaxed and could be themselves.

His mind raced back to her earlier declaration, wishing it was true, wishing there had been no mistake, wishing she really did love him.

CHAPTER 17

Having received a note with instructions to arrive promptly at eleven, Henry Weston hurried up the stairs to the office of Thorpe & Jones, eager for news regarding the return on his investment.

"Good day to you," he said with zealous enthusiasm as he stood at the open door of Mr. Bostock's room, desperate to lean against the jamb as his heart was practically beating out of his chest.

Mr. Bostock finished scribbling something in his ledger and then glanced up with a look of mild irritation. With hands like mallets and a neck as thick as his waist, he did not appear to be a man who enjoyed passing pleasantries. And so Henry simply stood, cane in hand, and waited. During which time he found himself becoming a little annoyed, as he doubted Viscount Harwood received the same lack of consideration.

"Come in and take a seat, Mr. Weston," Mr. Bostock finally said, nodding to the chair opposite while still clawing away with a pen held awkwardly between meaty fingers. When Henry peered over his shoulder towards the door to Mr. Thorpe's office, Bostock added, "As Mr. Thorpe's clerk, I deal with all payments and deposits."

Henry didn't really care who dealt with the financial aspects, so long as he got his money. "I received a note inviting me to call at eleven."

Bostock let out a tedious sigh, which sounded more like the irate snort of a bull. "I know. I sent it. Sit down, Mr. Weston." Reaching into the top drawer of his desk, Bostock removed a different ledger, opened it at the relevant page and scanned across with his chubby finger. "The return on your original investment is recorded at fifty-seven percent. I believe that means ..." His full lips twitched rapidly as he attempted to solve the mathematical sum. "You're to take receipt of four hundred and seventy-one pounds."

Henry's mouth turned up into a satisfied grin. "That is excellent news," he said, his face brightening as Bostock began counting out the notes. He would need to make a few more investments before he raised the thousand needed to rid himself of Lucas Dempsey.

"If you'll sign here." Mr. Bostock turned the ledger around, dipped the nib of his quill pen into the inkwell and handed it to Henry. "I believe that concludes our business, Mr. Weston."

It was at that precise moment that Mr. Thorpe opened the door to his chambers and proceeded to escort a rather elegant lady down the hallway towards the door of Mr. Bostock's office.

"Mr. Bostock will deal with all the necessaries," Mr. Thorpe said, bowing gracefully to the fiery-haired vixen. "Until tomorrow, Madame Saulnier."

"I cannot thank you enough, Monsieur Thorpe," she cried, an exaggerated gesticulation accompanying every word. "All that pretty silk, what a tragedy it would have been to waste it."

Madame Saulnier spoke with only the slightest inflection. The soft rolling burr of her French accent caused a frisson of excitement to run up the length of Henry's spine, as he'd often imagined himself partial to the exotic wiles of a foreigner.

Mr. Thorpe offered her an amused grin. "Made all the more appealing by a return of seventy percent," he said boldly. His gaze drifted past his pretty companion, and he acknowledged Henry with a curt nod of the head. "Mr. Weston, I trust things are in order?"

Not being a man to waste an opportunity, Henry stepped out into the hall and engaged Mr. Thorpe. "Perfectly, so." He gave a respectful nod. After all, the man deserved his utmost gratitude for providing such a lucrative return, even if his clerk was somewhat brusque and ill-mannered.

Madame Saulnier looked up at Mr. Thorpe in the subtle way ladies do when waiting for an introduction: with wide eyes and an inquisitive tilt of the head.

"Mr. Weston, may I present Madame Saulnier."

After dispensing with all the necessary courtesies, a demure Madame Saulnier resumed her dramatic protestations. "Such beautiful silk," she exclaimed. "Such a tragedy." She looked at Henry with a tear in her eye. "Please say that you, Monsieur Weston, are equally committed to rescuing this precious cargo."

Henry had never encountered a lady with such an overtly passionate nature, and it roused in him a great need to be cast as the chivalrous hero.

"Mr. Weston has only recently joined us," Mr. Thorpe interjected. "The stake for such an important assignment is rather more than we would ask of any new investor."

His gaze flicked to Henry with a look that suggested the words were meant respectfully. But the thought of being overlooked, of being deemed unworthy was too much for Henry to bear. "I'm sure allowances can be made, Mr. Thorpe," Henry began, spurred on by the look of gratitude bestowed upon him by Madame Saulnier. "I am more than satisfied with the service you provide."

Mr. Thorpe inclined his head. "Perhaps it would be wise to discuss the matter privately."

There was an air of condescension in Thorpe's countenance, and after years of feeling inadequate at the hands of Lord Banbury, Henry was eager to challenge any misconception. "Not at all. I am happy with the terms. You did say a return of seventy percent?"

Mr. Thorpe stared down his nose, and when he spoke his tone revealed a hint of arrogance. "A return of seventy percent on an investment of a thousand pounds, Mr. Weston. That is the minimum required."

Henry swallowed deeply, trying desperately to suppress the sense of panic that had taken hold of him. He could not refuse now. Not if he wanted to leave with his reputation intact and so he smiled confidently while his mind scrambled to think of a way to acquire the necessary funds. There was a man in Gower Street that he had used once before. His fee of thirty percent could easily be covered by a return of seventy.

"Very well." He nodded and offered Madame Saulnier a reassuring raise of the brows. "I presume you require the funds today?"

Mr. Thorpe took out his watch. "You have until three, Mr. Weston. Bostock will deal with the necessary paperwork."

CHAPTER 18

"I feel I must thank you again, Miss Ecclestone, for forgiving my rather uncouth comments," Mr. Huntley-Fisher said as he led her around Lord Berwick's dance floor.

Helena suppressed a frustrated sigh, wishing she had feigned an injury or thought of some other plausible excuse, but the man seemed determined to keep pestering her. It didn't help that he gave off a repugnant smell, as though he had fallen into a vat of peppermint oil.

"I have already accepted your apology," she replied, peering over his shoulder in the hope of locating Lucas. A whole day had passed since he'd escorted her back to her garden and kissed her until she was giddy. Yet her lips still tingled at the memory.

Gliding around the other dancers, she linked arms with her partner and he continued their conversation. "I'll be honest with you," he said, taking a deep breath that had nothing to do with the pace of his movements. "I must admit to having aspirations of there being an understanding between us. I was hoping to deter Mr. Dempsey with my rather coarse approach. Had I known he'd already made you an offer, then——"

"Let us say no more about it," Helena said impatiently,

feeling a strange frisson of awareness that drew her attention away to scan the tightly packed throng.

"Perhaps we shall be friends. That is if Mr. Dempsey will allow it."

Helena felt his words like the sting of a whip. "Mr. Dempsey does not dictate who I am friends with, sir."

Mr. Huntley-Fisher's eyes widened. "Oh, bravo!" he said, forsaking the elegance of his line to give an amused wave. "I do so admire a lady with gusto."

Helena gave a weak smile at the dandified gesture and tried not to show her relief when the dance finally came to an end.

With her sister's fondness for lingering around terrace doors, and the need to make a quick escape from her dancing partner, Helena pushed her way through the crowd in the hope of locating Amelia. Indeed, she spotted her sister next to the open door, waving her fan about as though swatting invisible flies.

"Were all guests required to drench themselves in gallons of perfume?" Helena said, inhaling the fresh air breezing in from the terrace as she came to stand at her sister's side. She wasn't sure whether it was the dancing, the sickly sweet smell or the thought of seeing Lucas that caused her stomach to do the sort of somersaults and flips that were worthy of an acrobatic display.

Amelia chuckled. "I think it has something to do with the heat, and Lord Berwick always attracts a seemingly larger crowd. Why do you think I'm standing by the door, waving a fan in front of my face?"

"At first, I thought it was a secret code to lure a suitor, or perhaps a ritual dance to ward off Mother."

"Oh, there's no need to worry about Mother," Amelia said, her face a picture of pure contentment. "Thanks to you, she has been bombarded with attention. Everyone wants to hear the heroic story of Lucas Dempsey saving you from a flying bust of Nefertiti." Amelia feigned a swoon. "Don't be surprised if Miss Linwood offers you an annual subscription as I hear the queue for the museum trailed all the way to Leicester Square."

"I am sure people have more important things to concern themselves with," Helena said, gazing across the crowd to see numerous pairs of eyes quickly averted.

"What with the terrifying accident and your betrothal to Lucas Dempsey, I believe you are quite famous," Amelia said, with only the slightest hint of bitterness in her tone. "I see you forgave Mr. Huntley-Fisher. I suppose where he is concerned we should expect a certain vulgarity of manner. After all, his mother was a courtesan."

"Who told you that?" Helena asked, doubting its authenticity.

"Mother. But she regards him as perfectly acceptable for his father is a marquess who can trace his lineage back five hundred years or more."

Their mother's hypocrisy knew no bounds. "Mr. Dempsey's brother is a viscount, yet she refuses to accept him."

"Mother is a follower of opinion. Had the Ratcliffe murderer been named the catch of the Season, she would have had us polishing his weapons and lining up to dance with him." Amelia suddenly changed the subject. "Mr. Dempsey arrived and did not seem pleased that you were dancing with Mr. Huntley-Fisher. He mumbled something highly inappropriate and stormed off in search of the refreshment table."

Just knowing that Lucas was in the same room caused her heart to skip a beat. She had that strange feeling again: as though she had spun around too quickly and her head was still trying to catch up with her body. "Then I had better go and see what I can do to lighten his mood."

As Helena squeezed through the crowd in search of Lucas, it became apparent that she had lost her beautiful cloak of invisibility. Now, every curious gaze, every nod of the head and weak smile was aimed in her direction. Amongst the suppressed titters, she heard her name wafting through the room as though carried back and forth on a breeze quickly gaining momentum.

Was this what Lucas faced every time he stepped out of his front door?

No wonder he didn't trust anyone. No wonder he stomped about like a lion with a thorn in his paw.

Feeling a sudden surge of anger, which dispelled all previous signs of embarrassment, she straightened her back, lifted her chin and presented her most self-assured smile. A smile that said *to hell with you all!*

When she reached the door leading out into the hall, Mr. Huntley-Fisher appeared at her side. "I cannot remember when I last witnessed such a crush," he said.

Even with his warm and friendly protestations, there was something about the man that left her feeling cold. "Forgive me. I'm just looking for someone."

"Yes. I saw you struggling through the crowd and thought you might be looking for your betrothed." He nodded in the direction of the hall. "Mr. Dempsey came through here a few moments ago."

Without any further comment, the gentleman cupped her elbow and steered her through the door. "There is no need to accompany me," she said, in an attempt to get rid of him.

"Nonsense, it would not do to have you wandering around these empty corridors, and there are certain rooms deemed unsuitable for a lady to enter."

With a shake of the head, Helena conceded. After scanning the room reserved for refreshments, Mr. Huntley-Fisher suggested continuing to the far end of the hall, to a room frequented by gentlemen who wished to smoke and drink copious amounts of brandy.

It was as they approached the last door on the left that they stumbled upon Lady Colebrook, huddled in an alcove, her palms resting on Lucas' chest, her mouth but a fraction from his ear.

Jealousy, like a wild and rampant vine, sprouted in Helena's stomach, creeping up through her body until it reached her heart, winding itself round with its tendrils until she found she could not breathe.

Mr. Huntley-Fisher pretended he'd not seen them, but Helena felt him stiffen at her side, felt the forced tremble in his hand as he feigned surprise. "My goodness!" he cried, putting a hand to his heart in an act worthy of royal acclaim. "Forgive me, Miss Ecclestone. I know a man keeps his mistress when he's wed, but this is highly inappropriate."

It was at times like these: when placed on the chessboard of life, that one's move meant the difference between winning and losing. There were those who chose to retreat and those who faced their adversaries head-on, determined to win the game. Suppressing all doubts, Helena tried to focus on what was logical, what was before her eyes.

Mr. Huntley-Fisher had lured her to the scene with the express purpose of stumbling upon Lucas and Lady Colebrook, who appeared to be engaged in a lovers' tryst. A point reinforced by Lady Colebrook's look of smug satisfaction.

Helena examined Lucas' countenance as he turned to see her standing there. She did not see guilt in his eyes or shock or even desire. She saw a mixture of anger, pain and frustration. He looked like a victim, not a perpetrator, and with that in mind she made her move.

"There you are, Lucas," Helena said, snatching her elbow free from Mr. Huntley-Fisher and walking towards them. "I believe you owe me the next dance."

With a look of relief, Lucas stepped forward, took her hand and brought it to his lips. "Then I shall not keep you waiting any longer, my love."

Upon hearing the endearment, Lady Colebrook sucked in a breath.

"I take it you have finished explaining to Lady Colebrook that you are not the sort of man who plays with the bones once he has finished with his meal."

Lucas pursed his lips. "I have," he replied, attempting to keep his expression impassive, yet his eyes were alight with amusement.

"Good." Helena directed her gaze at Lady Colebrook.

Lady Colebrook's mouth opened and closed a few times and then she said, "Better to dine on bones than to die of starvation."

Helena took a step closer and placed the palms of her hands on Lucas' chest, letting her fingers glide slowly up to his nape where she twirled a lock of his hair. Lucas let out a hum of appreciation.

"Oh, I would never let him starve," Helena said.

Lady Colebrook snorted, thrust out her overdeveloped cleavage and lifted her chin. "Well, he felt rather thin and scrawny when I kissed him yesterday."

Helena felt the vine tighten around her heart, a stab of pain rushing up to her throat. Just last night he'd been thoroughly devoted to her pleasure. She forced her mind to think rationally. Lucas would not lie to her. He couldn't possibly kiss her with such unbridled passion while still dallying with Lady Colebrook.

Helena looked up at Lucas' marred brow, his unsettled gaze revealing that Lady Colebrook was telling the truth. When it came to the habits of men, there was no doubt Helena was naive, but she refused to believe he was capable of such a thing. Her mind scrambled through the conversation. Lady Colebrook had not said that Lucas had kissed her, only she had kissed him.

When Lucas opened his mouth to speak, Helena placed a finger on his lips. "Lucas told me exactly what happened yesterday. He told me of your desperate attempt to seduce him."

Lady Colebrook had the courtesy to look embarrassed, confirming Helena's theory. "You won't be enough for him. He has a ravenous appetite," she hissed through gritted teeth.

Lucas looked up at the ceiling and cursed.

"Well, I believe he's quite sick of soggy old mutton," Helena replied, "and now craves lamb."

Lady Colebrook gasped. "You're a fool if you think you can tame him."

"Oh, I don't want to tame him. I find I like him exactly as he is."

Helena linked arms with Lucas and they took a few steps before stopping in front of Mr. Huntley-Fisher.

"Please tell me you object to my friendship with Mr. Huntley-Fisher," Helena said, looking up into the bluest eyes she had ever seen, eyes that made her legs shake and knees buckle. "Please tell me you refuse to allow us to be friends, and I must never acknowledge him again."

Lucas lifted his chin and puffed out his chest. "As your future husband, I forbid you to see or speak to Mr. Huntley-Fisher ever again."

"Excellent," she beamed before turning to the gentleman in question. "There you have it, sir. I am pleased to say I never wish to see or speak to you again. However, there is a lady I know who is desperate for someone to suck on her bones. Perhaps you will have better luck there."

Lucas calculated he had seen close to a hundred plays in his lifetime, yet he had never seen a show as entertaining as Helena's performance.

When he turned to see her standing in the hall, accompanied by that toad, Mr. Huntley-Fisher, her eyes fixed on Lady Colebrook's wandering hands, he expected her to make the natural assumptions. He expected her to storm off in disgust. However, it soon became apparent that faerie folk were woven from a much thicker cloth than ordinary folk. And Helena had used her magical tongue to show she was not a lady to be toyed with.

"I believe our dance is a waltz," he said as he led her out onto the floor, feeling a desperate urgency to hold her in his arms. "Could the night get any better?"

"Oh, I think it could," she said, raising her brow in a coquettish manner. "After all, we do not want you to die of starvation."

He should have chuckled, but he couldn't. His tongue had swollen, so it felt thick and heavy in his mouth. A beautiful ache filled his chest. He could think of nothing other than covering her with his body, feeling her hands in his hair, plundering her wet and witty mouth.

"I must thank you," he mumbled, trying to drag his thoughts away from the image of her soft thighs wrapped around him, from her breathless pants tickling his ear. "Most ladies would not have been so understanding."

"Was there any reason for me to behave otherwise?"

"Of course not!"

"Then there is no need to thank me."

Just like that, she trusted his word. Yet he felt he owed her an explanation. "Lady Colebrook heard about the accident at Miss Linwood's museum and called round to offer some comfort."

"I take it you refused her offer."

"Of course I did, but the lady wouldn't accept it, and I was forced to throw her out." He gave a frustrated sigh and pulled her a little closer, the familiarity of her potent scent, of her warm, pliant body, soothing him. "When I went out into the hall just now, she was waiting for me. She said she had some important news, and I feared … I feared the worst. Thankfully, it was just a ruse to make you jealous, to give you an opportunity to put an end to our betrothal."

"You thought she might be with child?"

She glanced up at him, her gaze penetrating through to his soul, calming him, telling him he could speak freely in her company without fear of reprisal. "Well, yes, though I have always been extremely careful in that regard."

Her lips curved into the beginnings of a smile. "You were not careful with me."

His thoughts flew back to the last magnificent thrust, to the moment where he felt a bone-deep level of satisfaction he'd never experienced before. "It is not the same," he said, as he twirled her around the floor.

No, it was not the same. He'd never wanted anyone the way he wanted her. He'd never wanted to fall in love or be loved in return.

"Everything is different with you," he whispered.

CHAPTER 19

Having spent the morning with his mother, Lucas ambled back home to Mount Street, his mind occupied with thoughts of Helena. He still felt somewhat disgruntled that her mother had whisked her away from Lord Berwick's without giving him a proper chance to say goodnight. He would have liked nothing more than to take her home to his bed and show her how much he appreciated her trust and her loyalty. Instead, he found himself creating vivid images in his head, walking about in a constant state of arousal, his brain barely able to form a rational thought.

On his return to Mount Street, he discovered his brother waiting for him in the study.

"He has been waiting for over an hour, sir," Gregson informed. Although he looked quite pleased that a male visitor had knocked on the door at last, and he had been able to be of service without fearing his master's wrath.

Anthony sat perched behind the desk, looking relaxed and comfortable as he scanned a copy of *The Times* while sipping from a steaming cup of coffee.

"Can I get you anything, my lord?" Lucas said, waving his

hand in the air to perform an exaggerated bow. "Ham and eggs, a fresh pot of coffee or perhaps a cushion for your back."

Anthony glanced up from his newspaper. "You seem more cheerful this morning."

"Well, I'm not."

He was miserable, frustrated and he had a constant pain in his chest that refused to go away. A desperate longing had taken hold of his mind and body, waking him at night to torture him with lurid thoughts of Helena Ecclestone. The other owner of the odd puzzle piece, the only one to fit with his.

"Sorry, do you need your desk?" Anthony asked.

"No," Lucas whispered, suddenly aware that it wasn't even his desk. His desk was in Boston, thousands of miles away from London, thousands of miles away from Helena. With each day that passed, he started to forget about his other life miles across the ocean. It was as though he had an identical twin. The man who lived in Boston was like kin to him. He looked the same, had the same mannerisms, but now they were intrinsically different. "No, I do not need to use the desk," he repeated, dropping into the chair opposite.

"I see Callingham is selling his gig," Anthony said, flipping back to the front page. "About bloody time. The man is a menace on the road. You know he almost ran over a nurse pushing a perambulator, I would lay odds his mother has—"

"I don't want to go back to Boston," Lucas interjected, surprised that he had spoken the words aloud. It felt good being honest and his thoughts were swamped with images of Helena again.

Anthony lowered the newspaper, sat up and gave Lucas his full attention. "You should never have been sent there in the first place."

"The people have been good to me. I have or did have a good life there." Indeed, he had responsibilities that required his attention, those whose livelihoods depended on him. "But I have changed and had forgotten how good it felt to be home."

"Am I right to assume this has something to do with Miss Ecclestone? After your waltz at Lord Berwick's the gossip is that yours is a love match."

Lucas sneered. "I do not give a fig for what the gossips say." Besides, it was easy to mistake lust for love.

Anthony sat back in the chair, steepled his fingers and after a moment of contemplation, said, "I agree. They obviously don't know that you plan to cry off. Talking of which, I thought we might ask Mr. Thorpe if he can help to solve the matter of your feigned betrothal. Apparently, he is a fountain of knowledge when it comes to legal matters and can—"

Lucas shot up from the chair. "I don't want to cry off." He flopped back down again, aware that Anthony's lips had curved into the beginnings of a smile. "I want to marry Miss Ecclestone. But I don't know if she wants to marry me." Could he take the chance that she would grow to love him, not just desire him, but truly love him?

"But I thought you didn't want to marry anyone?"

"I don't want to marry just anyone." No, he wanted to marry a wood nymph. He wanted to marry a member of the faerie folk who had ensnared him with her magical hands, her magical tongue, her magical … "I want to marry Miss Ecclestone," he repeated by way of dampening his desirous thoughts.

"Hallelujah." Anthony sighed. "It was obvious from the moment we sat down to take tea that you were in love with her. And I'll never forget the look on your face when I forced you apart at the museum."

Lucas jerked his head back. Was he in love with her?

His heart ached when they were apart; his loins ached when they were together. She was constantly in his thoughts, and the sight of her caused his stomach to do strange things. "Well, I do not know about that."

Anthony tutted and shook his head but said nothing.

Lucas poured himself a cup of coffee from the pot. "I cannot ask her to marry me until I have sorted out this problem with Mr.

Weston." There was also another pressing problem, one that grew larger with every passing day, but he forced it from his mind.

"That reminds me." Anthony reached into his pocket to withdraw a note, which he handed to Lucas. "We are to meet Mr. Thorpe this afternoon, at three."

Lucas scanned the note, flipped it back and forth a few times as though the movement would reveal some hidden clue as to Mr. Thorpe's character. "You're confident you can trust this Thorpe fellow?"

Anthony shrugged, removed his pocket watch and glanced at the time. "One way or another, we will soon discover the answer to that question."

They arrived at the office of Thorpe & Jones at three o'clock prompt and made their way up the stairs to the first floor. There was not a soul in sight. But a noise, which sounded like the wail of a banshee, could be heard coming from the room at the end of the corridor. Approaching the door with some caution, they hovered outside for a moment, in the hope that whatever was going on inside the room would soon become apparent.

"What are we waiting for?" Lucas mouthed as he pointed to the nameplate on the door, which indicated that it was Mr. Thorpe's office.

As Lucas raised a hand to knock on the door, Anthony thrust his arm out by way of a caution. "Just wait a moment. Are you this impatient with everything?"

Lucas thought about the question and then nodded.

"Then I feel sorry for Miss Ecclestone," Anthony whispered, his raised brow suggesting a more licentious meaning.

Lucas returned his look with a smug grin. "Miss Ecclestone is more than satisfied with my approach."

Anthony's eyes grew as big and as round as saucers, but

before he could comment they heard a thunderous roar, so loud it rattled the door. "Sit down, Mr. Weston!"

"Perhaps we should knock," Anthony said, and they both raised their hands simultaneously to carry out the task.

They watched with interest as the handle turned slowly and someone yanked the door open no wider than a foot. A large hulking figure of a man stood in the doorway, blocking their entrance. Lucas blinked a few times believing for a moment that the man was O'Brien. He had the same squashed face, a neck as wide as the Thames, and the fist that curled round the jamb had misshapen knuckles and a scar running from his wrist to the tip of his thumb.

"What can I do for you?" he said with a suppressed cockney twang.

"I am Viscount Harwood, and we have a meeting with Mr. Thorpe, at three."

The man looked at Lucas and then glanced back to Anthony before taking a moment to scan them from head to toe.

"What were your names again?"

"Just let them in Bostock," a voice shouted behind him.

Bostock muttered something and then stepped back, pulling the door open as he waited for them to enter. He did not leave the room and after closing the door, stood in front of it, his meaty mallets clasped behind his back.

A gentleman wearing a white wig, who they presumed to be Mr. Thorpe, sat behind a large desk, his fingers steepled together in a relaxed manner. Mr. Weston paced the floor in the corner of the room, his head bent low as he wrung his hands and muttered to himself.

"I shall need another seat, Bostock," Mr. Thorpe said. He nodded to them by way of a greeting and gestured to the two chairs in front of the desk.

"There's no need to trouble your man," Lucas said, "as I prefer to stand."

"As you wish." Mr. Thorpe nodded then turned to Mr.

Weston. "Will you please stop pacing and sit down, Mr. Weston."

As though woken from a trance, Mr. Weston looked up and upon noticing Anthony rushed over to him. "It's your fault," he said, saliva bubbling between his lips, white and frothy. "I should never have listened to you. I hope you're pleased with yourself, my lord, for you're looking at a dead man. I shall be surprised if I last the day out."

Mr. Thorpe looked upon the gentleman with a hint of pity. "I'm afraid Mr. Weston invested rather heavily in a shipment of silk. It was part of a cargo bound from Calcutta, which sadly met its demise in a storm off the South East coast." Once again, Mr. Thorpe gestured to the chair. "Please sit down, gentlemen."

Anthony sat down, and Lucas stood behind him. With a nod from Mr. Thorpe, Bostock stomped over to Mr. Weston and guided him into the chair before returning to his post.

"We were hoping to rescue the cargo and sell it for a profit. Unfortunately, as is the case with ventures such as ours, the silk is beyond repair."

Mr. Weston placed his head in his hands, his skeletal frame shaking as he began to sob. "I'll be found floating in the Thames come morning, with my throat cut from ear to ear."

Mr. Thorpe winced as though someone had asked him to hold a screaming baby. "I'm afraid he borrowed a proportion of his investment from a man in Gower Street who expects a thirty percent return. A thirty percent return on six hundred pounds."

Anthony whistled.

"That is unfortunate," Lucas said, not bothering to hide his disdain. He stared at the helpless figure, astounded that this whimpering wreck of a man was responsible for killing Lord Banbury, responsible for ruining his life. Then a thought struck him. What if Helena was wrong and Mr. Weston had nothing to do with the threats made against him?

"I do not expect you to offer any sympathy, Mr. Dempsey. After all, you've spent the last four years shouldering the blame for a murder that Mr. Weston committed. Is that not right, Mr. Weston?"

Mr. Weston sucked in a few deep breaths and then his head shot up. "Murder … what … I … I don't know what you mean."

Mr. Thorpe sat back in his chair and folded his arms across his chest. "Well, I should think very carefully before you open your mouth again, Mr. Weston. Bostock cannot abide liars, can you Bostock?"

Mr. Weston glanced over his shoulder as Bostock covered his fist with his other hand and cracked his knuckles. "No, Mr. Thorpe. There's nothing worse than a liar in my book."

"You've all gone mad," Weston cried, averting his gaze as he swallowed repeatedly. "I've done nothing wrong." His bottom lip trembled, and he yanked at his collar.

Lucas knew that Weston was lying.

Hot blood rushed down his arms, filling his fists until they were pulsing and throbbing. He darted forward, grabbing Weston by the scruff of his coat and dragging him from the chair.

"Bloody liar!" Lucas growled, his jaw clenched so hard that his teeth ground together. "Because of you, I believed I'd killed a man." Lucas pulled his fist back ready to unleash the devil's own fury, but Bostock caught his arm in his meaty paw.

"I understand your frustration, Mr. Dempsey," Mr. Thorpe said calmly. "But let me tell you that the man on Gower Street is known to cut out the tongue of those who cross him, and then we'd never be able to hear Mr. Weston's confession."

"Oh, Holy Mother Mary," Mr. Weston cried as Lucas released him and he crumpled to a heap on the floor.

Lucas yanked his arm free from Bostock's vice-like grip and straightened his coat. "Very well," he consented. "Let us hear what he has to say."

"We have a witness who overheard Mr. Weston discussing certain particulars with his accomplice, so I'm certain of his guilt," Mr. Thorpe said.

A wave of panic took hold, and Lucas prayed that Anthony had not revealed the name of their source.

Mr. Thorpe stood up and pointed to the door. "Bostock, take yourself off to Gower Street and inform Mr. Manning that Weston here cannot pay."

"No! No! I'll tell you. I'll tell you," Weston cried, jumping up from the floor. He rushed over to Mr. Thorpe, clutching at the sleeve of his coat like a drowning man would a piece of driftwood. "It was after the fight … when we brought Banbury home. I helped put him to bed and then Margaret … she said he'd found out about the money she'd given me and … and there wouldn't be anymore."

Mr. Weston ambled back to his chair and flopped down.

"Go on." Lucas thrust his arms behind his back for fear of throttling the man. "There's a damn sight more to the story than that."

"I … I don't remember any more. I fell asleep, and I remember opening my eyes. I was lying on the bed, and Banbury had a pillow over his face. Margaret was crying, and she said … she said …"

"What the hell did she say?" Lucas demanded.

"I can't … they will kill me if I tell you."

"I will bloody well kill you if you don't," Lucas roared. He pushed his hand through his hair as though the action would relieve the pressure in his head. "What I want to know is why the hell you chose to blame me?"

"Gentlemen, gentlemen, please. We shall get to that in a moment." Mr. Thorpe flapped his hands up and down in the air and then walked around the desk to the dressing screen in the opposite corner of the room. Pulling it aside, he said, "I assume you heard that, Lord Banbury?"

Lord Banbury stepped out from behind the screen. "I did, thank you, Mr. Thorpe." He continued across the room and came to stand in front of Lucas. "Please accept my apologies on behalf of my family, Mr. Dempsey, for the injustice that has been caused."

Lucas wanted to tell him to go to the devil, but somewhere in the back of his mind, he knew that Helena would expect better of him, so he offered Lord Banbury a respectful bow. "I am relieved justice has finally been served," he said, his words infused with a trace of resentment.

Mr. Thorpe cleared his throat. "Gentlemen, I do not wish to ruin the moment, but I am afraid to say that, in this case, justice has not been served."

Mr. Weston made an odd whimpering sound as all heads turned to face Mr. Thorpe.

"Calm down, Mr. Weston," Thorpe cried, "for we will need to hear your story once more and in as much detail as possible." He turned to face the rest of the group. "Gentlemen, I believe if you delve a little deeper you will discover that Mr. Weston did not kill Lord Banbury, either."

CHAPTER 20

Helena was out in the garden, tending to her roses when the butler informed her that Lucas was waiting to see her. Would her stomach always flutter upon hearing his name? Would her body always tingle in anticipation?

It felt as though she was connected to him by an invisible piece of twine that tugged painfully at her heart when they were apart, and made her feel light and free when he was near.

Leaving her basket on the terrace, she removed her gloves and dropped them onto the console table, before smoothing back a few loose strands of hair and shaking out her dress.

"Good afternoon, Mr. Dempsey," she said, yet the formal greeting was infused with a seductive undertone that felt as natural as taking a breath.

When he walked over to her and took her hands in his instead of offering a customary bow, she felt the heat begin to build within, her body besieged with a need she could not explain.

He glanced briefly at the door and then lowered his mouth to hers. Although expedited with speed and precision, the touch of his lips soothed her desperate soul and she felt almost bereft when he broke contact.

"I've lost count how many hours have passed since I last did that," he said, inhaling deeply as he stepped away to a more respectable distance though he held her hands for a moment longer.

She looked up at him: a lock of dark hair hung over his brow, and his blue eyes twinkled with boyish charm. How could anyone have ever imagined him capable of murder? It made her heart ache to think that his family had abandoned him, that he had been sent so far away from home.

"I have so much to tell you," he said, "but Anthony is waiting outside in his carriage. We have just returned from Mr. Thorpe's office, where Mr. Weston confessed to being involved in the murder of Lord Banbury."

"Oh, Lucas, that's wonderful news." Helena patted her hands together, but on witnessing his lack of enthusiasm, asked, "You have informed the magistrate?"

Lucas shook his head. "Mr. Thorpe is of the opinion that Mr. Weston did not kill Lord Banbury as he has no recollection of committing the crime."

Helena jerked her head back. "I don't understand. Why would he confess to being involved in a crime he cannot remember committing? Surely, you don't believe him?"

"That is what we need to ascertain. I know it sounds ludicrous, Helena, but the more time I spend in Mr. Weston's company, the more I believe he is incapable of murder."

Helena had a similar feeling when she met Mr. Weston outside Miss Linwood's museum. "Perhaps Mr. Weston is suffering from a disorder of the mind." When Lucas looked at her dubiously, she added, "It is possible his involvement in such a traumatic event caused him to block it out of his memory. I've read about such things before."

Lucas considered her words. "You mean he was so distraught after murdering Lord Banbury, he chose to forget all about it?"

"It's possible." Helena placed her hand on his arm for no reason other than to placate the need to touch him. "Can Mr.

Weston remember anything at all about his involvement in the event?"

"He remembers helping Lord Banbury to his chamber, remembers him regaining consciousness not long after."

Helena hugged her hands to her chest. "Well, that's a relief, as it proves you had nothing to do with his death."

"It does." He nodded and offered a weak smile. "But it does not explain why someone chose to use me as the proverbial scapegoat."

It was an excellent analogy, she thought, as he *had* been wandering around in the wilderness carrying the weight of other people's sins. "Did he tell you what happened after Banbury regained consciousness?"

"Weston helped Margaret put Banbury to bed. She suggested they watch over him, and so they sat in front of the fire and ate supper. It was while he was supping that he drifted off to sleep."

"Well, that does sound odd," she said, wrinkling her nose and shaking her head. "I've seen people fall asleep after a meal, but I have never witnessed anyone fall asleep during it."

"When Weston opened his eyes and became aware of his surroundings, he was lying next to Banbury on the bed, his hands gripping the pillow that covered Banbury's face. Margaret rushed to his side and accused him of suffocating Banbury."

Helena glanced up to the corner of the ceiling and tapped her lip with the tip of her finger. "So, Mr. Weston fell asleep during his supper and woke to Margaret's accusation. The question is, what was Margaret doing while Mr. Weston was sleeping?" As soon as the words left her mouth Helena's eyes widened as she loved working out complex puzzles. "What if Margaret drugged Mr. Weston and made him believe he killed Lord Banbury?"

Lucas smiled, and his gaze softened. "I think you should ask Mr. Thorpe if he needs an assistant as you are very astute, Helena."

"Why, thank you, Mr. Dempsey," she replied, unable to stop the blood rushing to her cheeks. It was not the first time he'd paid her such a generous compliment, but for some strange reason, a reason that defied all usual logic, she was desperate to hear praise of an entirely superficial kind. Did he admire her eyes or her hair? What did he think of her smile or her figure? What was it about her that roused his passion to such a degree?

"That is why I need you to accompany me," he said, his voice waking her from her reverie. "We need to call on Lady Banbury, and Anthony thought it would be better if it appeared as though we were making a social call. Lady Banbury has not been seen about in Society for over a week."

"You don't think something has happened to her?" Helena asked, remembering the conversation she overheard in the garden, hearing the ominous voice that said — *I will deal with Margaret.*

"I hope not," he said, his expression grave. "Margaret is the only person who can shed any light on the whole fiasco. Lord Banbury and Mr. Weston are to meet us there directly."

"Lord Banbury?"

"I know," he said, moving closer to cup her cheek, the pad of his thumb brushing softly over her lips. "It's complicated. I will tell you about it as soon as we're on our way."

Helena felt a rush of excitement. "Then I shall go and get my jacket."

As she turned to walk away, Lucas grabbed her by the wrist and swung her back round to face him. "Another minute or two won't hurt," he said, as his lips found hers again.

They arrived in Grosvenor Square to find Lord Banbury standing on the pavement next to his carriage, watching Mr. Weston partake in a rather animated conversation with his sister's butler. Mr. Weston shrugged, pointed and nodded to the hallway beyond the door and at one point threw his hands up in the air while the butler looked down his hooked nose and continued to shake his head.

"It's no good." Mr. Weston sighed as he joined the group. He appeared a little too cheerful for a man who'd confessed to a murder though his eyes were red and puffy. "Sedgewick insists that Margaret is unavailable. I mean there is doing one's job, and there's being downright stubborn."

Every member of the party turned to face Lord Banbury, and Helena took the opportunity to offer him a smug grin.

"Don't look at me," Banbury said, "I've already tried but to no avail."

"But is this not your house?" Anthony asked in a tone that made Banbury look somewhat weak and foolish. "I assume you do still own it."

"Erm … yes, yes," Banbury mumbled. "But it's the height of impertinence to barge into someone's home uninvited."

"Even if that person may have murdered your brother?" Anthony countered.

"Well, I have no qualms barging in there," Lucas chipped in. "Bad manners are considered rather tame when compared to my endless list of sins. Although now I can scratch murder off that list."

Banbury cleared his throat, and his face took on the appearance of an over-ripe tomato.

"Oh, for goodness sake." Helena sighed. "I will go and speak to … what did you say his name was?"

"Sedgewick," Lord Banbury and Mr. Weston chimed in unison.

"Perhaps we should wait inside the carriage," Lord Banbury suggested, glancing from left to right. "It wouldn't do to draw attention to ourselves."

Helena felt a sudden surge of anger. "Oh, I don't know," she said. "I'm sure the odd look here and there is a mere trifle when compared with four years of slanderous remarks and censorious glances. Wouldn't you agree, Mr. Dempsey?"

Lucas clapped slowly three times. "I would indeed, Miss Ecclestone," he said, his eyes full of warmth and admiration.

"Now please wait here," she said, "I will be but a moment."

After a brief conversation with Sedgewick, Helena informed

the butler that unless she was able to see Lady Banbury and check that no harm had befallen her, she was going to have to fetch a constable and be forced to make a scene on the doorstep. She reminded the man that malicious gossip could render someone unemployable and so, with a few grumbles and groans, Sedgwick agreed that a maid would accompany Helena to check on Lady Banbury.

"You're not going in there on your own," Lucas said, shaking his head vigorously by way of reinforcing his point. "As far we know Lady Banbury is involved in her husband's death."

"Surely not," Mr. Weston cried, his gawky frame shaking with unsuppressed emotion. "I cannot believe Margaret would let me take the blame for something I didn't do."

"Why not?" Lucas said through gritted teeth. "Thanks to you, I've spent four years shouldering the blame for something I didn't do. In fact, I don't know what's stopping me from pounding you into a pile of pulp."

Mr. Weston made an odd whimpering sound, and his bottom lip quivered.

"Because you're a better man than that," Helena said, "and I feel confident Mr. Weston will pay the price for his misdeeds." She drew on every ounce of love she had for Lucas in the hope of conveying it in her tone and in her eyes. "You must trust me, Mr. Dempsey. I shall be perfectly safe knowing you are out here waiting for me." She wished she could kiss his furrowed brow, could rub her hands over his tense shoulders, could find some way to ease his tortured expression.

Lucas let out an exasperated sigh. "I shall give you five minutes and then I'm coming in. And in the meantime, I shall do my best to keep my hands from Mr. Weston's neck."

Sedgewick escorted Helena into the hall and requested that she wait while he located a maid. Helena took the opportunity to peek around the door to the parlour. The fire had been swept and laid; there were new candles in the sconces and a vase of freshly cut flowers on the side table, giving the impression they expected their mistress down anytime soon.

Helena was staring up at the ceiling in the hall, feigning interest in a Greek-inspired architrave when Sedgewick returned with the maid, Martha.

"Martha has just informed me that Lady Banbury has taken to her bed suffering from one of her migraines." Sedgewick gave a few slow nods and then held his arm out to usher Helena towards the front door. "If you would care to return tomorrow, I am certain that …"

Helena folded her arms across her chest. "I am not leaving this house until I have seen Lady Banbury."

The butler huffed and puffed. "Surely, you cannot expect to gain access to her private chamber?"

Sedgewick did have a valid point: Helena's request was highly inappropriate, but there was something amiss in this house. Besides, if unsuccessful in her task, Lucas would rip the place apart searching for answers, and he didn't need to be embroiled in another scandal.

"In precisely ten seconds I am going to open the front door and do two things," Helena said, glaring at them with a look of steely determination. "I will request that Viscount Harwood call a constable, for I believe you are both guilty of endangering the life of your mistress. And I will insist that Lord Banbury turn you both out without references."

"We could just let her peer around the door," Martha whispered to Sedgewick. "I don't see what harm that could do."

Helena watched the pair exchange glances, their distinct facial movements suggesting they had the power of telepathy and were conducting their own silent conversation.

"I shall escort you to Lady Banbury's chamber." Sedgewick's tone was icy-cold. "If you would care to follow me."

Helena followed Sedgewick's methodical plodding up to the first floor. They stopped outside Lady Banbury's chamber.

Martha scurried forward to open the door, her hand trembling as she turned the handle.

From the moment the maid forced the door from its jamb, Helena was aware of the sickly sweet smell and she forced herself to inhale deeply so she could determine its origin. It was an odd concoction: a mixture of brandy, honey, some sort of spice and vomit.

Helena peered around the door. The heavy curtains blocked out the light and so she narrowed her gaze, locating the still figure lying huddled under the coverlet on the canopy bed. It didn't feel like the room of someone who had just taken to their bed with a headache or for an afternoon nap. The room felt bleak and desolate, devoid of any real life. Despair lingered in the shadows, watching and waiting, as if the occupant were a mere moment from death.

"Thank you," Helena said, swallowing deeply as she stepped away from the door. "I do not need to see any more."

There was something familiar about the smell. As she descended the stairs, her mind scrambled to assemble all the relevant bits of information.

When she reached the front door, Sedgewick rushed forward and held it open, but Helena did not step out over the threshold.

"Gentlemen, hurry. You must come quickly," Helena cried, and Lucas was at the door before she had time to take another breath.

"What is it?" he said, concern marring his brow as he cupped her cheek.

"I believe Lady Banbury has been drugged. She may even be dead."

CHAPTER 21

Mr. Weston pushed and shoved his way past everyone in a bid to be the first to reach his sister's bedchamber. While Anthony ushered Sedgewick and Martha into the study, ignoring their protests that the mistress was just ill and nothing sinister had taken place.

"Mr. Weston must care for his sister very much," Helena whispered as Weston tripped on one step and caught his knee on the next.

"I'm not so sure," Lucas replied as Lord Banbury squeezed past them and raced up ahead. "I think he cares more about the health of her purse."

"Are you always so cynical?"

Lucas raised an arrogant brow. "Most definitely." His answer was short and succinct. What else was he supposed to say? That he believed everyone to be insincere, that assuming the worst in people was the only way to protect oneself from disappointment. Although Helena had never disappointed him. He believed every word that came out of her luscious mouth—well, almost every word. "I do not find it easy to trust the motives of others," he added, as she deserved a more truthful explanation.

What happened next would be ingrained in his memory for the rest of his life.

As they neared the top stair, Helena removed her glove and placed her tiny hand in his. She squeezed gently so that their palms touched; an innocent gesture that shook his body like nothing else had ever done before. A hard lump formed in his throat as some undefinable energy shot up his arm, obliterating the lock on the iron chest that held his heart. He must have been holding his breath, for he exhaled deeply as his heart sprouted wings and flitted around freely in his chest.

"Helena," he said with a sigh. There was so much he wanted to say. But he didn't know where to begin.

She looked up at him. "You can trust *me*, Lucas," she said with a smile before removing her hand and placing it back in her glove.

"I know," he whispered. He knew he could trust her, that she'd never lie to him. But emotions were complicated things, easy to mistake, easy to confuse.

"Miss Ecclestone is right. Margaret's been drugged," Lord Banbury said as he rushed to meet them at the door to Lady Banbury's chamber. He looked less pompous, more capable, as though he'd climbed the stairs a boy and would descend a man.

"Please tell me that we're not too late," Helena implored.

"No, she's conscious, but heavily sedated."

Helena sighed. "It is laudanum, isn't it? I noticed the smell as soon as Martha opened the door."

"I'm not sure. There is a tincture on the table beside her bed, but the label has been removed." Lord Banbury turned to Lucas. "I must go and get help. Are you able to wait here until my return?"

"Of course," Lucas replied, forcing his thoughts back to the matter at hand. Satan himself wouldn't be able to drag him away, not until he had discovered what the hell was going on.

They entered the bedchamber to find Mr. Weston crouching by the side of the bed, his hands clasped together in prayer.

"Please wake up, Margaret," he cried, rocking back and forth. "Wake up. Wake up and I promise you everything will be right again."

"The man's a wreck," Helena whispered. "I see what you mean when you said he's not capable of murder. I doubt he's capable of tying his own cravat." She looked up at Lucas with her silver-green faerie eyes. "I confess I do not know whether to pity the man or hit him over the head with a chamber pot."

Lucas gave a weak chuckle. "I feel the same though I tend to sway more to the latter. I can forgive the fact he wanted me dead," he replied, "but I will never forgive him for what happened to you at the museum."

"I can forgive him," she said, placing the tips of her fingers lightly on his chest. "Had it not been for Mr. Weston's desire to have you killed, I would not have called on you in Mount Street. I would not have had the opportunity to know you. I would not have fallen in love with you."

Without waiting for a response, she walked away from him, over to the listless figure of Lady Banbury. "We will need fresh water, Mr. Weston, a warming pan and see if you can find extra blankets. We must do everything we can to make her comfortable until Lord Banbury returns."

Mr. Weston jumped up, took two paces to the right then four paces to the left.

Helena huffed, removed her gloves and jacket and placed them on the end of the bed. "The pitcher, Mr. Weston. Go down to the kitchen and refill the pitcher."

Lucas watched Mr. Weston scurry from the room. "Perhaps we should let in some air," he said, feeling the need to do something useful, and so he pushed back the curtains and pulled up the sash. "I don't know what's worse. The acrid smell in here or the choking fog outside."

"I should leave it open. Her breathing is shallow and a little hoarse, but I think that's due to the effects of the laudanum." Helena picked up the brown bottle, removed the dropper and sniffed the liquid. "I wonder if she administered it herself," she said, jerking her head back sharply. "Her withdrawal from Society does seem to coincide with your return to London. Perhaps seeing you roused feelings of guilt and she used this to blot it all out."

"Then why do the servants look as though they've just been sentenced to the gallows?" he said, his fingers brushing against hers as he took the bottle from her hand and put it back on the table.

"If anyone were to see her like this, Lucas, it would inevitably cause a scandal."

He gazed upon the ghostly apparition in the bed, the lady bearing no similarity to the one he once knew. Her eyes were but tiny red circles buried in a powder-white face, her lips thin, flaky and a deathly shade of blue. He could understand why someone would want to erase painful memories. A bottle of brandy had been his friend and ally in those first few months in Boston, and he would often take to his bed for days in a state of total intoxication. "I can understand her motives," he said, "but to go to such extreme lengths. I know from experience that drugging oneself is not the answer."

"Lady Banbury did not administer the drug herself." Anthony's voice echoed through the room. He came to stand on the opposite side of the bed, inhaling audibly at the sight of the wraith-like creature as pale and as still as a stone statue. "Lady Banbury receives the same gentleman every evening at seven. I believe he's the one responsible for this."

Lucas snorted. "I take it Sedgewick squealed."

"Like a pig on market day when I threatened to have him arrested as an accessory."

"Do you think it's the same gentleman who met with Mr. Weston in the garden?" Helena asked.

"Undoubtedly," Anthony said. "Weston refused to disclose the name of his accomplice, but it all fits together. The gentleman has been a regular visitor here for the last six years. I would guess that his relationship with Lady Banbury is rather more than that of a physician. He's convinced the staff that he is treating Lady Banbury for her various ailments, paying them handsomely for their cooperation."

"Look at this." Helena lifted Lady Banbury's arm from the coverlet and pointed to the lines of lumpy red scratches. "It appears as though she's fought with a bramble bush, but it is a classic symptom of laudanum addiction."

Lucas stared at her, a mixture of burning curiosity and admiration filling his chest. "How do you know so much about it?"

Helena placed Lady Banbury's arm under the coverlet. "I read a book on herbology," she said with a mischievous grin. "I had to do something while I was waiting to save you."

There was a creak on the landing, and Mr. Weston entered the room carrying the pitcher. He scuttled over to the washstand and poured the water into the bowl, soaking the linen square that he found draped over the rim.

"Thank you, Mr. Weston," Helena said. She took the linen out of his hand and wiped Lady Banbury's brow, wiped her cheeks and around her dry mouth. "Did you manage to find blankets?"

"I shall go and get them." Mr. Weston glanced at the bed, his face twisted with anguish. "Will she live?"

"I'm sure she will," Helena nodded and waited for him to amble out of the room. "Under the circumstances, he's proving rather helpful."

"I think he's desperate to know if he really did murder Banbury," Anthony said. "And Lucas told him that the investment opportunity was bogus, that Thorpe would reimburse him for the money he thought he'd lost in the venture. I have never seen a man look so relieved."

"That was good of you," Helena said with a look of adoration. "You could have made him wait before you put him out of his misery."

"Oh, I wanted to," Lucas said. He'd wanted to be petty and

resentful, wanted to let bitterness twist its barbed knife around in his gut, for he was comfortable with that feeling. But Weston was just as much a pawn in this game as Lucas. And so some strange urge to be noble and magnanimous took hold of him, and the words tumbled out of his mouth before he could change his mind. "Well, perhaps I'm a more compassionate man than even I knew."

"I have always known that," she said, and there was a level of tenderness in her tone that touched him deeply.

Anthony cleared his throat. "Let us get back to the matter at hand." He paused and waited for Lucas to tear his gaze away from his woodland enchantress. "As I said, the gentleman has been Lady Banbury's physician for years. He is a man of some eminence, educated at Eton and Cambridge, well respected in Society, albeit on the fringes. Ironically, he was an adviser to the committee who petitioned for the Apothecaries Act ... for the use of medicine to be regulated."

"Sedgewick told you all that?" Helena asked with some astonishment.

Lucas suddenly felt cold. "No, Sedgewick didn't tell him," he replied bluntly as he knew the man his brother spoke of. "My brother is familiar with the gentleman because he was also our father's physician."

Anthony's gaze softened. "You know that Frobisher prescribed our father laudanum for his gout. That in the weeks before Banbury's death he'd been a frequent visitor."

It all made a little more sense now, Lucas thought. It was Doctor Frobisher who poisoned his father's mind, who invented gossip and scandal and his father had believed every word. Lucas swallowed deeply in a bid to dislodge the hard lump blocking his windpipe. He had found it easy to despise his father, to shape him into the image of a cold-hearted beast capable of betraying his kin. It made it easier to deal with the pain. It made it easier to cope with the loss.

"It is fair to say that our father may not have been in charge of his faculties when he sent you away, Lucas," Anthony continued.

"Perhaps." Lucas shrugged. There was no point in dreaming about the possibility as he would never know the truth. The focus now was to determine Frobisher's motives and to tear him limb from limb as a warning to all those who attempted to cross him.

"Do you think this Frobisher fellow is responsible for Lord Banbury's death?" Helena said, patting the patient's brow with the tips of her fingers before pulling the coverlet up a little higher around her shoulders.

"I believe he's responsible in some way, whether he killed him with his own hand, well, that's another question." Anthony removed his watch and checked the time. "We have an hour until Frobisher makes his daily call, so we need to decide how best to proceed."

There was a gasp and a dull thud from the doorway as Mr. Weston dropped the bundle of blankets on the wooden floor. "It wasn't me," he cried. "I didn't tell you anything."

"We are already acquainted with Frobisher," Lucas said, feeling bile rise from his stomach when he recalled seeing the man in Lady Colebrook's garden on the night of the ball.

Mr. Weston did not have the opportunity to reply as Lord Banbury arrived, bursting into the room with his physician, Doctor Hargreaves.

"Thankfully, Hargreaves was at home," he said, gasping for breath as he held his hand over his heart. "It was … was quicker to run. We … we can be assured of his discretion."

Hargreaves didn't look a day over twenty, but he made a thorough examination of both the patient and the bottle of reddish-brown liquid. "Her pupils are constricted, her breathing shallow and these marks on her arms are indicative of an excessive use of laudanum. I'm afraid the weaning process will be long and drawn out, and she will need constant supervision."

Lucas turned to Helena and gave her a respectful nod, which she returned with a satisfied grin.

"Could you spare a moment, Lord Banbury," Anthony said. Lord Banbury nodded and accompanied the group out onto the landing, leaving Hargreaves and Weston to tend to Lady Banbury.

"I believe the man responsible for this," Anthony said, nodding towards the chamber, "will be arriving shortly to administer the usual daily dose. If we are going to uncover the truth behind your brother's death and the subsequent treatment of his wife, then we must act quickly."

Anthony explained what they knew of Frobisher.

"Without an admission of guilt we have no hope of proving any of this," Banbury replied. "Frobisher only has to say that his patient has an addiction and he is helping her through it. It is not unusual for a physician to make regular house calls or to enlist the services of the hired help. Then it will simply be a case of Frobisher's word against Mr. Weston's."

Everyone looked at the floor in silent contemplation. Lucas knew he would just need a minute alone with Frobisher to gain a confession.

"I have an idea," Helena said, all heads looking in her direction. "We will need Hargreaves' approval as it will mean moving Lady Banbury to another room so that *I* may take her place."

Lucas felt as though someone had slit him open from neck to navel and the contents of his stomach had splattered out onto his boots. "The hell you will!" he roared.

CHAPTER 22

"No, Helena," Lucas cried, oblivious to the fact he had used her given name. "There's every chance Frobisher has already killed one person." He turned away from the group and thrust his hand through his hair before swinging back round. "Look what he's done to Lady Banbury. There are people lying on the mortuary slab with more life in them. No, I can't let you do it. I won't let you do it."

Helena stared up at him, his tortured expression visible for all to see.

Could he not understand she was trying to help him?

"I shall be perfectly safe, Mr. Dempsey," she said, trying to find the right words to bring him peace and comfort, "as you'll be in the room with me. You can hide behind the curtains and I shall call out to you should I need assistance."

Lucas looked at her as though she had said the sky was green and the grass was blue.

"Miss Ecclestone does have a point, Lucas," Viscount Harwood interjected. "If she could convince Frobisher that she's Lady Banbury, we might be able to gain a confession or, at the very least, some idea as to what is going on." He placed his hand on Lucas' upper arm. "It is worth a try."

"And how on earth is she supposed to do that?" Lucas replied, jerking his arm away in protest. "No. Find some other way."

As determined as he was to protect her, she was as determined to help him solve this mystery, and she had a feeling the battle was not going to be pleasant.

"There is no other way," she said firmly. "I will don a mobcap and bury myself under the coverlet. If we keep the room dark and I alter the tone of my voice, it should not be too difficult to fool him. Frobisher will not expect his patient to be coherent, and will be so concerned with what has gone wrong he'll not even consider the possibility I'm an impostor."

Lucas covered her elbow with his hand and steered her to the other end of the landing. "Excuse us a moment," he called back over his shoulder. "For heaven's sake, Helena, what are you trying to do to me?" he whispered, turning his back to shield her from prying eyes. "Frobisher has taken everything from me. He has robbed me of my family, robbed me of my reputation." He closed his eyes briefly and exhaled. "If anything should happen to you …"

Helena placed the palm of her hand flat against his chest and she could feel his heart racing. "Lucas, nothing is going to happen to me. You must trust me when I tell you I can do this." Although she was still trying to calm her nerves, still trying to stop her body from shaking at the thought of coming face to face with a murderer. The thought that Lucas had endured four years of injustice gave her the strength she needed, and she was determined to find a way to bring an end to the matter. "I've shown that I trust you, now you must do the same."

Lucas shook his head. "It is not the same," he whispered.

He was right, of course. "No, it is not," she conceded, "but I am asking for your support. I am asking you to help me."

He was silent as his gaze fell beyond her shoulder to some imagined place in the distance.

"Lucas." When he didn't answer, she added, "Please have a little faith in me."

He sighed, looked down at her hand resting on his chest and covered it with his own. "The moment you feel uncomfortable, the moment you think he may—" he broke off abruptly and turned his head away. "I cannot believe I am saying this."

She placed her hand on his cheek and forced him to look at her. "Look, let us come up with a plan and then you may feel better about it. Will you, at least, do that?"

He sighed as his gaze fell to her mouth. "Very well. But you're going to have to find some way to soothe my delicate sensibilities."

Helena moved behind the dressing screen to change into one of Lady Banbury's nightgowns while Hargreaves, Banbury, and Mr. Weston busied themselves with moving the patient and making her comfortable. Viscount Harwood had gone downstairs to give Sedgewick and Martha their instructions and to secure their cooperation.

"Do you need any help?" Lucas asked from the other side of the screen. "I have very nimble fingers that make the removal of ladies undergarments a much less tedious affair."

Helena smiled to herself, as she loved to hear his witty banter and knew he used it to mask his real feelings. "I don't intend to remove everything," she said, dismissing the desire to feel his arms around her. "But thank you, I think I can manage. Besides, we don't have much time, and I have a feeling you would be a distraction."

"Only if you want me to be," he said, and she almost hit the ceiling when she turned around to find him standing behind her. "I see I'm too late." His gaze drifted over the plain nightgown. "How disappointing. You know how partial I am to cotton. I like the way it glides through the air, the way it lands softly on the floor."

Helena's face flushed as she recalled the last time she'd worn such an unflattering gown, when she'd dragged it up over her head only to discard it in shameless abandon. "I always aim to please," she purred.

He stepped closer, slid his arm around her waist and pulled her to his chest. "Isn't that my line?" he said as he lowered his mouth to hers.

Helena could gauge his mood and interpret his thoughts by the way he kissed her. There was something intense, something possessive about the way he claimed her mouth, the way he deepened the kiss with such desperate urgency, as though the end of the world was imminent and every single second might be the last. As his tongue thrust wildly against hers, desire coursed through her body, accompanied by the familiar tightening of her abdomen that begged for release. When his breathing grew ragged, she knew it would not be long before their passion claimed them and they lost control.

"You see," she panted, forcing herself to break contact. "I knew you would be a distraction."

He did not pull away but touched his forehead to hers and inhaled deeply. "If Frobisher lays so much as a finger on you, I am going to kill him."

"No, you're not," she replied. "You're going to restrain him until a constable arrives."

Lucas sighed. "Is this the way of it now?" he asked feigning melancholy. "Am I to be a toothless lion who's had his claws ripped out, who can do nothing but yawn and patter around on useless paws?"

Helena pursed her lips but snickered as she tried to suppress a grin.

"It is not funny, Helena."

There was a knock on the door. "Miss Ecclestone, are you ready? Frobisher will be here in ten minutes."

After a silent debate that involved lots of pointing, nodding and raised brows, Lucas stepped out first, his broad shoulders acting as a shield. "Don't mind me. I'm only here to help Miss Ecclestone into bed," he said in a rather salacious tone and Helena prodded him in the back. "I mean, I'm here to assist Miss Ecclestone prepare for her role."

"I see," Viscount Harwood said, raising his brows. "Well, perhaps you should hurry up and get on with it."

Lucas settled Helena into Lady Banbury's bed, tucked in the coverlet and handed her the mobcap.

"How do I look?" she asked, shuffling down under the covers and pulling the cap down around her ears.

"Like an old maid," Lucas whispered, his warm breath tickling her neck as he moved closer, "a rather enchanting old maid." He turned and directed his question to Viscount Harwood. "What more is there to do?"

The viscount stepped back towards the door to survey the room. "We need to close the curtains and remove all the candles, just leave one in the sconce. It will cast some light without giving Frobisher the freedom to walk about with it."

Helena watched the gentlemen hurry about their business and tried to focus on the matter at hand. It was only like acting, she thought. How difficult could it be? All she had to do was draw out her words in a grumbling sort of tone.

"Margaret is secure, and Frobisher will be here any moment," Lord Banbury said as he rushed into the room. He looked more terrified than Helena did. "Where do you want me?"

"Behind the curtains," Viscount Harwood replied. He scanned the room and nodded before walking over to Helena. "We will only be a few feet away, Miss Ecclestone. Are you sure you're happy with the arrangements?"

Helena nodded.

"You do not need to say anything, but I want you to know

that I shall be forever in your debt." The viscount smiled and walked over to Lucas. "Come," he said, grabbing his brother by the arm and pulling him towards the curtains. "Let us give Miss Ecclestone a few moments alone to prepare for her role."

It was as though Lucas was sleepwalking as he allowed his brother to draw him away, although his eyes never left hers.

"I shall be right here," he mouthed and then he closed the curtains while she lay in wait for a murderer.

Ten minutes felt like three hours. The sickly smell that clung to the bedsheets made her feel nauseous and light-headed, yet her initial sense of relief upon hearing footsteps on the landing was soon forgotten.

The door opened with a creak. "That will be all. You may leave now, Martha."

The sound of Frobisher's voice caused all the air to leave Helena's body. His tone lacked any warmth or variation of pitch. It had no harmonious melody to indicate meaning, just stone-cold words that caused a frisson of fear to flash right through her.

"As you wish." Martha's voice was even and honest and did not reveal that anything untoward was about to take place.

Helena heard the light patter of receding footsteps followed by a click as the door closed. She swallowed deeply in a bid to lubricate her vocal cords. "Is that you," she said, the low croak a little louder than a whisper. It occurred to her that Lady Banbury would surely use his given name, but she could not recall hearing it mentioned. "Martha? Is Frobisher here?"

"Mar-Margaret?" There was a hitch in his voice as he took a hesitant step towards the bed. "You're awake."

Helena could not risk him walking up to the bed. "Don't come any closer or I will scream." She lowered her voice and with some vehemence, added, "I know what you have done to me. I know you want me dead." Helena let out an anguished whimper.

Frobisher's gaze flitted to the brown bottle on the nightstand. "Do not be ridiculous. Your medicine is causing delusions," he said with a dismissive wave of the hand. "You're ill, Margaret, and I am here to help you."

He took another step closer.

"No, you are trying to kill me." It was not wise to say too much, but she needed to find a way to rattle his resolve. "I have sent a letter to Viscount Harwood explaining your involvement in Banbury's murder—explaining your involvement in everything."

Frobisher gave a chilling chuckle. "And who agreed to deliver your letter, Margaret? Perhaps Martha or Sedgewick? I think not."

Helena had forgotten that he'd bribed the staff, and so she coughed while she waited for inspiration to strike.

"Sedgewick knows it would not be wise to alert others to your condition. He knows what a terrible scandal it would be," Frobisher continued. "No doubt, I shall receive the letter upon my departure."

"Henry took it," Helena blurted, grateful she had paid attention and took note of Mr. Weston's name. "He forced his way in here, earlier today."

"I don't believe you. Henry has more important things on his mind."

Helena lowered her chin and used the coverlet to muffle her voice. "He told me that he asked you to kill Lucas Dempsey. He told me he offered you a thousand pounds."

Frobisher's eyes widened, and he glanced around the room as though he was expecting Mr. Weston to appear. "Y-your letter proves nothing," he said, regaining his confidence. "Who is going to believe the word of an opium addict? And as for Henry, well, it is only a matter of time before he is found floating in the Thames. Or perhaps he will never be found and will rot away in the bottom of some pauper's pit."

Helena was relieved Mr. Weston was not hiding behind the

curtains for she had a vision of him dashing out in a fit of apoplexy. Frobisher took another sly step closer, and she scoured her mind to think of a way to drag a confession out of him.

"I thought you loved me," she said, feigning a sob. "I thought … I thought you killed Banbury so we could be together."

"And I did, but things have taken an unexpected turn now Lucas Dempsey has returned. I cannot afford any undue attention."

Helena coughed again. Her mouth was dry and her throat hurt. "Mr. Dempsey will hunt you down when he discovers you were the one who killed Banbury."

Frobisher chuckled again. "I will tell him Henry did it. Henry believes he is the murderer and it will not take much to extract a confession. I will tell Dempsey you confessed on your deathbed and the letter was a ruse to divert suspicion. He will not think to question my word. After all, I was his father's physician."

A cold chill settled in Helena's bones and she did not have to feign a stutter. "On my deathbed … after everything … you plan to kill me?"

"My dear, I have enjoyed your company immensely and enjoyed your money a lot more. But I'm afraid you are the only one who knows the truth, which leaves you in a very precarious position."

He turned his back to her and walked over to the dressing table, put his brown leather case down and flicked open the brass catches. The sharp clicking sound resembled a pistol being cocked, and she imagined the contents were just as deadly.

"If you mean to administer more laudanum then … then I must tell you I will fight you till my last breath."

Frobisher laughed. "Under the circumstances, laudanum would not be appropriate." He removed a pair of black gloves from his case and put them on.

Although Lucas stood just a few feet away, Frobisher

appeared unpredictable, and Helena wondered if she had made a terrible miscalculation in suggesting the switch. Her thoughts flitted briefly to the wraith-like image of Lady Banbury, to the woman who had foolishly believed Frobisher's protestations of love and nearly paid the ultimate price.

"What are you doing," she said, failing to disguise her voice as Frobisher took a few slow, steady steps towards her, pushing his fingers into his gloves to ensure a snug fit.

"It would not do to have you claw at my hands as you take your last breath. I do have other patients to consider and—" He stopped abruptly and narrowed his gaze. "Remove your cap."

Helena froze.

When she failed to answer, Frobisher cried, "Who the hell are *you*?"

She barely had time to take a breath before he darted towards her. In a panic, she slid down under the coverlet as he lunged at the bed and braced herself for the painful impact. But all she heard was a heavy thud, loud groans, muttered curses and then Lucas' voice.

"You gutter rat. I should gut you, skin you and hang you out to dry."

Helena shuffled back up the bed and peeked out, to find Frobisher lying on the floor. He had a cut on his lip and blood trickled from his nose. He held his arms across his stomach, and as he brought his knees to his chest, Lucas raised his arm to punch him again.

Viscount Harwood stepped forward. "Lucas, we'll take it from here," he said, putting a hand on his brother's shoulder. When Lucas ignored him, Viscount Harwood said, "Lucas, you must think of Miss Ecclestone."

Lucas straightened and turned to look at Helena, his face red and puffy from anger and overexertion. His eyes had lost their brilliance and were like round black pebbles in the darkness.

The viscount grabbed Frobisher by his lapels and pulled him

up off the floor. "I'm afraid we all know the truth now. Isn't that right Lord Banbury?"

"Indeed, it is," Banbury said, walking from behind the curtains to face his brother's murderer. In a move considered highly uncharacteristic, Banbury pulled his arm back and punched Frobisher in the stomach. "That is for my brother and for me, as I do not like being taken for a fool."

Frobisher coughed and spluttered, but when he straightened, Viscount Harwood punched him again. "And that is for my brother," he said, his words conveying a combination of emotions—bitterness, anger and sorrow. "And this, this one is for our father."

Lucas came over to the bed and sat on the edge. "Are you all right?" He removed her cap and smoothed out her hair, stroked her cheek and then picked up her hand and held it in his while she just lay there and watched him. "My God, you're shaking," he gasped.

"I'm fine," she replied. "It is just a little cold in here."

He looked at her dubiously and then began rubbing her hands between his. He should have been relieved, even ecstatic at the prospect of clearing his name, at the prospect of bringing the real culprit to justice. But he looked lost, like an orphan boy who had no idea where he was going to lay his head at night.

"You must be relieved," she said, trying to bring him out of his melancholic mood. "At least, you now know the truth."

He was silent while his brother dragged Frobisher from the room and then he glanced over his shoulder as the door closed. "I cannot find the words to express how grateful I am to you, Helena. For doing this," he said as he waved his hand over the bed, "for everything. Had I not left Boston, had I not met you, I fear I would have been left to waste away in a ditch of self-pity."

"There is no point dwelling on the past, Lucas. You must think ahead. You must think about the future."

He averted his gaze and pushed his hand through his mop of black hair, and she had the suspicion there was something he wasn't telling her. "I know it's not fair to ask, not after what you have been through and I know the hour is late, but will you come home with me, just for a little while."

She sat up and brushed her lips against his. "You must know I would do anything for you."

CHAPTER 23

Lucas decided to wait on the landing while Helena dressed. Partly, because he wanted to give her a moment of privacy, a moment to catch her breath after her encounter with Frobisher. Partly, because he didn't trust himself around her: not while this all-consuming need overpowered every rational thought and every logical action.

He was still trying to make sense of his chaotic emotions.

Was it natural to feel such a desperate need to protect another? He had certainly never felt that way before. Was it natural to feel such acute discomfort in her absence? It was an odd feeling, almost as though his lungs were being compressed and her presence provided the air he needed to breathe. Indeed, the image of Frobisher lunging towards the bed caused all the air to leave his body. The lack of oxygen inducing a minor memory lapse for when he regained focus he was but one step away from ripping the man's throat out.

He let out a heavy sigh.

"Please tell me you're not still brooding about what happened in there."

Helena breezed out of the room as though she'd only nipped in to admire the new curtains. But as he studied her more closely, he noticed the faint red circles beneath her eyes, noted that her complexion lacked its usual brilliance.

He forced a smile and waited for the Lord to rain fire down upon him for his selfishness. "Come, let me take you home," he said, hiding his disappointment that she would not be sharing his bed. "You're tired and no doubt you will need to rise early tomorrow. Lord Banbury has asked if you will make some sort of formal statement, but I have suggested it's possible to secure a prosecution without your testimony."

"Thank you," she said. As she stared at him, her gaze drifted over his hair, over the breadth of his chest and up to his mouth. "But I'm not tired. I shall come home with you. If only for a little while."

Home.

The word usually roused feelings of resentment and bitterness, images of a dank stone prison cell. Yet it sounded safe and warm when it fell from her lips, and he had a vision of a heavenly sanctuary, of brilliant blue skies, green meadows and an abundance of white blossom trees. A place where children laughed and ran freely on the grass and in the dark depths of his private chamber, Helena lay naked in his bed.

He forced the image from his mind. "It was wrong of me to ask. Your mother will be worried, and you've not eaten for hours."

"What time is it?"

"It's almost eight."

Her eyes widened, and after a moment of contemplation, she said, "If you were to invite me to dine, I think I could stay until ten. I will send a note to say we're dining with Lord Banbury. Under the circumstances, it should not be a problem. Mother will be so thrilled to hear that Lord Banbury is now in your debt she'll probably not care a hoot."

"You're sure you feel able?" he asked. Although he had no idea how he was going to survive the next two hours, not when all he wanted to do was bury himself inside her and forget all about the world, forget all about Boston.

She won't want you when you tell her.

The voice of his conscience rang loudly in his ears and he shook his head in a bid to drown out the sound.

"Feel able? You say that as though you have planned something wicked and sinful," she said, offering him a coy smile. "I hope I'm not going to be disappointed."

He forced a smile. "When it comes to sin, Miss Ecclestone, I believe I am more than capable of meeting all of your expectations."

Her face flushed a pretty shade of pink. "You must be hungry, too," she said, attempting to lead the conversation back to the matter at hand.

"Hungry?" he repeated, moistening his lips. The word did not even begin to describe how he felt. "I'm utterly ravenous."

They used Anthony's carriage to travel back to Mount Street, although he believed Lucas was taking Helena home and had been full of praise for his thoughtful actions.

Lucas spoke with Gregson on their return and escorted Helena into the study where he lit the candles and pulled the chairs closer to the fire.

"Would you care for a glass of sherry?" he asked, before pouring a mouthful of brandy into a glass and swallowing it down in one. As he watched her take a seat, his gaze moved down to the Persian rug where the memory of her naked form writhing beneath him, swamped his thoughts.

"You have sherry?" she replied with some surprise.

"I do."

A brief silence ensued while she studied him and he felt a pang of guilt for being so presumptuous as to assume he would be entertaining her here again.

"That would be lovely."

"Are you cold?" he asked handing her the glass before dropping into the chair opposite.

"No. I'm fine, thank you."

"Can I get you anything else?"

"No."

"I imagined you would not want to dine formally, so I took the liberty of ordering a light supper and asked that it be served in here."

Now he was home, the weight of his burden pressed down upon him. Consequently, his voice sounded cold and detached. When she searched his face, he knew the little cogs were working away in a bid to decipher the reason for his reserved manner.

"A light supper sounds perfect although I have lost my appetite."

He wasn't hungry, either. Well, not for food at least.

"I don't suppose I will be able to eat a thing," she continued, taking a sip of sherry, "not until you have told me what it is that plagues your thoughts."

His traitorous gaze flicked to the desk, to the ticket that would take him thousands of miles away from her. He should have told her before, but he'd forced the knowledge from his mind. He should tell her now, but he didn't know where to begin.

"Helena." He paused as the demon inside urged him not to speak, to wait until he'd held her in his arms. Until he'd sated this all-consuming need. "Words cannot express how grateful I am to you for your help with Frobisher."

"You do not have to keep thanking me, Lucas." She placed her glass on the side table and sat forward. "But that is not what you wish to say to me."

"Am I so transparent?" He wished she had some magical faerie ability to see into his soul, to understand his motives and his feelings for it would save him the pain of saying the words aloud. He pushed his hand through his hair and sighed. "Helena, I have to go back to Boston. I have matters of business to attend to that have been neglected. I only ever intended to stay for a month and well—"

"You're going back to Boston?" He saw his own pain reflected in her eyes, and she swallowed visibly. "When will you go?"

The muscles in his stomach twisted into knots. "I'm to sail on the tenth."

Her bottom lip trembled, and she took a deep breath. "In … in five days, then?"

"No, in three. I must leave myself enough time to travel to Liverpool."

"Oh, I see." She looked down into her lap and began fiddling with her fingers. "How long will you be gone?"

"It's difficult to say. I hadn't planned on returning, but things are different now."

Should he say he would be back as soon as he was able? Should he offer some explanation, some reassurance that his affections were genuine or would she feel obliged to wait for him? If only he could trust the truth of her words, but it would break him to discover that what she thought was love, was nothing more than infatuation and desire.

Before he could speak, she stood abruptly. "I'm sorry, Lucas. I … I should go," she said, her gaze fixed on the floor and he could hear her voice quiver. "You're right, it's late, and I'm a little tired after the incident with Frobisher."

In the time it took to draw breath, she was at the door, her hand gripping the handle.

"Helena, wait." He rushed over to her, pressing his body against her back to prevent her from turning or opening the door. "Don't go, don't leave me," he muttered into her hair.

"I am not the one leaving."

He heard pain, fear, and resentment in her voice: a heady concoction that stabbed at his guilt-ridden heart. What was he supposed to say, that he was doing it for her? That he didn't believe she loved him? That he was convinced her desire for him would wane in his absence?

He turned her round to face him. "I don't want to be thousands of miles away from you, but there are things I must attend to, things that need to be clarified." A stray tear ran down her cheek, and he'd spill blood to stop another from falling. "While I'm away, you should think about what you want. If you don't want me to return, then you must write to me."

She looked up at him as though he'd spoken in a foreign tongue and his words made no sense. "I love you," she cried as she flung her arms round his neck.

~

He was leaving.

It was as though he'd fired a blunderbuss at her chest, the lead ball tearing through her heart, ripping it to pieces. "I love you," she repeated, and as her lips found his, he returned her kiss with the same burning intensity. He pinned her against the door, his frantic hands caressing her body as he delved deeper into her mouth.

"Don't leave," he whispered, his words wafting like a breeze against her neck as he rained kisses along her jaw, before ravaging her mouth once again.

The loud rap at the door woke them from their passionate union and Lucas tore his lips away from hers. "What do you want?" he barked.

"To serve supper, sir," Gregson replied.

They stepped back and straightened their clothing. Helena wandered over to the window, touched the walnut bookcase to steady her balance, as her legs were shaking and she could barely rouse a coherent thought.

Lucas yanked open the door. "You may leave it over there," he said, thrusting out his arm in the direction of his desk.

Gregson nodded, and when he moved closer, Helena whispered, "I'm sorry, Gregson. He is not himself this evening."

She didn't feel like herself, either, and the thought made her wonder if she was ridiculously naive and if she really knew Lucas' true character at all. Did he mean it when he said he didn't want to be so far away from her? Or was he using the opportunity to distance himself? Her thoughts flashed back to the first time she told him she was in love with him. Remembering the look of disbelief on his face, she recalled his comment that desire was a powerful emotion, that he trusted no one.

Why wouldn't he believe she loved him?

Did it all come back to fear and doubt in the end?

Helena watched Gregson push aside some papers to make room for the tray: a platter of cold meats, cheeses and fruit. Her eyes followed the trail of paper until she spotted the ticket. It wasn't difficult to read the words Boston and Liverpool or that he had booked passage on the *Sachem* with Holland & Co.

Seeing the words written in ink banished any thoughts of a misunderstanding. In five days' time, he would be sailing away —leaving her alone with nothing but a gaping hole that would never be filled.

"Thank you, Gregson," she mumbled, her gaze drifting beyond the platter as an idea popped into her head, her mind now occupied with assessing its merit.

The butler gave a respectful bow and without comment vacated the room.

Helena dragged her thoughts away from her proposed plan. She looked up at Lucas, at the deep furrows across his brow, at his pursed lips and rigid stance and she forgot all about her own fears and insecurities.

She was going to have to take control of this situation, and so she strolled over to him, placed her hand on his cheek and watched him close his eyes as he covered it with his own.

"Before I leave this room," she began, knowing her words would induce him to open his eyes and focus his attention. "I want you to know that love is not some silly game to me. I want you to know that I am not so overcome with desire that I do not know my own mind. You, more than anyone, should know I value honesty above all things, and so I want you to listen carefully to what I am about to say."

Lucas swallowed deeply and then nodded.

"I'm in love with you, Lucas, and a lifetime apart would not change that." She wanted to say he was breaking her heart. For her, there would never be another, and so she would live the rest of her life alone if she couldn't be with him. "Now," she said with a sigh, "I think it's time to go."

As she struggled to pull her hand away, she could sense his torment, but took the necessary steps towards the door.

"Helena, please wait," he said, not bothering to hide his desperation. "Can you not just stay for supper?"

Helena glanced back over her shoulder. "Well, I was hoping you were going to carry the tray and follow me upstairs. Your bedchamber is the second door on the left?" she asked as she sauntered from the room.

CHAPTER 24

Lucas stood at the bottom of the stairs with the silver tray in hand, his gaze fixated on the gentle sway of Helena's hips as she neared the top. The anticipation of their coupling was like nothing he had ever felt before. Hot blood raced through his veins like a bittersweet madness, a delicious delirium that only she had the power to cure.

He took the stairs two at a time, and practically threw the rattling tray onto the console table, before grabbing the candlestick.

It was dark in his chamber, so he set about lighting every candle and sconce until the room was alight with a golden glow. During the long voyage back to Boston he would remember this moment. He would conjure up the image of Helena's face glistening with pure pleasure so that it filled his waking hours and revisited him in his dreams, too.

"Is it not a little bright in here?" she asked, and he could hear the nervous hitch in her voice.

Lucas walked over to her, took hold of her chin and stared into her eyes. "It's perfect." He pulled the pins from her hair and discarded them on the floor. Her earthy locks tumbled down around her shoulders, and he felt the deep physical ache that accompanied his desire. "You're perfect," he continued as he cupped her face and kissed her gently on the mouth.

"It will be easier if you help me with this," she whispered, glancing down at her dress. "Perhaps we will finally be able to put those nimble fingers to the test."

Lucas raised an arrogant brow. "I believe you will be so impressed that you'll want to hire me as your lady's maid." He turned her around and undid the row of pearl buttons before turning her back to face him. As he bunched her dress up to her waist, she raised her arms in the air so he could lift it over her head.

"You would soon tire of doing this twice a day," she said, placing her dress neatly over the back of a chair.

"Oh, I would never tire of bedding you, my love."

Knowing he had deliberately misconstrued her meaning she gave him a playful grin. "Did I say twice? Well, on certain occasions it can be as many as four times."

"In one day?" Lucas said, feigning surprise. If his throbbing manhood was any indication, he was confident he could rise to the challenge. "You're making the job sound more appealing by the minute."

She came back to stand in front of him, her expression a little more solemn. "You do know that if I were to hire you, you'd have to stay."

It crossed his mind to drop to his knees and beg for the position. To say to hell with his business in Boston, to settle in Shropshire and accept the allowance his father had provided for him. Then his thoughts were drawn back to the men who worked for him, to their families and to those who'd believed in him and who he owed a great debt. With a sigh of regret, he drew Helena closer and cupped her cheek once more. "Or perhaps you will weave that faerie magic of yours, and I shall wake to find you curled up next to me in my cabin."

Helena wrinkled her nose and gave him a quizzical look. "My faerie magic?"

"Did I say that out loud?" When she nodded, he added, "Well, you have bewitched me, Helena. And all the best dreams are magical."

They stared at each other for the longest time. The same undeniable attraction charged the air between them and he could feel a torrent of emotion bursting forth as his mind, body, heart and soul cried out to join with her.

Helena made the first move; her hand moved up over his shoulder to draw him closer and he needed no further inducement.

He tried to kiss her softly and slowly, tried to prolong the sensation, but his mind and body were possessed by a raging frenzy that threatened to consume him, lest he gave way to it. The feeling was contagious as she was just as determined to plunder his mouth while her fingers fumbled with the buttons of his waistcoat. It wasn't long before she was tugging frantically at his shirt. When they were both naked, they stopped to catch their breath, and he took the opportunity to let his gaze travel over her luscious form.

"You're so beautiful, Helena," he whispered, and her face flushed at the compliment. "If only there—"

She put her finger to his lips. "Let's not talk, Lucas. Let's just think about the here and now and not worry about the future. Let me show you the depth of my affection. Let me reveal to you what is real, what is honest and true."

He would do that, too, he thought. He would show her what was in his heart, all he struggled to express with words. With that thought, he gathered her up in his arms and carried her to his bed.

As she looked up at him from the depths of the mattress, she appeared every bit the frolicking wood nymph. With her hair cascading over his pillow and her eyes filled with mischievous delight, the image drew him back to their first meeting in the garden. If he'd remained in Boston, they would never have met. If he'd not stormed out of the ballroom looking for sanctuary, he would never have bumped into her. It felt painful to give such thoughts merit.

But he *had* found his sanctuary that night. In the shape of a dainty woodland creature with a heart of Goliath proportion.

"You are my salvation, Helena," he heard himself say as he followed her down, his voice revealing the strain it took to maintain control.

Against the demands of his jutting arousal, he rolled onto his side, draped his leg over hers and began a slow rhythmical assault on her senses. He rained featherlight kisses along her jaw and down her neck until a delicious hum resonated from the depths of her throat.

He brushed his lips against hers, gently coaxing them apart as he trailed the tips of his fingers down her neck, down the valley between her breasts, circling her navel. His touch roused a pleasurable moan as her body responded. As his hand edged down between her thighs, she arched up to meet him while his tongue simultaneously traced the line of her lips. When the tip of her tongue met his, his heart slammed against his chest, his manhood jerking against her leg in response. The low growl emanating from the back of his throat seemed to spur her on. She delved deeper into his mouth, her hand wandering over his shoulder, down across his hips to curl around his hard length.

"Helena," he panted, breaking contact as his head fell back. He tried to focus, tried to maintain the rhythm as he stroked her back and forth, knowing that her climax was near. Indeed, her breath soon grew ragged as she bucked against him.

"Lucas," she pleaded, her voice a breathless whisper. "I need you."

The words sounded like the song of an angel, and he rose above her nudging her legs wider apart. "Tell me you want me," he heard himself say.

Helena wrapped her legs around him and gripped tightly. "I want you, Lucas. It will always be you."

That first slow stroke felt heavenly as her warm body

welcomed him, drew him deeper and he closed his eyes and relished the feel of her, locked it away in his memory never to be erased. With each subsequent movement his overwhelming need to sate his soul, his desperation to ease this delicious torment, drove him harder. Despite his silent plea for restraint, his thrusts became more wild and erratic. Helena clung to him so that they moved together with each undulation.

When his release came, it was spectacular. Ripples of pure pleasure shot through his body rebounding back to his heart until it swelled, ready to burst.

He should have moved to lie at her side; he should have given her a chance to catch her breath. But blissful waves still coursed through him and the only thought that presented itself was a need to be buried deep inside her for all eternity.

"Forgive me," he panted. "I could wait no longer."

"Are you all right?" she whispered as her fingers trailed down his back, and as he focused his gaze on her bright eyes and swollen lips, he couldn't resist one final stroke.

The wave of ecstasy experienced from that small movement was evident on her face, and she sucked in a breath as she welcomed him. Once more, maybe twice and he knew they would be at the mercy of this mad passion.

He bent down and kissed her gently. "I wish there were no restrictions. I wish we could lie here until morning and everyone be damned. I hope morning never comes."

"It would be lovely," she replied, "and I don't want to break the spell, but if you don't move soon I'll be as flat as a farthing."

It took him a moment to comprehend her meaning, and then he eased himself away to lie at her side. "I'm sorry. There are other positions to experience, ones you may find more comfortable," he said, trying to dismiss the image of her sitting astride him.

"You tell me that now," she said, with a mischievous grin as she turned on her side to face him. "Though I do like it when …"

she blushed and looked down at the coverlet. "I mean, I feel safe and protected when you're above me."

He knew she would enjoy other positions, too. He wanted to say he would show her every single one of them, once they were married, but he didn't want her to feel obligated to wait for his return. Besides, the crossing could be treacherous. What if he was struck down with some debilitating illness while on board? No doubt, she would feel duty-bound to care for him, and he could not live with that.

"If only we had more time," he said, his tone a little melancholic as he gathered her to his chest. "I think you would enjoy having me at your mercy."

She did not reply, and he wondered if her mind was occupied with thoughts of him leaving.

"I know you will not like what I'm going to say," she said, twirling her fingers in the dusting of dark hair on his chest.

"When did that ever stop you," he chuckled.

She pulled one of the hairs and laughed at his pained response.

"Whatever happens, Lucas, I want to thank you. It probably sounds terribly crass, but I want to thank you … well, for this." She waved her hands back and forth between them. "For such a wonderful experience, for your companionship, your friendship, for making me feel needed and desirable and for—"

She stopped abruptly, and he was overcome with the sudden urge to shower her with compliments, to lavish her with gifts, to spend the rest of his life giving her anything her heart desired.

"That is the nicest thing anyone has ever said to me," he replied honestly as he brushed a strand of hair from her face. But then he wanted to kick himself for not saying he had every intention of returning, that if he had his way, there would be no end to this beautiful thing that had grown between them.

"I will miss you," she said, swallowing visibly.

"And I you."

A heavy silence settled upon them, and after a time, Helena asked, "Are you hungry? Shall I bring in the tray?"

Perhaps it was her way of offering a distraction, a way to lighten the solemn mood. But as his gaze lingered on her mouth, he knew there was only one way to ease his torment. "I'm only hungry for dessert," he said as his mouth claimed hers.

CHAPTER 25

Helena woke to the news that the statements from Lord Banbury and Viscount Harwood were more than adequate to proceed with a prosecution against Frobisher. And as such, she would be spared the embarrassment of her involvement being made public.

Not that it mattered. She would gladly do it all again if it meant clearing Lucas' name and restoring his reputation. Still, the expectation of a house call had forced her to rise early. With her mind and body plagued by a heavy sadness, she had not slept well at all.

Tapping on the door to her father's study, Helena straightened, took a deep breath and waited. The curt reply to enter did not deter her, and she stepped into the room before closing the door firmly behind her.

"Helena," Mr. Ecclestone said with some surprise as he glanced up from his ledger. He removed his spectacles as his gaze searched her face. "Forgive my abruptness, but I thought Amelia had returned to berate me over her clothing allowance. Do you know how much that girl has spent on gloves in the last three months? It is enough to finance a whole army."

Helena smiled at his frustrated expression. She also felt a little sorry for him. With a kind heart and warm nature, he deserved more respect than he was duly given. "You'll be pleased to hear I am more than happy with my allowance, but there is a matter of some import I would discuss with you."

He gestured to the empty chair. "I assume it relates to Mr. Dempsey's impending departure?"

Helena felt an ice-cold chill run through her body at the mere thought of it. "You know about Mr. Dempsey's trip to Boston?"

"Of course," he replied, somewhat surprised by the question. "One does not leave their betrothed to travel miles across the ocean without offering some justification. I received his letter yesterday morning and have already sent my reply."

While Helena knew a betrothal was a legally binding agreement, it hadn't occurred to her Lucas would need to explain his movements. She supposed some people would see such a timely departure as abandonment; some would see it as an excuse to escape marriage. Such gossip would tarnish both of their reputations.

"I don't mean to sound impertinent," she said, "but I need to know what Mr. Dempsey said. Does he mention the reason behind his trip?"

The lines on her father's forehead became deep furrows as he drew his brows together. "You mean he has not discussed this with you?"

"No … well, yes he has, but I'm not sure I understand his motives." Helena could feel her composure slipping, and her heart began to ache at the thought of such a lengthy separation.

"Helena, you know I cannot disclose the contents of a private letter. But suffice to say, there is nothing untoward about his need to consolidate his investments, not if he is to move back home to England."

Her heart jumped up into her throat. "He's told you that he's moving to back England?"

"Well, he has intimated it but has made no mention of you relocating to Boston. Helena, you're starting to worry me. You do want to marry Mr. Dempsey?"

"Of course," she said honestly, acknowledging the truth aloud for the first time.

"And it is quite obvious to everyone that the gentleman is besotted with you, so I do not see a problem here."

Was Lucas besotted with her? Could he ever love her the way she loved him?

"I am pleased that you think so, as I would like your permission to go with him."

Her father shook his head and sighed. "But have I not just told you he is moving back to England. There is no need for you to relocate to Boston. Honestly, Helena, you're starting to sound like Amelia."

Helena swallowed deeply. "I mean, I would like to go with him before we are wed. I would like you to book me passage on the *Sachem*, departing from Liverpool on the tenth."

Mr. Ecclestone flew to his feet. "Have you gone mad, girl? Have your wits all but up and left? How can you ask such a thing, for you must surely know my answer?"

"We could marry on the ship or … or in Boston," Helena replied, knowing that it sounded ludicrous, pathetic, knowing she might follow him only to find he didn't want her. But she was drowning, sinking into the depths of despair and clutching desperately at anything to keep her afloat.

"Marry on a ship? Do you want to put your mother in Bedlam?"

"I know it sounds ridiculous and a trifle improper—"

"A trifle? Only a trifle?" He flopped back down into the chair and pressed his fingers to his temple as though alleviating some imagined pain. "You must love him a great deal, and I can see that it pains you," he said a little more calmly. He sat forward, his arms resting on his desk as he studied her. "Love can blind us, Helena. It can make the wisest man behave like a blithering idiot, so you must listen carefully to what I am about to say to you."

Helena simply nodded as the hard lump in the back of her throat prevented any comment.

"While you are prepared to make such a sacrifice, and believe me, it would be so as you would be ruined in the eyes of Society, the sacrifice is not yours alone. The scandal would destroy your sister's reputation. Your children would bear the scar, a scar as damning as the Devil's mark. The repercussions of your actions would last for generations. Do you understand what I am saying to you?"

Helena sighed. "Yes. I understand."

In truth, she didn't give a damn about her reputation. She'd donned a wig and visited the home of an unmarried gentleman. She'd experienced a level of intimacy reserved only for married women. She'd climbed into Lady Banbury's bed and used her wits to lure a murderer. There was a difference now, though. Her actions would affect the lives of many, and she could not live with that on her conscience.

"I understand," she repeated, "but to think of him being so far away. To think I may never see him again, that he could be lost to me forever."

Her father's eyes softened. "My dear daughter, it warms my soul to know you have found someone who makes your heart sing so beautiful a song. We are not all so fortunate. Do not cheapen so precious a gift. Lord Banbury has sent word that he wishes to pay his respects to you both at a ball tomorrow evening. Treasure the time you have together, and I am sure it will not be long before your Mr. Dempsey sets foot on English soil again."

Helena stood, choked back the tears and offered her father a weak smile. "As always, I thank you for such wise counsel."

"How easy life would be if everyone else shared your sentiment," he said, his mood melancholic as he stared beyond her shoulder. But then with a sharp shake of the head and a succession of rapid blinks, he refocused. "Now barricade the door on your way out, there's a good girl. And tell your mother I'm revising the clothing allowance and will need at least three hours' peace to complete the task."

CHAPTER 26

It had been years since Lord Banbury had hosted a ball. He'd not even had the inclination to hold a dinner party or soiree, which was probably the reason why the queue of carriages trailed all the way around Berkeley Square. Indeed, Helena witnessed more than a few gaping expressions as guests surveyed the exterior, eager to see what marvels were hidden inside.

"At last," their mother said with a sigh as she stepped down to the pavement to join them. "I have been sitting in the same position for so long that if you stuck a pin in my leg I doubt I would feel it. I'm afraid you can forget all about me dancing this evening."

"But you never dance," Amelia said, sounding somewhat bemused.

"That is not the point. Banbury is an intelligent man and should have anticipated such a crowd. You cannot mention that you have a room named after a sultan and not expect a crush."

Amelia wrinkled her nose. "I do not see what's so special about that. From what I hear it has nothing to do with a sultan and is just some silly old curtains."

Their mother gasped. "I would not call Persian silk silly,

Amelia. Lady Crawford said it's a marvel and Lord Banbury has spared no expense. She said the walls are covered in reams of rich, red fabric that make you feel as though you have been spirited away to the desert, to one of those exotic bedouin tents."

"You mean, Bedouin," Helena corrected. She glanced up at her mother's garishly pink turban and could see her happily holding court in such a place. "Let us hope Lord Banbury has not invited a real sultan, for I hear they trade their wives for cows."

Her father suppressed a chuckle. "I think I would settle for an empty water skin and a camel's toe," he whispered as he followed them inside.

As Helena pushed her way through the bustling throng, it became apparent that her mother was right. The atmosphere in the house buzzed with excitement as guests scurried about between the downstairs rooms, frantically searching for the mysteries of the Orient. Lacking experience in such matters, Lord Banbury had opened all the doors to allow the air to circulate. To a consummate gossip an open door was an explicit invitation to snoop, and the *ton* could boast of having many a gossip in its numbers.

Any ideas Helena had of escaping to the terrace were hampered, as Lord Banbury insisted on introducing her to numerous guests.

"I shall forever be in Miss Ecclestone's debt," Lord Banbury said to the group gathered around him. "It was her actions that first led me to question Mr. Dempsey's role in my brother's death."

Helena's heart skipped a beat. Lord Banbury had promised Lucas he would not mention her involvement in the capture of Frobisher. Even so, she would like to hear Banbury explain why a lady would jump into someone else's bed while three gentlemen watched from behind a curtain.

"She is an impeccable judge of character," Banbury continued, "and was able to see quite clearly that to which the rest of us were blind."

"And it all worked out splendidly for you, Miss Ecclestone," Lady Fanshaw remarked. "In the process of promoting the merits of Mr. Dempsey's character, you knew he would make an excellent husband."

"Indeed." Helena smiled, dismissing the fear that she may never see Lucas again, let alone call him her husband. "I am extremely fortunate and count myself lucky to have been given the opportunity to know him."

Helena did not need to see Lady Fanshaw's flushed cheeks or wide eyes to know Lucas was standing behind her. The aura that radiated from him drifted over her shoulders like a warm mist, caressing her skin until it tingled in response.

"I've been looking for you." His words were but a soft whisper, causing a shiver to run all the way down to her toes and as he moved to stand at her side his fingers brushed against her back. "I believe I am the lucky one, Lady Fanshaw," he said, inclining his head to the group.

"Well, I will not disagree with that," Banbury chuckled.

"I hope you will forgive me," Lucas said, "but I must speak to my betrothed."

Like all the other members of the party, Banbury failed to suppress a grin, "Of course, of course," he said as he waved them away. "Do not stray too far. Remember you are to lead the floor in the waltz."

Lucas threaded Helena's hand through his arm and led her away. "I cringe at the thought of dancing while the crowd looks on," he said with a frustrated sigh. "I'm surprised he doesn't want me to don a hat with bells, sing songs and recite poetry."

"He did ask, but I told him metrical verse wasn't your forte."

"Oh, I understand rhythm. I just choose to apply the principles in a far more pleasurable way."

Helena's stomach did an odd little somersault. "I can testify to that," she said coyly. "You are an exceptional dancer, as I recall."

When he stopped near the terrace and turned her round to face him, her knees almost buckled. The look of longing in his eyes caused a fire in her heart that blazed through her body to warm a more intimate region.

"I would like nothing more than to put my talents to good use. After all, dancing is a prelude to seduction, Miss Ecclestone. I just wish the location was a little more private."

Each word dripped with desire and the memory of his bare skin pressed against hers caused her face to flush crimson. "I doubt there is a quiet place in the whole house," she said as she tried to quell the craving for him. "Tell me, were you not tempted to go in search of the mysterious sultan room?"

"Neither a sultan nor a king could drag me away from your bewitching beauty." His gaze moved over the silver flowers in her hair, over the diaphanous sleeves of her gown before dropping to linger on the low-cut bodice. "You look every bit a queen of the faeries, and I have a sudden urge to see your bare skin glisten in the moonlight."

She turned her head and looked out beyond the doors to the terrace. The moon was full and only obscured by the faintest shadow. "I believe you're in luck, Mr. Dempsey. If you could wait but an hour I think we may find an opportunity to tour the gardens."

At the mere mention of the garden, a feeling of sadness coursed through her as she recalled their first meeting. How fitting that their last night together should end in a similar vein.

He took her hands and brought them to his lips. "I would wait a lifetime for one more kiss, Helena. Always remember that."

They stared into each other's eyes, the spell only broken by the sound of a lady clearing her throat. Helena turned, her gaze darting to the vibrant coiffure: a fiery mass of red curls, a loose tendril or two tickling the lady's neck. With her eyes shining like lush green fields in the height of summer, the contrast was striking.

"Mr. Dempsey." The lady nodded as she turned to face Helena. "And Miss Ecclestone, I presume."

Lucas bowed and then cast Helena a mischievous grin. "Miss Ecclestone, allow me to present Miss Linwood."

Helena didn't know what to say.

In her mind, she imagined Miss Linwood to be middle-aged with streaks of white hair and spectacles. A studious type whose wrinkled skin was a consequence of being out in the midday sun. As in Egypt, it was said to be blisteringly hot. She had also heard reports that Miss Linwood was, in fact, a gentleman. What lady could have such vast experience in matters of the Orient? Helena's eyes fell to the generous bosom strapped tightly into an emerald-green gown. No, Miss Linwood was definitely not a gentleman.

"It's a pleasure to meet you, Miss Linwood."

"The pleasure is mine," she replied gracefully. "And may I take the opportunity to express how sorry I am for the terrible mishap at the museum."

"I've not had the chance to tell you," Lucas began, "but I met with Miss Linwood yesterday, at the museum. She believes the place is cursed, that our accident was in some way connected."

Helena's eyes widened with delight. "A curse," she whispered.

"I knew you would be intrigued," Lucas said, showing pleasure at her response.

"Have you managed to locate Mr. Stone?" Miss Linwood asked. "The man is practically a recluse, but you seemed confident he would attend this evening."

"From what I remember, Gabriel has a tendency to lurk in the shadows," Lucas replied as Helena watched the exchange with an open mouth. "But if he is here it will be in the hope of examining the parchment."

Noticing Helena's bemused expression, Lucas said, "I went to school with Gabriel Stone. He had an unhealthy interest in Egyptian relics, even then. Miss Linwood believes he is the only person with the knowledge required to break the curse."

Miss Linwood's demure countenance suddenly changed and she grasped Lucas by his sleeve. "You must help me, Mr. Dempsey. I cannot sleep at night. I see things and hear things. Oh, you must persuade Mr. Stone to speak to me."

"Please, calm yourself, Miss Linwood." Lucas sighed and pushed his hand through his hair. "I'm sorry, Helena," he said, "but I must try and find Stone. It will not take long. I'll be back with you before the hour is upon us." He cast a devilish smile as his eyes devoured her. "Will you wait for me?"

Helena stood up on her toes and whispered in his ear. "I would wait a lifetime." Straightening and offering a reassuring smile, she added, "Now, be gone and find this Mr. Stone. Miss Linwood will keep me company and will begin by telling me all about this dreaded curse."

Lucas pushed his way through the crowd, although there were still those who doubted Banbury's account of recent events and avoided any contact with him at all, stepping out of his way when witnessing his approach. He wondered what sort of reception he should expect to receive from Gabriel Stone. After all, he had not seen the man for years.

As expected, he found Gabriel in the library, towering over a glass display case, absorbed by whatever was inside. Of course, Lucas knew what it was: it was a sixteenth-century parchment, a study by Becanus relating to the deciphering of the pictographic script of the ancient Egyptians.

"I see you still have a morbid fascination with the dead,"

Lucas said as he came to stand at Gabriel's side. The man straightened. Lucas had forgotten what a large and imposing figure he cut.

"And you're still creeping up on people." He removed his spectacles and pushed a lock of black hair from his brow. When he glanced behind, he seemed surprised to discover the room was empty. "As you're so light on your feet, perhaps you could use your talent to help me slip out with this thing. It is almost impossible to study it with all this noise and disruption, and though I have tried, I cannot persuade Banbury to part with it."

"This is a ball, Gabriel. There must be fifty ladies eager to get their hands on such a virile specimen. You should be dancing not hunched over some ancient scroll."

"You know I'm not the sort to waste my time on such frivolities."

Lucas suppressed a grin, as he was hoping Gabriel would say that. "If you would rather spend time in the company of musty old paper then perhaps I could speak to Banbury. I think I could persuade him to allow you a little more time to study it."

Gabriel narrowed his gaze. "And why would you do that?"

"Oh, I don't know." Lucas shrugged. "Perhaps because one good deed deserves another. I believe Lord Banbury would allow you to spend the day in his library, where you will have the opportunity to study it, undisturbed."

"And what would you have me do in return?"

"I would have you speak with Miss Linwood. She has tried to make contact with you on numerous occasions. Miss Linwood has a problem at her museum and believes you are the only one who can help."

Gabriel sneered. "I do not have time for fakes and frauds."

Lucas removed his pocket watch and glanced at the time. "That is a shame. Well, as much as I enjoy discussing your interest in antiquities, I have an urgent desire to stroll around the garden, and I'm afraid it cannot wait."

Lucas turned and made for the door. He estimated it would take no more than a few steps for Gabriel to change his mind.

"Dempsey," Gabriel called out as predicted. "I'll speak to this Miss Linwood, but nothing more. In return, I want two whole days with no disruptions."

Lucas smiled to himself. "Done."

CHAPTER 27

The exchange in the library was not Lucas' only unexpected encounter of the evening. As he strolled past the ladies retiring room, he heard his name mentioned and so stopped outside to listen. It appeared that his relationship with Helena was the topic of conversation, and it was not difficult to determine that the instigator was Miranda Colebrook.

"Well, I heard Viscount Harwood say Mr. Dempsey must return to Boston for reasons pertaining to his business."

"He would say that," Miranda chirped. "Mr. Dempsey would not want Society to know he has no intention of marrying a silly chit like Miss Ecclestone. He is using the trip as a means to put some distance between them and in truth is kicking himself for getting embroiled in the whole affair." Miranda snickered. "He told me so only last night."

There were numerous giggles and high-pitched titters.

"You still see him then?"

"Well, we are very close, if you take my meaning."

Lucas' blood coursed through his veins like a turbulent river, saturating every muscle until they felt heavy and engorged. He was primed, ready to attack, but this was to be a fight with

213

words, and so he took a moment to regulate his breathing before striding into the room.

"Ah, good evening, ladies," he said, thrusting his hands behind his back to stop them from pulsating. "Forgive me for entering your private sanctuary, but I found my ears burning and upon hearing your conversation thought it only polite to correct a few misconceptions."

Miranda Colebrook sat in the middle of the sofa, flanked by two young ladies. The two matronly figures sitting opposite, Lucas recalled, were Lady Brunson and a Mrs. Howes. The whole party appeared shocked to see him. Miranda Colebrook's face turned a deathly shade of white while her chin decided to take a journey southward.

"I am afraid I must correct you on two points," he continued. His calm and controlled manner did not reflect the anger boiling beneath the surface.

"Th-there's no need to say anything," Miranda stuttered.

"I insist," Lucas said forcefully as he held up his hand to silence her. "I will start by clarifying that I have not been on *friendly* terms with Lady Colebrook since meeting Miss Ecclestone. And I most certainly was not with her last night, as she claims. I'm afraid that Lady Colebrook does not understand the word *no*. Indeed, she has used various devious methods in an attempt to add credence to her claims and has even taken it upon herself to force her way into my house."

Lady Colebrook gave a nervous chuckle. "And I seem to remember you were wearing nothing but your breeches."

Lucas clenched his jaw. "You force me to be blunt, madam, and so I say why would I sup on cheap ale when there is champagne?"

Lady Brunson gasped and put her hand on her heart.

"And now to my second point. I must travel to Boston to address urgent business matters, so I may return and marry Miss Ecclestone. We plan to reside in Shropshire as soon as we are wed." He gave a half-hearted bow. "I hope that has answered any doubts you may have regarding the credibility of my betrothal."

Not bothering to wait for a reply, Lucas turned and marched towards the door, but then stopped abruptly, compelled by a need to make a declaration, a need that burned deep inside him.

"Just so we are completely clear," he said, swinging back around to face the group. "As I know how easily gossip can be twisted and distorted. I am in love with Miss Ecclestone, deeply in love, to the point that I can think of nothing other than her. She means everything to me, and I will release the Devil's wrath on anyone who so much as looks at her in the wrong way. Do I make myself clear?"

When they all stared at him with open mouths, he bellowed, "Do I make myself clear?"

"Yes ... yes."

"Completely."

"Perfectly, sir."

Miranda Colebrook said nothing, but her face turned scarlet as she drew her bottom lip into a taut, thin line.

Lucas turned his attention to the other ladies in the group. "Society tolerates gossips. It does not, however, tolerate liars. Should I hear of such slanderous remarks made against myself or Miss Ecclestone again, then I will know exactly where to come."

All the ladies made their apologies and skittered from the room.

"Don't push me, Miranda," he said through gritted teeth. "Else I shall be the one to spread malicious gossip so that no gentleman will ever touch you again."

As Lucas strode out of the room, he flexed his fingers as they were still throbbing and twitching with a need for vengeance. Bloody hell. If Miranda were a man, he would have ripped her head from her shoulders. Helena did not deserve to be the topic of tasteless conversation. She did not deserve to be viewed as inadequate, as someone unworthy of his attention. She deserved to be adored, to be loved, to be cherished and—

He came to an abrupt halt.

Every word he'd spoken in that room was the truth. He loved Helena Ecclestone deeply. In her arms, his soul was sated. With her, his life was a picture of heavenly possibilities and she damn well deserved to know it.

When he entered the ballroom, it was with a renewed sense of purpose.

"Lucas, you will never guess what just happened," Helena said, almost skipping with delight as she came to meet him. She appeared happy and carefree, and he wanted to nurture the feeling. "I was talking to Miss Linwood about the curse, and suddenly her eyes widened. When I looked over my shoulder, there was a gentleman standing in the doorway. It was most strange for he beckoned to Miss Linwood as though she were nothing more than a disobedient dog."

So, Gabriel had already fulfilled his part of the bargain.

"Perhaps you should take a breath," Lucas teased as he drank in the wondrous sight. Her eyes shone like brilliant stars, and her luscious lips reminded him of soft, ripe peaches. A warm fuzzy feeling filled his chest, and he felt his heart beat with pure joy. "I assume Miss Linwood went with him."

"Well, I told her no one should be treated in such a manner. If he wanted to talk to her, she should wait for him to approach."

"Which he did not."

Helena's brows knitted together. "How did you know?"

"The only way Gabriel Stone would set foot in a ballroom was if Anubis appeared and waved his crook. I assume it was Gabriel."

Helena glanced up and to the left as though revisiting the scene. "The man was so tall he almost filled the doorway. He seemed quite strong and powerful and not at all the studious type."

"You are making me feel somewhat inadequate," Lucas replied, feeling a small stab of jealousy.

"Oh, I could not love a man like that, he's far too handsome."

Lucas laughed and was overcome with a burning desire to banish all thoughts of Gabriel Stone from her mind. "Come then, let us take a stroll in the garden. We shall find a quiet corner so you may study my imperfections."

"You have a way of making the most common of occurrences sound positively sinful, Mr. Dempsey." Helena smiled and was about to take his arm when Lord Banbury made an announcement.

"I swear that man has the most ridiculous sense of timing," Lucas groaned.

"My lords, ladies, and gentlemen," Banbury began. "I will not bore you with a lengthy speech, suffice to say, I wish to pay my respects to Mr. Dempsey and Miss Ecclestone. To congratulate them on their upcoming nuptials and ask they lead the floor in the next dance."

The floor emptied as guests bustled around the outside and amidst the hum of activity, all heads turned in their direction. How different things were now, he thought, as he took Helena's hand and led her out onto the floor. There were no snubs or scowls, no fearful eyes or trembling lips, just a group of people who appeared pleased to watch and applaud—appeared being the operative word. It took nothing more than a juicy piece of malicious gossip to influence this fickle lot, and he would use the next few minutes to make sure there was no confusion regarding his feelings for Helena Ecclestone.

"Are you ready?" he asked as he gathered her into his arms. Holding her in such close proximity caused a bolt of desire to tear through him and his abdomen tightened in response. He allowed the feeling to consume him, to radiate from him like a bright beacon. "Remember, this dance is to be a prelude to something far more sinful."

In her eyes, he saw his own desire reflected back at him. But she did not have a chance to answer, for the music began and they were soon twirling round the floor in fast succession.

"I must say your line is faultless, Mr. Dempsey," Helena said with some amusement. "Although your beat is slightly off, as I find myself somewhat breathless."

"I should get used to it," he replied as his gaze fell to the delicious creamy flesh that called out to him from the confines of her bodice. "I intend to spend the rest of the evening eliciting the same response."

He felt a shiver ripple through her body.

"And I thought I had saved the sinner," she said, although her expression suggested that was what she loved about him.

"If what I feel for you is sin, then I don't want to be saved," he said, and as they whirled round and round again, his heart swelled until it filled his chest. "I'm in love with you. I have been in love with you from the moment you yanked the sleeve of my coat in a desperate bid to find your sister."

As she looked up at him, her eyes brimmed with tears. "Lucas, I … I don't know what to say. I mean, I hoped you would but …"

"But nothing, Helena. I love you, and if we were not spinning around the floor, I would take you and kiss you so deeply you would feel the truth of my words."

Helena's cheeks flushed. "I know you speak the truth, Lucas. I just wish you hadn't mentioned kissing me because now my head is spinning and I cannot think of anything else."

Lucas' head fell back and he laughed. "I may not be able to kiss you, but I can do this," he said as he lifted her off her feet and swung her round and round in the air.

"Lucas!"

By way of covering up such an unprecedented breach of etiquette, numerous couples took to the floor, concealing what would no doubt later be regarded as a mishap with a dancing slipper. Although when the dance ended and they joined Lord

Banbury, Lucas discovered there were those who had noticed the sentiment in such a public display.

"There is no finer thing than the folly of two people in love," Lady Fanshaw said, patting Lord Fanshaw on the arm with her fan.

"I didn't know you were a gentleman prone to such an excess of sensibility," Lord Banbury said with some amusement.

"Only where Miss Ecclestone is concerned," Lucas said with a respectful nod.

Helena blushed. "Come, let us find some refreshment. All that twirling around has left me thoroughly parched."

She took his arm and steered him through the crowd towards the terrace.

"I thought you were in need of refreshment," Lucas said, although he was more than pleased with the course of their direction.

Helena's fingers brushed over the muscle in his arm, the tips circling the sinew in such a way as to cause his manhood to stir. "I am in need of refreshment," she said in a rather inviting tone. "And I am thoroughly parched. But not for ratafia."

As they made their way down the stone steps, Lucas wondered what he'd done to deserve such a precious prize. Helena Ecclestone made him feel complete. He did not know how he was going to survive the next few months without her.

They wandered down the gravel path, past a row of trimmed topiary and continued around the perimeter. They talked about the events surrounding Lord Banbury's death and about the relief Lucas felt at finding the real culprit.

"I think it is fair to say your father may not have known how much he hurt you when he sent you away," Helena said.

Lucas sighed. "I've spent the last four years refusing to acknowledge him, but now I can take comfort in the fact that Frobisher manipulated him." He drew her behind another row of tall topiary and turned her round to face him. "I could not have done it without you, Helena," he said as he bent down and kissed her softly on the lips. "I should have professed my love before. I should not have left it so long."

Helena shook her head. "It doesn't matter now."

"I want you to know, for me, this was never a feigned betrothal. I wanted you from the moment I saw you, and I will want you until I draw my last breath."

Helena threw her arms around his neck and pressed her body against his. "Do not talk about drawing your last breath, Lucas, not when you must travel miles across the ocean."

A sob burst from her lips.

Lucas held her face in his hands and used his thumb to wipe away a tear. "I am so in love with you it's killing me. But I have to go to Boston. I have—"

He lost all train of thought, then, as Helena kissed him. It was a wild, desperate plea to numb the pain and he welcomed the feel of her hot mouth as it plundered his. A fire ignited in his chest and spread quickly through his body until he could think of nothing other than burying himself deep inside her.

He would not take her here, not in Banbury's garden.

"I love you, Lucas," Helena panted, and his body groaned with need.

"And know that I love you," he said as his hand drifted up her bare thigh to explore a more intimate place. He would help her to forget her sadness. He would help her to remember him.

CHAPTER 28

Helena scrambled around the wreckage, determined to follow the length of the shoreline. The wind howled around her, biting at her face and blowing strands of damp hair to hinder her vision. She struggled to move on the wet sand, for her shoes were sodden and sank into the saturated grains as though it was thick, oozing mud.

But she would not give up.

She would never give up.

"Lucas. Lucas."

Helena called out to him, but only the waves answered her. The sibilant whispers suggesting they were party to a secret and the knowledge wasn't fit for the ears of a mere mortal.

"Lucas, where are you?"

She saw it then, floating towards her, only to be dragged back by the greedy waves. It came again, closer this time and she charged into the water to retrieve it. The salty solution splashed her lips as her hand curled around the wooden figure.

As she studied the carving, she noticed it was the head of a dragon, the body nothing but chipped jagged edges. The waves came again, crashing against her in their anger and she lost her footing, the figure flying from her hand only to be pulled under down to the bottom of the murky depths.

"No!" she cried.

"Miss Ecclestone. Miss Ecclestone, please, you must wake up."

Helena squinted under heavy lids and gasped at the sight of the dark figure looming over the bed.

"Lucas, is it you?" she whispered.

"No, it's me, it's Emmy," the maid said holding the candle up to her face. "You've been dreaming."

It took a moment for the words to penetrate her addled brain and as her eyes grew accustomed to her surroundings, she gave a sigh of relief. "Emmy. Oh, you don't know how happy I am to see you."

"I'm sorry, miss, but I had to wake you."

Helena placed her hand on Emmy's arm. "It was Lucas. I thought … I thought he was lost." She shook her head and remembered to breathe. "It doesn't matter now. What time is it?"

The maid bent down. "It's almost one. One in the morning."

"But I've been asleep most of the day!"

Helena lifted herself up on her elbows and then flopped back down. Her arms felt shaky and weak as though the muscles had wasted away in her sleep, leaving nothing but skin and bone. It was hard to believe she'd slept for so long. Yet the thought of passing the days in blissful ignorance seemed so appealing.

"Do you think the apothecary sells a remedy to help one sleep, to sleep for a few months I mean?" It was a serious question, as Helena could not bear the pain of such a lengthy separation.

Only one day had passed since Lucas Dempsey declared his love for her. The words had caused her head to feel light and fluffy, a feeling that coursed through her body leaving a trail of joyous rapture in its wake. Now, hours after his departure, the declaration was marred by a deep sadness, which only served to highlight that the precious gift was so far from her grasp. She'd never experienced grief and in her ignorance wondered if such intense sorrow, such feelings of utter uselessness and despair were in any way similar. It seemed impossible to perform even the simplest of tasks when her heart ached and when Lucas occupied every thought.

"Sleep for months?" Emmy said. "Only way to do that is to dose yourself up on laudanum." She placed the candle on the dressing table and picked up a tray. "Besides, I bet sleep is the last thing you'll be thinking about."

Emmy placed the tray on the bed.

"It is far too late to eat, Emmy," Helena said, glancing down at the plate of sandwiches and the piece of fruitcake. "And I seem to have lost my appetite."

"I did call you for dinner, but you were fast asleep, and the master said just to leave you where you be. You should try to eat something, miss, as you'll be on the road for hours before you get a chance to stop."

Emmy gave a mischievous little grin and then set about removing various items of clothing from the armoire.

Helena shook her head and rubbed her eyes. "Emmy, am I still dreaming, or are you saying and doing the oddest things?"

"The answer's neither, miss."

The faint clopping of horses hooves echoed up from the street below, which in itself was nothing out of the ordinary, but Emmy rushed over to the window and peeked out from between the closed curtains.

"You'll have to eat while you dress, miss, as Viscount Harwood is here," Emmy said, flapping her hands about as though that would speed up the process.

No one made a house call at one in the morning, not unless something disastrous had happened. Curiosity brought with it a renewed burst of energy and Helena scrambled from the bed to inspect the scene for herself. Emmy was right. Viscount Harwood's carriage had stopped directly outside the house.

A frisson of fear shot through her.

"Has something happened to Mr. Dempsey?" The words came out like a garbled cry.

"Shh," Emmy said, putting her finger to her lips as she came closer. "You'll wake the whole house." She took Helena's hands in hers and gave a little squeeze. "Nothing has happened to Mr. Dempsey. Your father's purchased tickets for the *Sachem*. You're to travel to Boston. Oh, it's going to be wonderful, miss."

Helena's heart was beating so fiercely she could feel the pounding in her throat. "I ... I am going to Boston?" she repeated slowly.

Emmy twirled away, patting her hands together in silent applause as she struggled to contain her excitement. "Yes, yes. Your trunk is all packed and ready. Although I had a right old job hiding it from your mother, and Amelia wanted to borrow your green Spencer, and you know how she ..."

Emmy's words faded into the distance as Helena's mind wandered back and forth like a lost child, flitting to and fro, but not really knowing which train of thought to follow. What had happened to change her father's mind? Was Lucas aware that she was to join him on board the *Sachem*? Why was she leaving in the dead of night?

"Now quick, you must hurry and please be quiet, miss."

Helena grinned. "Emmy, you are the only one talking," she said as she pulled her nightdress up over her head.

It took no more than five minutes to get dressed, and they exited the room as though on a military exercise, their primary mission being to evade the enemy. It didn't help that Emmy banged into the console table, causing the porcelain vase to rock on its base and Helena was somewhat relieved when they finally tiptoed down the stairs.

As they reached the bottom, Emmy pulled Helena into an embrace. "Good luck, miss. Have a safe journey and mind what you eat on board. The fish will be safe enough, but don't eat the beef."

Helena narrowed her gaze. "But you said tickets, Emmy. I

assumed you were coming with me."

A figure appeared in the doorway. "No, I am the one coming with you, Helena." Her father's voice held a hint of amusement. He stepped out from the shadows into the hall and Helena rushed over to him.

"But how ... why ... what did Mother say?"

Mr. Ecclestone nodded to Emmy, who curtsied then skipped off in the direction of the servants' quarters. "I have not told your mother or Amelia of our plans. They would do everything in their power to stop us, Helena. I am sad to say that they serve no one but themselves."

Helena wanted to throw her arms around him and hug him until his face turned blue. With her father acting as a chaperone, she need not fear for her reputation. "But it's so far away. I cannot ask you to make such a sacrifice, I ..."

He cupped her cheek and offered a smile that spoke of love and pride. "It is not a sacrifice, Helena. I could not bear to watch you wither away in Mr. Dempsey's absence and I long to see your face glow with joy and happiness, as it did at Lord Banbury's ball." He gave a little chuckle. "Besides, I have always wanted to travel, and it would not be wise to be within a hundred miles of your mother when she learns I have reduced the clothing allowance by a third." He raised a brow and then added, "Well, how else was I to pay for our trip to Boston."

There was a gentle rap at the front door.

"That will be Anthony, come to take us on our grand adventure."

"Anthony?" Helena asked.

"Viscount Harwood despises formality amongst friends," he said as he ushered her out of the door.

"So you're friends, now?"

"No, Helena. Soon we will be family."

At that moment, Helena felt like the luckiest person alive; to be loved by two such wonderful gentlemen was more than any lady could ask.

CHAPTER 29

"If it was me, I'd have the beef stew."

The tavern wench gave Lucas a coy smile as she bent down to reveal generous mounds of pasty-white flesh. If she offered him dumplings, he would not be able to hide his amusement. "It's been cooked fresh this morning," she whispered, inhaling his scent like a crossing sweeper sniffing a sprig of lavender after a day spent scooping *shite*.

"Very well, I'll have the stew."

"And if that don't satisfy ya, I know something else that might."

"I'll be sure to let you know," Lucas said in a neutral tone. It was best not to insult the person who brought your food.

With an exaggerated sway of the hips, the wench sauntered off in the direction of the kitchen and Lucas was left alone with his thoughts.

Of course, there was only one thought on his mind.

Three days had passed since he last saw Helena; each one was like a notch carved into his soul as a permanent reminder of his pain. He wondered how he would feel when the number reached eighty or ninety. Would the passage of time lessen the blow or would it always feel as painful as that first deep cut?

It was all rather ironic.

When he first arrived in Boston, he could think of nothing other than his home in England. When he came back, over a month ago, all he could think of was his home in Boston. Now, his home was with Helena, wherever that may be.

"Here you go. Hot and tasty, bet that's just how ya like it."

The wench was right. The food was hot, edible and brought a modicum of comfort and so he made sure he gave a generous tip.

Upon leaving the tavern, he wandered over to the office of Holland & Co. where, after squeezing past thirty or so other passengers, he presented his ticket. Thankfully, there were no delays as both cargo and mail had arrived on time. Having booked one of the ten exclusive cabins he was directed on board before all the poor souls booked in steerage.

The cabins opened out into a private saloon, a place where the captain would dine with all his prestigious passengers, a place where they could mingle and enjoy the conversation.

"Yours is the one at the end there, sir, on the right."

Lucas spent the next few hours drifting in and out of sleep, images of Helena filling his dreams. He woke to the sound of voices, the clattering of plates and the sweet smell of mutton and pearl barley. He took a moment to make himself more presentable but having no appetite for dinner decided against leaving his cabin.

Some fifteen minutes later, there was a light rap on the door; even the gentlest of knocks making it shake on its hinges.

"Dinner is served, sir," said a boy who didn't look a day over twelve, his high-pitched tone confirming the assessment.

Lucas breathed a sigh. He did not want to be in company this evening. With his mind so distracted, he would struggle to follow the line of conversation and could not partake in idle chatter, not when his heart was engaged in more serious matters. But three weeks was a long time at sea, and he would soon tire of his own company.

"Good evening, Captain Hart," Lucas said as he joined the

other passengers at the table, suppressing his frustration at having to pass pleasantries.

The captain, a broad-shouldered man with curly red hair and long side-whiskers, set about making the introductions to the other passengers seated around the table. Lucas was pleased to discover that both the ladies on board were of middling years and married. Even so, he was quick to note that the two spaces opposite were empty.

As he took his seat, Mr. Grimshaw, a gentleman to his right, commented on the general purpose of his trip. "I'm not sure how long I'll be staying in Boston. I have matters of business to attend to," Lucas replied. It sounded better than saying he was running away to give his betrothed a chance to change her mind. Although, in truth, he had come to accept that Helena's feelings were genuine, and he did having pressing business in Boston.

Mr. Grimshaw nodded. "I'm a milliner, and my wife is a modiste. We had premises on Bond Street, but my sister moved out over a year ago, and we were keen to follow. I hear French lace fetches a pretty price across the water."

"Perhaps we may have an opportunity to talk more on the subject," Lucas said in an attempt to be civil. "I have a textile company and may be able to offer advice if you plan to acquire new premises."

Mr. Grimshaw replied, but Lucas' attention was drawn to the cabin boy who knocked on one of the other doors and said, "Dinner is served, miss."

He groaned inwardly, as he'd spent the best part of the journey to England avoiding matchmaking mothers and their eager daughters.

"Forgive me, Mr. Grimshaw," Lucas said, turning to give the man his full attention. "You were talking about your shipment of silk."

The captain cleared his throat. "This is Mr. Ecclestone and his daughter."

Lucas shook his head. His thoughts had begun to take on a voice of their own.

"Mrs. Brocklehurst will introduce you to everyone," Captain Hart added.

Lucas heard her voice then, her warm, husky tone penetrating the coldness, caressing him and stimulating his senses. His head shot round, and he drank in the glorious sight.

"Thank you, Captain Hart," she said with a beaming smile, "although we are already acquainted with Mr. Dempsey."

It took every ounce of strength Helena had not to scramble over the crude table and jump into Lucas' lap. She imagined the cries of protest, soup bowls flying in the air, numerous cups of wine being caught in desperate hands, but in her vision she didn't care. She wanted to kiss him, run her fingers through his hair and tear at his clothes like a wildcat, all in the hope of alleviating the pain his short absence had caused.

The look in Lucas' eyes, accompanied by his short ragged breaths, suggested he was thinking a similar thing.

"Mr. Ecclestone," Lucas gave a respectful nod. "I trust you're well." His gaze drifted to Helena's face, which he proceeded to give a slow perusal. The beginnings of a devilish grin formed at the corners of his mouth. "Miss Ecclestone, what a pleasure it is to see you again."

"The pleasure is mine, Mr. Dempsey," she replied as she took her seat, aware that the other people around the table were following the conversation with marked interest.

"It is always preferable to be in the company of friends when faced with such an arduous journey," Mrs. Brocklehurst said during the soup course. "I remember my first trip back in ninety-eight. What a treacherous voyage. To this day, I have never seen a storm like it. The clouds were as black as coal and the thunderous—"

"Let's not talk about storms and treacherous voyages," Captain Hart interjected.

They ate in silence for a few minutes, while everyone contemplated the terrifying prospect of the ship being caught in a storm. Sensing a feeling of unrest, the captain struck up a conversation with a portly gentleman to his right and others soon followed his lead.

"Do you have family in Boston, Miss Ecclestone?" Mr. Grimshaw asked.

Lucas put down his cutlery and waited for her answer.

"No, we do not. But my father has longed to travel, and one must make sacrifices for those we love." She glanced across at Lucas. "What of you, Mr. Dempsey, are you pleased to be returning to Boston?"

Lucas smiled. "In all honesty, Miss Ecclestone, I was dreading the prospect of such a lengthy voyage, of being cooped up in such close quarters. But now I am on board I find I have warmed to the idea."

"Well, we shall try our best to entertain you, sir," Helena replied.

They continued their meal in the same manner, and as they moved away from the table, Mrs. Grimshaw tapped Helena on the arm.

"I think Mr. Dempsey has taken a liking to you," she said with a little chuckle. "He did not take his eyes off you at dinner. Look, there he is now trying to attract your attention."

The captain encouraged the gentlemen to play cards, and after having a private conversation with Lucas, her father appeared more than happy to oblige. "It will give you a chance to speak with Mr. Dempsey," he said by way of an explanation.

Indeed, Lucas made his approach as soon as the captain dealt the first hand.

"You don't know how pleased I am to see you." He panted the words as though he'd been holding them in for a month and was suddenly able to release them. "I shall be forever in your father's debt."

"Only pleased, Mr. Dempsey? Well, I shall have to do something to rectify that."

Lucas smiled, his blue eyes twinkling with pleasure. "I was going to change my assessment to ecstatic, but will stick with pleased as I am more than intrigued to discover what you intend to do to sway my opinion."

Mrs. Brocklehurst walked past them on her way back to her cabin.

"And I trust your brother is well," Helena asked in a neutral tone.

"Do you know how difficult it is to make small talk?" Lucas said as Mrs. Brocklehurst closed her cabin door. "All I want to do is take you in my arms and ravish you senseless."

His words sent a delicious shiver down her spine.

"I quite enjoy watching you struggle under the pressure of restraint. In fact, I cannot wait for breakfast, so I may tease you some more."

The sound of raucous laughter drowned out their conversation.

"If you think I can spend three weeks in your company and not touch you, then you're mistaken." His gaze fell to her lips. "There must be someone on board I can bribe."

"There's no need," she said with a mischievous grin. "I have spoken to the quartermaster, and we are allowed to stroll on the upper deck tonight. There'll be clear skies, and I recall you were curious to see my skin glisten in the moonlight."

He moved closer and whispered. "I need you in my bed, Helena, but will happily settle for a kiss beneath the stars."

Helena inadvertently moistened her lips at the thought. "Wait until everyone's asleep and I will meet you up on deck."

"I shall look forward to it," Lucas said in that deep drawl that made her body tingle. "I always enjoy our illicit liaisons. I suppose it does make a change from meeting in the garden."

The mere of mention of the word *garden* brought a flurry of scandalous images to her mind. Although the most memorable was the night at Lord Banbury's when Lucas told her he loved her and when she clutched at his lapels and cried his name with resplendent pleasure.

"Until later then," she said softly.

Helena bid him goodnight, retired to her cabin and ferreted around for her copy of *The Old English Baron*: the medieval battle between good and evil being the only thing that would prevent her from falling asleep. In fact, she was so absorbed in the Gothic tale she almost missed the gentle tap on the door.

"You're wanted up on deck, miss," the cabin boy whispered.

Helena grabbed her shawl and followed the boy up the stairs. He pointed to the dark figure staring out over the ocean, and Helena stopped and stared at the magnificent sight before moving to stand at his side.

"I still cannot believe I'm here with you," she said, glancing out over the inky-black ripples. "It just doesn't feel real somehow."

He turned to face her, pulled her shawl more tightly around her shoulders, kissed her until she trembled with need. "Does it feel real now?" he asked.

Helena pondered the question. "No, I think I need you to try again."

He turned her around so she was facing the ocean, his large body pressed against her back, acting as a shield. He rained kisses down her neck and along her jaw as his hand snaked down into the bodice of her gown, to tease and tempt her bare flesh.

The breeze from the ocean heightened her senses, and she pressed herself against him and relished the pleasure of his touch. He removed his hand and turned her back round, claiming her mouth again, the kiss wild, reckless and unrestrained.

"Marry me, Helena," he said, breaking away from her with a gasp. "Marry me."

He looked so vulnerable that she could not help but tease him a little. "I was under the impression we are already betrothed," she said, her teeth chattering as the temperature on deck was much cooler than expected.

"Here, take this," Lucas said, removing his coat and draping it over her shoulders.

It smelt divine: all woody and warm and thoroughly masculine.

"Although we're betrothed," he continued, "I have not asked you formally."

She slid her arms around his waist and snuggled into him. "There is no need for formality between us, Lucas."

"Then say you'll marry me. Say you will marry me as soon as we get to Boston." He took hold of her chin and tilted her face, looked deeply into her eyes. "I love you, and I want you to be my wife."

At that moment, Helena felt like she was living in a dream.

"We can have a blessing in St. George's when we return," he added. "And just think how much fun it will be to share a cabin on the way back to England."

"I love you, Lucas, and I would marry you here and now." She caressed his cheek and pushed the lock of hair from his brow. "I don't need a blessing or any other inducement to say yes. Besides, what choice do I have when your dragon bite has rendered me helpless?"

He smiled at that. "And you, my darling little nymph, have rendered me besotted to the point of madness." He bent down and brushed his lips against hers. "And thankfully there is no cure."

EPILOGUE

SHROPSHIRE, 1822

"Have you seen Lucas?" Helena said as she walked into the parlour to find Anthony bouncing little George up and down on his knee. "He disappeared after luncheon, and I have not seen him since."

"He went out into the garden," Anthony replied without lifting his gaze from his nephew, oblivious to the look of horror on the nursemaid's face as she hovered at his side.

Helena smiled. "Mind he doesn't ruin your coat," she said, pursing her lips when the nurse mouthed *thank you*.

"He'll be fine. He has a strong constitution." Anthony raised George up in the air, and the child laughed. "Oh, Lucas said you're to wait for him on the terrace."

Helena narrowed her gaze. "Has he said what he's up to?"

"He may have."

Anthony was beginning to sound like Amelia, but she decided against complimenting his eyes. Helena walked over to them and kissed her son on the temple. "Then I shall go and sit outside and await further instruction."

She walked out onto the empty terrace and scoured the lawn, but there was no sign of Lucas, and so she sat on the wooden bench and stared out over the rolling Shropshire hills. The sun was shining, and she felt content just to sit and admire the spectacular view.

The view improved tremendously when Lucas opened the iron gate to her left, his stride strong and purposeful as he walked towards her. The image roused memories of the first time she saw him, when she thought him arrogant, thought his character lacked kindness and compassion. When she had been completely wrong about him in every way.

"Good afternoon," he said, taking her hand and pulling her into his arms. His mouth met hers, and he kissed her in the wild and untamed way that was always a precursor to something far more sinful.

"With that sort of greeting, I give you permission to disappear after luncheon every day."

"With such an eager response, I think I will," he said with a wide grin, his eyes gleaming like a child who had just been given a biscuit from the cook. "Come. I've got something to show you. Close your eyes."

Lucas took her hand and led her down the path, whistling a little tune to himself amidst the birds' chorus.

When she opened her eyes to see where they were going, Lucas pulled her into his chest. He put his arm around her shoulder and covered her eyes with his hand. His warm masculine scent caused her heart to flutter.

"If you look again I will have to think of a suitable punishment."

"I was frightened I would fall," she said to appease him and then regretted the words, as she was intrigued to know what sort of punishment he had in mind.

"I would never let that happen."

"Where are we going?"

"To the ornamental gardens."

Helena gasped. "The garden is finished? No wonder you look so pleased."

With their feet no longer crunching on gravel, she listened

out for any familiar sounds. "The fountain is working!" she cried, hearing the trickle of water.

"It is," he said, his tone brimming with masculine pride and she wrapped her arms around his waist and hugged him.

"There," he said, dropping his hand, "you may open your eyes."

At first, she could see nothing other than bright lights swimming about in front of her, but when she blinked her vision cleared, and she found herself in a secluded corner. An eight-foot topiary hedge surrounded them on all sides. In the middle, there was a large stone statue standing on a six-foot plinth.

"Do you like it?" he asked moving to stand next to the statue as though it would make the whole scene more pleasing to the eye. "I decided against Hercules and picked one that reminded me of you. It is Minerva, the goddess of wisdom."

"It's beautiful, Lucas," she said, her eager gaze drinking in the sight. But the look of pure joy on his face affected her much more than the pleasant scenery. "Although I am just wondering why it is on such a tall plinth," she continued, trying her best to suppress a grin.

He sauntered over, devouring her with his licentious gaze. "I think you know the answer to that," he said, brushing his lips against hers. "I thought we could try it out, just for size." He nodded to the far corner, to the willow tunnel connecting the entrance to the rest of the garden. "I thought we could try that out, too."

Her mind conjured an image of them in her parents' garden, when her body throbbed with need for him and when she knew she loved him. "What did you have in mind?" she said, desire evident in her tone.

"I thought we could sneak out later tonight. There is a full moon, and with any luck, the sky will be clear." He put his hand over his heart. "I am not thinking of myself, of course, only of George. He desperately needs a playmate."

"Well, we must not disappoint him," she said, glancing up at the statue. "But if it's a girl don't think I am calling her Minerva."

"Don't you like the idea of naming a child after the place it was conceived?" he teased.

"No. Not when you think George would have been called after the *Sachem*."

Lucas laughed. "I agree, somehow it doesn't seem appropriate."

He looked so happy, so relaxed and carefree that her heart soared, and she had a sudden urge to treasure the moment.

With her hands on her hips, she walked around to the back of the plinth. "Are you sure it is large enough for what you have in mind? It looks a little short to me."

"Of course it is. I have measured it myself."

When he followed her around, she grabbed him by his lapels and pulled him into an embrace. "Good, as I have a desperate desire to see your bare skin glisten in the daylight."

Lucas raised an arrogant brow as her hands drifted over his shoulders and up into his hair. "When have you ever known me to disappoint?"

THE END

Made in United States
Orlando, FL
21 June 2023